A GIUSEPPE BIAN

AFTER THE STORM

By Isabella Muir

Published in Great Britain
By Outset Publishing Ltd

Published December 2020

ISBN: 978-1-872889-33-7

www.isabellamuir.com

Cover photo: by Gavin Kelman on Unsplash
Cover design: by Christoffer Petersen

1964

CHAPTER 1

Some of the locals reckoned Bexhill-on-Sea had gained its name and reputation from the wind. The nickname, 'Windy hill', was tossed around. And yet on the September day that Giuseppe Bianchi first noticed Edward Swain, there wasn't even a sea breeze.

Even so, the temperature wasn't enough to tempt Giuseppe to sit outside. The milky sunshine creeping through the blanket of clouds covering the Sussex sky offered light without warmth. Spending any time outside in the unhelpful English climate required preparation. As each week passed following Giuseppe's arrival in Bexhill back in July, he had added an extra layer of clothing, a vest beneath his shirt, a jumper under his jacket.

Now, from the smoky atmosphere of the café, he peered through the glass, misted with condensation, at a man who reminded him of another man, of a similar age, both grey-haired, both wearing their life's experiences in the lines on their face. Outside the café were just two tables, and the man was sitting at one of them, upright, ram-rod straight back, square shoulders. The man had turned the chair, and was facing towards the café, with his back to the sea, looking directly at Giuseppe. The man's charcoal grey eyes were wide open, fixed, unblinking. It wasn't the first time Giuseppe had seen him, but it was the first time he had really noticed him. Perhaps his observation skills were fading, alongside all the other things he'd abandoned when he chose to retire.

Giuseppe closed his own eyes for a moment to clear the memory that pressed in on him of that fateful day at the start of the year. His flat in Rome. A man he had known for many years. Not a friend perhaps, but more than a neighbour. Carlo Prezzi. The expression he had seen in Carlo's eyes on the day that triggered all the choices Giuseppe had made since, was the same expression he saw now on the face of the man sitting outside his cousin's café in Bexhill.

As Giuseppe's short holiday stretched into a longer stay, he became more familiar with the daily routine of the Rossi family. On weekdays Bella Café opened early, offering a hot drink or some buttered toast to workers on their way to work, or on their way home. This morning there were just two customers; a railwayman looking weary at the end of his night shift, and a postman grabbing a cup of tea before continuing his round.

Giuseppe's cousin, Mario, invariably took the early shift in the café, while Anne chivvied up their grandson, Stevie, who preferred to linger over his cornflakes rather than dressing for school.

Giuseppe and his cousin woke at a similar time. Mario's focus was work. For Giuseppe it was an espresso, carefully prepared and drunk strong and hot, before setting off on a brisk walk along the seafront with Max. The arrival of the lively Beagle in the Rossi household, shortly after Giuseppe's own arrival in England three months earlier, had meant changes for everyone. When Giuseppe offered to take on responsibility for the early morning walk, everyone was grateful, not least Max, who was waiting now in the back kitchen, pacing, pushing his paw against the door to no avail. The Italian would not be rushed. He savoured his espresso, as he savoured the peace. Then, he placed the empty cup down onto the saucer and rose, moving away from the table. All the while, the elderly gentleman outside did not alter his focus. It was almost trance like in its intensity, as if the man had fixed his mind on a particular memory, his steady gaze helping him to concentrate. An ex-military man, perhaps. Neat in his attire, a grey woollen jacket with a dark blue cravat tucked in around his neck for warmth. Giuseppe thought of the man as elderly, perhaps it was the thinning grey hair. His own hair had stayed thick and black, with just the odd peppering of silver around the edges of his hairline, rich waves that turned to curls whenever the English rain caught him out, as it did all too frequently.

Upstairs he collected a jumper and jacket from his bedroom, still speculating about the gentleman. Downstairs again, he clipped a collar and lead onto an excitable Max and stepped out onto the pavement, only to find the gentleman no longer there. He tutted at Max, yanking the dog back as the Beagle strained to pull forward.

'No, Max. *Aspetta*. Wait.'

They crossed the road onto the seafront, no traffic to navigate, just a double-decker pulling into the nearby bus stop. Fifty yards ahead, Giuseppe noticed the café customer once more. He let Max bounce forward. The man ahead of him had slowed, then stopped. He was leaning on the iron railings, looking out across the shingle beach towards the horizon.

Max was temporarily distracted by the smell of a nearby rubbish bin, allowing Giuseppe to approach to one side of the man, although several feet away. Giuseppe mirrored the man's pose, leaning on the railings and looking straight ahead.

'Good morning.' Giuseppe didn't turn as he spoke.

The man didn't respond.

'No wind today. It is unusual for Bexhill. They say the

town got its name from the wind. I don't know if that's true,' Giuseppe continued.

'You are Mario Rossi's cousin.' The man turned towards Giuseppe, holding out a hand by way of greeting.

'Giuseppe Bianchi. You know Mario? You are one of his regulars?'

'Your Italian accent is much stronger than your cousin's.'

'He has lived here so long, I think he is more English than Italian.'

'Edward Swain. I run the lodgings round the corner, along Sea Road.'

Edward turned back to face the sea. Perhaps the conversation was over for now. But then Edward spoke again. 'It surprised me when they took on the dog. Seems to me they have enough on their plate, what with the café and little Stevie to look after.'

'And now a visitor who may have outstayed his welcome.'

'Surely not.' Edward shot a questioning glance at Giuseppe.

'I try to help by walking Max.'

'He's spirited alright.'

'Max or Stevie?'

'Both.' Edward's expression softened a little.

'No breakfast to prepare for your guests?'

'No, it's not a bed-and-breakfast, just lodgings. They each have their own room and shared use of the kitchen. They can please themselves what they eat and when. It suits me that way.'

Max had been watching two seagulls pecking at a dead fish down at the water's edge. As the gulls flew away, so Max tugged at his lead.

'He believes he can chase the gulls,' Giuseppe said.

'That's one of the great things about dogs, they are ever hopeful. It's a shame we can't match them for optimism.' And then, without waiting for a response, Edward fell in step beside Giuseppe. 'I'll walk along with you, if you don't mind.'

They walked in silence. The only sounds were the occasional passing car, the gulls cawing overhead and the waves jostling the shingle up and back.

'You are not missing Rome?' Edward was the first to break the silence. 'It is Rome you come from? I heard Mario mention it one time.'

'Rome. *Si*. And yes, I am missing the city, but most of all the weather. I am still adjusting to your English climate.'

'Ah. There's no adjusting to it, I'm afraid. That's the thing about the English weather.'

'In Italy it is easier. We have spring, summer, autumn and winter. Seasons we can rely on.'

'I had a wonderful geography teacher when I was a lad.'

'Geography?'

'That was what Mr Weston was supposed to be teaching us. Instead, he taught us about bees.'

'Honey bees?'

'That's it. According to Mr Weston, you just had to watch the bees to know what the weather was going to do. When the bees spend more time out of their hive, it's a sure sign of rain to come. The great thing about it was that once we got him talking about his bees we didn't have to learn about the boring side of geography - soil erosion, oxbow lakes and the importance of salt marshes. Although, I'll admit I don't find any of it boring now. But when you are twelve years old...'

'The bees forecast the weather?'

They reached the end of the promenade. To walk any further, they needed to turn down Cooden Drive and away from the sea.

'Shall we turn back?' Edward said, glancing again out to the horizon. 'I don't like the look of those clouds.'

'There is no wind today to move the clouds. They will remain out there, perhaps drift over to France.'

'You might be right. Although you know we have a saying in English - the calm before the storm.'

'We have something similar in Italy. But also we say, *la quiete dopo la tempesta*. The calm after the storm.'

'Not sure I'd agree with that. A storm usually leaves devastation in its wake.'

'And from the ruins there are often new beginnings.'

A sideways glance from Edward suggested Giuseppe's philosophical stance surprised him.

'Well, regardless of Mr Weston's teaching, I don't rely on bees,' Edward said. 'Instead, I listen to the shipping forecast every morning. It gives me a sense of certainty for the day ahead.'

They returned to silence for the rest of their walk. Max was constantly up ahead, tempted on by the knowledge that as soon as they were back home he would have his breakfast. Once they were in sight of the café Giuseppe noticed his cousin out front, with a bucket and chamois leather, washing the windows and door.

'Your cousin is always working. In all my time here, I don't think he has ever taken a holiday.'

'Mario does not believe in holidays.'

'He'll be pleased to have you here though, I'm sure. It's true what they say about blood being thicker than water.'

Giuseppe still had to go through a process of internal translation, checking he had the right word and the right meaning, then stringing them together to see if he had grasped the sense of the phrase. Often it meant he didn't respond immediately.

'Family.' Edward added. 'There's nothing quite like it.'

'Ah, *si*.'

As they reached the café Mario mumbled a greeting while continuing to dip the leather into the soapy water, wringing it out and then wiping it across the windows. Then he stopped briefly and turned to his cousin. 'Found someone to walk with, eh?'

'I've been learning about bees,' Giuseppe said. '*Signor* Swain, I will be walking again in the morning, and every morning. If you care to walk with me, I would enjoy the company.' He left the statement hanging, nodded at Edward, then went inside.

CHAPTER 2

Each morning for the next few weeks Giuseppe and Edward walked Max along Bexhill seafront. Starting at Bella Cafe, they strolled east as far as Galley Hill, letting Max scamper across the grassed area beside the promenade, before taking the path up and over the headland. Then they would sit for a while on one of the benches that faced directly out at the French coast, before making the return journey.

On the cooler mornings, as September tipped over into October, Giuseppe added an overcoat to his jacket and scarf. He'd never intended to stay in England for so long. The luggage he'd brought had seen him through late summer, the jumpers coming out of their wrappings, worn on a daily basis. But now not even a jumper was enough, so he'd visited the local gentleman's outfitters in Devonshire Road and picked up an overcoat. Soon he would have to decide whether to leave the overcoat here, give it to Mario maybe, or take it back with him. He had a perfectly serviceable coat at home in his Rome flat, where he planned to be by the end of the month. November was bound to bring with it the beginnings of an English winter. Even his new overcoat wouldn't provide sufficient comfort from dropping temperatures, maybe even snow.

Giuseppe had told no one of his recent decision to return to Rome. He had yet to book the ticket, but when he did, he was determined he would book two more tickets, one for Mario and one for Anne. But he had yet to persuade them it was time. It would be Mario's first return visit to the place of his birth since arriving in England some eighteen years earlier. The shadows in Mario's past hovered like an invisible barrier between the cousins. Mario avoided the topic, perhaps, Giuseppe suspected, even with his wife. And so Giuseppe needed to find the right words to encourage Mario to open up, to shine a light on the shadows, confront them and then let them go. Giuseppe's return home was for him to do the exact same thing. Carlo Prezzi and his grandson. A tragedy that remained unresolved in Giuseppe's mind, because he had allowed it to, by retiring, by walking away.

For now though, Giuseppe was enjoying his early morning walks. On weekdays the seafront was quiet, apart from other dog walkers. The summer holiday season had ended, children were back at school, parents at work, or busy with household chores. There was little time on a busy weekday to saunter along the promenade, unless you were retired, or responsible for walking a dog, or both. Like Giuseppe.

Weekends were different. On Sundays, in particular, the beach was often populated with fishermen, who took advantage of their rest day to set up their rod and line at the water's edge and sit for a few hours, enjoying the peace of a deserted beach. Perhaps there was an unspoken protocol that all the fishermen followed, because it was rare to see two men sitting close together.

Giuseppe remarked on it to Edward.

'That's why they fish,' Edward said. 'Because they want time alone. If they wanted company, they'd take up bowls or cricket.'

'What would you choose?'

'I've never tried fishing, and the idea of cricket reminds me of my schooldays. I was never any good at it, not at any sport. And you?'

'A kick of a football, perhaps. Although now I would

9

be in danger of twisting an ankle or getting out of breath.'

'It's strange to think back, to remember how we were as young boys.' Edward's expression softened. 'I loved school, not the sport, but all the rest of it. The routine. I think that's what I loved the most, that and the friendships. I remember a cross-country run where my friend, Patrick Booker and I had taken a short cut, trying to avoid a muddy patch of forest, only to be caught out by the schoolmaster who gave us both detentions.'

'I think that running through the English countryside on a cold wet day would be punishment enough,' Giuseppe said.

'I can imagine your childhood pursuits involved a little more sunshine. Days on end playing on a sandy beach, swimming in a warm sea.'

Now it was Giuseppe's expression that softened as his thoughts flitted back in time. 'A long time ago.'

'I was reminded how long just recently when I took on another lodger. Daniel Forrest. He's probably twenty, maybe a year or two more, but he's like a child. Reminds me how old I am.' Edward gave a rare smile, as if he was relishing the thought of being old.

'You are not old.'

'Older than you.'

'*Sì*. But that does not make you old. Closing your mind to new ideas. That's what makes you old.' As he said the words, Giuseppe felt he had held up a mirror that reflected back at him a side of his nature he'd rather not admit to.

'Well, it seems that young Daniel Forrest is full of new ideas. He's recently started working as a typewriter salesman of all things.'

'Will he sell typewriters here in Bexhill?'

'I asked him the same thing. He came back at me with

such certainty. *There's Hastings and Eastbourne,* he informed me. He's certainly not short of enthusiasm.'

'He could visit Christina's office. The *Eastbourne Herald.*'

'Christina Rossi? Your cousin's daughter?'

'*Si.*'

'I might mention that to him. Although I wouldn't be surprised if he hasn't got his sights on it already.'

'And now you have no more vacancies?'

Giuseppe had passed Claremont Lodge many times. Sea Road offered the easiest route to the newspaper shop, as well as the other small shops that made up Bexhill town centre. He'd barely glanced at the three-storey town house, but since his regular walks with Edward he'd taken a little more interest in it, noticing how the dark green painted front door caused it to stand out from the neighbouring properties.

'I've space for more, but I'm content with two. There's a young married woman - Mrs Lorna Warrington. She's been with me a few months now. I'm not sure how long she's staying, but if she moves out, then I'll advertise again.'

'You have many rooms?'

'The place is too large for me, that's why I take lodgers. Kitchen and breakfast room on the ground floor, a dining and sitting room that are barely used. Three bedrooms on the first floor and one in the attic. I let the lodgers have the two front bedrooms. They're almost too big for me, what with the bay windows as well. I'm in the attic room. Doing the stairs is my penance, a reminder that I need to at least try to keep fit.'

English houses were an anathema to Giuseppe. He'd only ever lived in a flat, as did everyone he knew back home, with families of several generations often sharing a one-bedroom home with a tiny bathroom. Parents sleeping on makeshift beds in the living room, while children shared their bedroom with grandparents. It was what he'd grown up with.

'In Rome my flat is on the fourth floor, but we have a lift. When I return, I will try to use the stairs. Improve my fitness.'

'Have you plans to return?'

'Of course. One day I must return. But which day… I have yet to decide. And the longer I stay, the more possessions I acquire. A few weeks ago I bought a wireless.'

'Ah, yes. I couldn't be without mine.'

'I have taken your advice. I have been listening to the shipping forecast on the wireless. But I understand nothing. Just strange words that seem to flow together. It is almost like a song,'

'It's a language of its own, that's for sure. *Veering* - that's telling you the direction of the wind, veering north-westerly, for example. And when they say *Good*, it doesn't necessarily mean good weather. They're talking about the visibility, how much fog or mist. It's critical for sailors, of course. And the place names - *Dogger, Fisher, German Bight* - they are the names of the coastal areas around the British Isles.'

'Did your geography master teach you to understand it?'

'I've picked it up over time. It's been a godsend for sailors for nearly a hundred years. Saved lives too, I'm sure. Although sadly the man who thought it all up - a chap by the name of Robert Fitzroy - committed suicide before he had the chance to see it in action.'

Giuseppe shook his head. 'It is a desperate man who chooses to take his own life.'

Edward didn't respond, looking away into the distance.

Then, after they had walked a little further, he said, 'Doesn't Mario have a wireless?'

'*Sì*, but I decided it was better to have my own. They have recently rented a television set. I sit with Christina sometimes in the evenings, although her choice of programmes is not mine. There is a weather forecast after the television news but it does not have the detail of your shipping forecast.'

'I wish it was mine. I'd love to take the credit for such a great innovation. I've always been a plodder. Slow and sure wins the race.'

'And did you?'

'Win the race? Far from it.' There was a weight to Edward's words, tempting Giuseppe to prod a little to find out more.

Instead, Edward continued. 'I'm not keen on the idea of television, I've never been one for moving images. With the wireless you can use your imagination.'

'I am the same. At home I have a wireless, but also a gramophone.'

'Ah, a music buff.'

Giuseppe looked askance, reminded that many English words still caught him out.

'What's your passion?' Edward said. 'What am I saying. You're Italian, so it must be opera.'

'Verdi, Puccini, they were the geniuses of their time.'

'I agree, but also Gustav Holst, Benjamin Britten, not opera, but still wonderful composers. Then there are the big bands, Joe Loss, Glen Miller. I'd be happy to loan you some records. See if we can't get you attuned to something other than opera. I'm sure Mario has a gramophone, although if Christina monopolises it there'll be nothing but pop music blaring out in the Rossi household. That's the way of it nowadays. Youngsters wanting to shout about all they think is wrong with the world. It wasn't the done thing when I was that age. We learned to put up and shut up, so to speak.'

'You are right. Christina loves her music, but also the news. She questions everything. I have told her, with such a forensic brain, she is wasted in journalism. She should join the police force.'

'Now there's a thought.'

When they reached the bench on the top of Galley Hill, they both fell silent. Giuseppe looking nowhere in particular, occasionally gazing at the ground, other times closing his eyes. Even as a detective, Giuseppe had never been one for incessant questioning. He preferred to leave space for a suspect to offer their own account, in their own time. He had learned that silence could be the enemy of the guilty. Leave a space and they would find the need to fill it.

Not that Edward was a suspect of course. But there was something that Giuseppe couldn't quite pin down about his new acquaintance. A hidden layer beneath the smartly dressed gentleman who chatted easily about diverse subjects, from music to the habits of bees. Now and again a darkness crossed Edward's face. It was as if he had a cloak he carried on his shoulders at all times, and whenever the need arose he brought it up and over his head, shielding him from interrogation.

'This town is so empty of people,' Giuseppe said. 'Even in the village where Mario and I grew up there was more noise, more movement.'

'Yes, I can imagine there's quite a difference. Blame it on our cold, damp weather. On days like this most folk will want to be huddled up in front of the coal fire, closing their curtains on the world.'

'If I go outside after five o'clock in the afternoon, I see no one,' Giuseppe continued. 'The first time I visited my cousin - some ten years ago - I told him he lived in a town of ghosts.'

Edward smiled and nodded. 'And now you live in Rome - the Eternal City - it must be a wonderful place, so full of history.'

'It is the perfect place to learn about the past. Every road, every building tells a story.'

'I spend most of my time trying to forget the past,' Edward said, his voice dropping down so low that it was as if he had forgotten Giuseppe was there beside him.

'You have regrets?'

'Don't we all?' Edward was looking at the ground beneath the bench and he didn't raise his eyes, but continued. 'Your cousin has adjusted well to a quiet English life?'

'He has adjusted. *Sì.* If he has adjusted well, you will have to ask him.' A mischievous smile crossed Giuseppe's face. 'And you, Edward. Have you travelled?'

'The war, of course. Although I don't think that counts as travelling. We were sent to wherever we were needed.'

'And where were you needed?'

'I was forty-three when war broke out. At first it was just the young men who joined up, but later they were pleased to have everyone who was prepared to come forward, even us old chaps.'

'Hardly old at forty-three?'

'Perhaps if they'd taken us from the beginning, more young lives could have been saved. It doesn't seem fair, does it? A whole generation wiped out.'

'There is nothing fair about war. Innocent people die,

fear turns into hatred.'

Giuseppe stood, stamping his feet on the ground. 'Shall we walk back down? Even with my scarf and coat I can feel parts of my body becoming numb.'

Max had been lying beneath the bench, but now with the promise of a return journey he sprang into action.

'We have much to thank the Allies for,' Giuseppe said, as they made their way back down Galley Hill towards the seafront. 'It is strange to think we might have fought beside each other.'

'I never made it to Italy. I was involved in northern France mostly.'

'And now, twenty years later, there are still many places at war. It seems we do not learn.'

'The tenth Commandment tells us, *Thou shalt not covet.*'

Giuseppe stopped walking, waiting for Edward to explain.

'Wanting something that belongs to someone else,' Edward continued. 'It's at the route of every disagreement, every battle, every war.'

They fell in step again. Once they were opposite Bella Café Edward pointed towards the window at the front of the Rossi flat. 'You have a room at the front or at the back?'

'The front. But it means I wake early to the sound of the milk deliveries. Your attic room is quiet? Deep sleep is a prize that does not come so easily as we get older.'

Edward continued to look up at the flat as he said, 'They say good sleep only comes to those with a clear conscience. I think it was Charlotte Bronte who said, *A ruffled mind makes a restless pillow.*'

'I find it helps to close my eyes.'

'It's a pre-requisite to sleep, isn't it?'

'In the day, I mean.'

'We call it a cat nap.'

'No, not to doze, just to think.'

'Or not to think?'

'We are of a similar mind.'

The morning had started grey, cloud sitting heavily across the sea and land. Looking out towards the horizon, it was difficult to see where the line of cloud ended and the sea began. The wind had been building since early morning. Now, as Giuseppe watched, it grabbed at the waves, turning their tips to the colour of mud. Overhead, a flock of black-legged kittiwakes gathered. Two of them suddenly swooped down to catch a fish. An argument ensued. The larger bird won, hastily carrying off its prize.

'Bit of a brute, that one,' Edward said. 'Survival of the fittest, I suppose,' he added, as if speaking to himself. 'Mario tells me you were a detective.'

'*Sì.*'

'Were you good at your job?'

'I tried to be good at my job.'

Edward was quiet, and then he said, 'There are events in my past that seem to weigh more heavily on me as the time passes.'

'The more years we go forward, the more years gather up behind us. Memories, regrets…'

Edward turned to face Giuseppe. 'I'd like to tell you something. You are a good listener and I'm certain you will understand.'

Giuseppe didn't know if it was for him to reply. He waited for Edward to continue.

'Tomorrow morning,' Edward said.

'On our walk?'

'After our walk. Come back with me to Claremont

Lodge. We can share a pot of tea.'

'I don't drink tea, but a visit to your home would be very welcome, thank you. But the forecast? They suggest it may not be walking weather tomorrow.'

'Who knows what tomorrow will bring. There's no such thing as certainty.'

'What about the bees? Don't they know?'

'Not even the bees.'

CHAPTER 3

The first rumble of thunder woke Giuseppe from a rare patch of deep slumber. Since moving into the front bedroom of his cousin's flat above the café, he had yet to enjoy a continuous night's sleep. The rattle of the milk delivery around 5am often woke him, unless his own dreams or lack of them had done so already.

He rolled over, turning to face the clock on the wooden chair beside his bed. The clock was shaped like an apple, the bright green luminous numbers confirming it was 2am. The clock was one of the few items left behind when Stevie moved into the smaller bedroom across the hall. Clearly, the apple-shaped clock was no longer favoured by the six-year-old. Superseded perhaps by a tomato or an orange.

The thunder was not the worst Giuseppe had heard. He had watched electric storms from his balcony in Rome countless times. The sky changing colour with broad sweeps of lightning, followed by booming thunder circling around the Seven Hills. On those nights it was as though the storm was captured, forced to roll around, often for hours. And not a drop of rain fell. Until finally the hills would release their captive and the thunder and lightning would trail away into the distance.

But this was the first English storm Giuseppe had experienced. Seconds after the first crash of thunder, the rain began to fall, pummelling on the roof immediately above his bedroom. It was as if half a dozen horses were galloping across the tiles. There was a rhythm to it, increasing to a crescendo, before decreasing again. Then, seconds later, the clouds above threw all they could muster onto the buildings below. The horses' hooves were no longer running across the roof, they were stampeding on Giuseppe's head. At least that was how it felt, as his eardrums were filled with the mix of rain, thunder, and now wind. The intensity of it blocked out any other thoughts. He was at the window, drawing back the curtains, which did little to prevent the draught from whistling through, chilling the room and its occupant.

Then, in a momentary easing of the rain, he heard movements within the house. Barking from Max, and then a knock on his bedroom door.

'Giuseppe. Are you awake?' It was Mario.

'Of course. What about Stevie? Is he afraid of storms?'

'There isn't much that frightens Stevie. But this is a bad one. Here on the seafront we often get the worst of it. It comes straight across the Channel from France, with nothing to break its journey.'

'Christina? Anne?'

'Still sleeping.'

'But you are awake.'

'I worry about the café. The front windows. The shingle gets thrown up and across the road. It happened once some years back, smashed the glass, cost a packet to repair.'

'So now we are both awake. Shall we go downstairs? Have a drink?' Giuseppe's silk dressing gown offered little extra warmth, nevertheless he lifted it from the chair and pulled it tight around him.

'No espresso for me. Not at 2am. If I can't sleep now, then coffee will only make it worse.'

'You are so English. You have your tea, but I will pass, maybe I will have a glass of something stronger.'

Giuseppe followed his cousin downstairs to the back kitchen of the café. Max greeted them with a growl, which developed into an occasional bark each time the thunder sounded. They were having to raise their voices to be heard over the roar of the storm, while at the same time trying not to speak so loudly they would wake the rest of the household.

Drinks of any kind were temporarily forgotten as Mario pushed open the swing door leading from the back kitchen into the café. Although the place was in darkness, the streetlights on the pavement outside shone a sulphurous glow over the empty tables and chairs. Patches of dull yellow blended with the shadows to create a patchwork of light and dark.

Mario flicked the switch beside the counter and the overhead fluorescent tubes lit up, bathing the whole place in light, dismissing the shadows. He stepped towards the café windows, passing his hand over each of them, and then the door. It was as though he didn't trust his eyesight, which was telling him there was no damage, nothing was broken, nothing cracked.

Giuseppe was behind him, but his gaze wasn't on the shop front. Instead, he looked beyond the glass, through to the street scene outside. He struggled to reconcile what he was hearing with what he saw. The downpour continued, still with the occasional rumble of thunder and crack of lightning. But now the strength of the wind had increased to such an extent it seemed to be building into a gale. Giuseppe saw something flash past the café, with the speed of an arrow from a bow. Then another and another. He narrowed his eyes, trying to focus as objects continued to fly past, some high in the air, others rolling along the pavement.

'Rubbish,' Mario said. And just as he spoke, a dustbin clattered past, tumbling along the road as though a giant had put his foot against it in some sort of game.

The storm had coincided with a low tide; the waves crashing heavily on the shore, but not throwing the shingle up high enough for it to reach the promenade. The cousins watched in silence for a few moments, the only noise coming from the crescendo of wind and rain outside.

Then, just as Giuseppe turned to go back into the kitchen, he caught sight of something much larger in his peripheral vision.

'*Mamma mia.* What is that?'

'It's someone's flat roof - asphalt,' Mario said.

The piece of roofing - some four feet square - landed right beneath the lamppost. The torn edges suggesting the wind had ripped it away from a nearby shed or outhouse. Seconds later, a gust picked it up again and flung it towards the railings where it lodged, stuck, as if temporarily exhausted.

'Thank goodness folk are all in their beds,' Mario said. 'Anyone in the path of flying debris like that - well, the hospitals would be having a busy time of it.'

As they went through to the kitchen, there was another sound. Footsteps on the stairs, followed moments later by the appearance of Stevie, the legs of his pyjama bottoms ruffled up. His voice contradicting his appearance. 'Granddad. Come and look.' Here was a child ready for adventure.

Mario picked Stevie up, letting him wrap his legs around his waist. Max ran towards his lead. If Stevie was up, then it must be time for a walk.

'Granddad,' Stevie continued, ignoring the excited Beagle. 'You have to come. You too, Uncle Giuseppe.' The urgency in his voice raising the volume above the sound of the storm.

'Ssh now. Your grandma and Auntie Christina haven't

woken and it'll be better for them if they don't. How about I take you up and tuck you in? The storm will ease soon enough.' Mario said.

Stevie wriggled free of Mario, dropping to the ground, then grabbing his granddad's hand, pulling him towards the staircase. 'Come on, I've seen something outside.'

'I'll come too,' Giuseppe said. 'We can settle him together.'

But there was to be no easy settling of Stevie that night. Once in his bedroom, Stevie tugged Mario towards the window, where the curtains were pulled open.

'Look down there. Do you see?' Stevie jabbed his finger on the glass.

All three looked down at the back garden of the café and then raised their gaze a little to see beyond, into the back gardens of the houses that ran along behind the café. There were no streetlights overlooking any of the back gardens, so it was only when a fork of lightning briefly lit the darkness that Giuseppe could see what Stevie was pointing to.

There, in the garden of Claremont Lodge, was an old timber summer house. At least it used to be an old timber summer house, until the willow tree that stood beside it had been uprooted and was now lying across a pile of timbers. The summer house had been flattened.

'*Santa Maria.*' Giuseppe didn't wait to see if Mario was following. He raced back to his bedroom, threw his dressing gown aside, tugged trousers and jacket over the top of his pyjamas, swapped slippers for shoes, without delaying to put socks on.

Downstairs he pushed past Max, who was still hopeful of a night-time adventure. Once out in the street the full force of the wind seized him, making him turn sideways into it to try not to lose his footing. Faced with a gale force wind, even a six foot, broad-framed man could be wrong footed. He tugged his jacket collar up, but it offered little protection against the sheeting rain, which had soaked his hair and clothes in seconds. Contents of dustbins flew around him, paper bags, empty crisp packets, catching under his feet, while tin cans and glass bottles rolled in the gutter beside him.

It was barely fifty yards from Bella Café to Edward's lodging house, yet by the time Giuseppe reached the green front door he felt as though he had run a mile. His breath was coming in gasps as he thumped on the door. Then he crouched, pushing at the letterbox, shouting Edward's name, before banging on the door again. He tried to blank out the noise of the wind, attuning his hearing to what was happening inside the house. But it was impossible; all the elements of the storm combined to be as loud as a train approaching, or several trains, coming at him from all directions. After what seemed like forever, but could only have been minutes, the door opened to reveal a young woman, a quilted dressing gown pulled tight around her, a startled expression on her face.

'I saw the tree is down. I have come to help.' Giuseppe's breath was still laboured as he tried to speak.

'It's the middle of the night.'

The woman seemed oblivious to Giuseppe's appearance, which now resembled a sodden scarecrow.

'The summer house. It's been badly damaged. Destroyed.'

'You're Italian. I'm right, aren't I?'

'*Signora*. This is not the time to speak of nationalities.' He stepped from the porch into the hallway. 'Perhaps there is other damage too? You are alright? And Edward's other guest? The young man. I forget his name.'

'It's very kind of you to be so concerned. But really, it's just a storm. And as Mr Swain has clearly not heard you banging on the front door, it would appear he has slept through the whole thing.'

Suddenly Giuseppe felt stupid. What was he thinking of? He barely knew Edward. They had walked and talked together, but they weren't related, not firm friends, just casual acquaintances. He turned to go, but something in the pit of his stomach kept him riveted to the spot. He had made a considerable noise banging on the front door, and he had been standing in the hallway for several minutes. Wouldn't Edward have heard something?

He looked beyond the woman, imagining for a moment that somehow Edward would appear as if by magic, with no advancing footsteps, no opening or closing of doors.

'Perhaps we should knock on *Signor* Swain's door. Let him know about the summer house.'

'Can't it wait until morning? There's hardly much we can do now in the darkness, in the middle of a storm.'

'You are *Signora* Warrington? Edward mentioned that you are one of his lodgers.'

'Lorna.'

Giuseppe considered Lorna's words. She was right, of course. There was little point in attempting to fix anything while the gale continued to blow, the rain cascading down as though God had released Heaven's flood gates.

The last time a neighbour had needed his help, Giuseppe was a detective. There were rules, he couldn't get involved. It was all too close to home. Reasons that were convenient. Excuses that allowed him to walk away. *This is different. It is just a broken building. Not a broken child.*

'I will see for myself.' He edged past Lorna. He was a

stranger to her, turning up in the middle of the night, demanding to see an elderly man who was sleeping. It was no surprise to Giuseppe that she had tried to bar his way.

He remembered Edward explaining that his was the attic room. He flicked the switch at the bottom of the first flight of stairs. Wall lights, shaped like seashells, cast a pearly light up towards the top of the house. Three flights of stairs took him to a small landing with one door which was open. Peering inside, he needed first to adjust his eyes to the darkness. He felt for the light switch beside the door. The bed was empty, the covers thrown back as if the occupant had left in haste.

He had climbed the stairs slowly, conscious that he was disturbing a household, for no real reason other than a fallen timber building. But now he ran back down to the ground floor where he found Lorna still standing in almost the same place he had left her moments before.

'Have you woken Mr Swain?' she said. 'I hope he doesn't think it was my fault. That I let you in when I had no right doing anything of the kind. I don't even know who you are.'

'He is not in his room.'

Once again, Giuseppe left Lorna standing as he made his way along the hallway, sensing the kitchen would be at the back of the house and beyond that the way to the back garden. He didn't ask Lorna to direct him, but was aware of her following him.

'A torch. We'll need a torch,' Giuseppe said, with a force to his voice, but low in tone, not shouting.

The kitchen was in darkness, but moments later, Giuseppe had switched on the lights, found the key hanging beside the back door. As he unlocked the door a powerful gust of wind caused it to slam towards him, almost catching him in the face. Peering out into the garden Giuseppe could scarcely see anything in detail, just shadows - flowers, bushes, branches of trees - looming shapes that the gale was forcing to bend low and then just when it appeared they would snap off at the roots, they shot back up again.

'*Signor* Swain. Edward,' Giuseppe shouted into the darkness. If Edward wasn't in his bed, he must be here in the garden, perhaps already attending to the damaged summer house.

'Did you find a torch?' Giuseppe turned to Lorna, who stood immediately behind him. It was as if they had formed a partnership, although barely ten minutes ago he had never even met her.

She thrust a heavy rubber torch into his hand. He fumbled with it for a moment, before locating the button to switch it on. The torchlight was penetrating, shining some ten feet into the distance. When he had looked at the broken timbers of the summer house from Stevie's bedroom window, they seemed to form a distinct shape, a rectangle of timbers laid out on the grass, with the uprooted willow tree lying across the bottom part of the rectangle. Everything neatly ordered and precise. But now he was at ground level, he could see the individual timbers were spread in a haphazard way, some sticking up at an angle, others tossed to one side, lying on their own as if discarded. The roof of the summer house had come down in one piece, lying centrally over the pieces of wood that once formed the walls. And glass, everywhere.

'Edward.' Giuseppe shouted again, finding it increasingly unnerving that his friend had not responded.

He was close to the wreckage now, shining the torch across the site, as though he was a building inspector, checking that all protocols had been followed. When, of course, there was no longer any building to inspect.

And that's when he saw the slipper. It was just to one side of the main pile of timbers, lying in a puddle that had been created by the rain falling into a dip in the lawn. As the pellets of rain continued to hammer down, they bounced on the puddle, making the slipper dance. A one-legged dance.

Giuseppe crouched down, shining the torch at a lower level around the edges of the timbers. Another slipper, but this time not floating, not moving at all.

'Edward, it's me. Giuseppe. Can you move?'

One large timber lay across the lower half of Edward's body, pinning him to the ground. Small timbers covered his chest and right arm and shoulder, leaving his left arm exposed, but unmoving.

The howling of the storm was unrelenting. Even as Giuseppe shouted Edward's name it was as if the wind caught the words and blew them in the opposite direction. And if Edward was saying anything, his words were also lost.

'*Signora* Warrington. Go now. Telephone. We need an ambulance. The fire engine perhaps. We need help.' He didn't turn to see if Lorna had followed his instruction. His focus was on calculating what he could do to free his friend from his wooden prison.

Giuseppe was kneeling now, edging closer to Edward's face, taking care not to kneel or press on a timber that might push down further on his friend. If he could get close to him, lean down to within inches, then he might be able to hear words that he imagined might be said. *I'm in pain.* Of course the man was in pain. *Can you help me?* That's what Giuseppe dearly wanted to do, and yet he felt as

28

helpless as he had that day when Carlo looked across the balcony at him and then down at the devastating event unfolding on the street below.

'Help will be here very soon. We will get you to hospital. All that is broken will be mended. But not the summer house, eh?' Giuseppe delved into his memory to find the right tone, the perfect level of joviality to calm a victim, for Edward was a victim of the storm. And of the dreadful and unlucky decision that caused him to come into the summer house, moments before the willow tree crashed to the ground, flattening all within its path.

'You were right, of course,' Giuseppe continued. 'The shipping forecast said a strong wind, some rain, a gale, but this is more like a hurricane.'

The tree had fallen onto the building and then the building timbers had collapsed as if they were nothing more than a pile of matchsticks, trapping Edward's body. None of the debris touched his head or face. There were no signs of cuts or grazes, although any blood on his cheeks or forehead would have been quickly washed away by the rain. Edward's position, lying on his back, meant that Giuseppe couldn't tell if the underside of his friend's head had sustained an injury and he was loath to move him, lest he cause further pain or damage.

Giuseppe kept the torch shining on Edward's face, willing his friend to open his eyes. Then Edward's lips moved. He was alive, he was speaking. But the words were caught and blown away by the wind. Giuseppe leaned closer to Edward's face.

'Again, tell me again. What is it you want to say?' Giuseppe said.

It was as if Edward used his remaining breath to push the words out once more. 'Josephine. It was my fault.'

29

Later, when Giuseppe reflected on the evening's events, he recalled hearing sirens long before the ambulance finally arrived. The storm would have caused damage across the town, the emergency services were busy that night. So busy that by the time the ambulance men joined Giuseppe in the garden of Claremont Lodge, Edward Swain was dead.

CHAPTER 4

During his years as a detective, Giuseppe had learned that people are composites of many different behaviours. A joyful event may trigger laughter in one person, tears in another. He'd seen men behave like children, and young girls take on the yoke of responsibility as if they were born to it. He had also reflected on his own personality, trying to understand which strengths and weaknesses led him to make the choices he'd made. But amid his reflections, he'd never been able to anticipate his reaction to trauma.

It seemed his responses were random, it didn't matter if the victim was young or old, male or female. There were times when he'd been called to a murder scene and he would stand emotionless, his gaze taking in every inch of the scene, objectivity at the forefront of every action, every thought. Yet on other occasions, seeing a dead body resulted in an overwhelming desire to flee. He had to force himself to remain rooted to the spot, while he memorised the position of the body, the clothes, any potential weapons lying nearby. Later, away from the scene and back in his office, he would make patchy notes, recalling every detail, using all his senses to recreate what he had seen, heard and smelled. He barely referred to his notebook again, all he needed to do was close his eyes and he could return to every crime scene that he witnessed in all his years as a detective.

That night, when the ambulance men knelt beside him in the back garden of Claremont Lodge, confirming what he already knew – that Edward Swain was dead – there was no hesitation, no desire to flee, but a raging anger flaring up inside him, flung out with full force at anyone who cared to listen.

'You took too long,' he shouted.

'I'm very sorry, sir. Was he a relative?' The youngest ambulance man went to take Giuseppe's hand, the hand that until minutes ago was holding the torch. Giuseppe couldn't even remember throwing it down. Had it flung it away, or dropped it? There was no need for it now. No need for the ambulance.

'Can you tell us the gentleman's name, sir? Miss?'

It was only when the ambulance man addressed Lorna that Giuseppe realised she was there, standing behind him. It was the strangest tableau. A woman – Lorna – in her early twenties, wearing a short, quilted housecoat, pulled tight around a short nightgown. Both items now clinging to her body as if she had stepped into a bath fully clothed, stepping out moments later onto the back lawn. Beside her a man – Giuseppe – tall, broad shouldered, a blue jacket and dark grey trousers, worn over a pair of striped pyjamas. The jacket surely ruined, rain dripping from the bottom edge onto the trousers that could no longer absorb more water, allowing it to run down Giuseppe's legs into puddles at his feet. The two ambulance men in their uniform, kneeling either side of Edward Swain. And Edward, who was covered by lengths of timber from a summer house, crushed under the branches of a willow tree still in full leaf.

It may have been ten minutes or an hour before Giuseppe was back at Bella Café, sitting in his sodden clothes, while Anne passed a cup of hot, sweet tea into his hand. Mario had sought to persuade his cousin to change into dry clothes the moment he came through the door into the café. But Giuseppe waved him aside, choosing instead to sit and stare at the steaming liquid that he had no intention of drinking.

'You left so quickly. I was going to follow.' Mario said. 'But then Anne woke, then Christina. By the time we all tried to settle Stevie down and encourage Max to stop barking, it was too late. I heard the sirens and saw the ambulance pull into Sea Road. I thought, I hoped...' Mario shook his head.

'It was already too late when I arrived.'

'Poor man.' Anne laid her hand on Giuseppe's arm, as if an offer of comfort to the living would somehow ease the fate of the dead. 'And you don't know why he was out there? Why he'd put himself in such danger?'

Giuseppe looked out through the rain-spattered glass, across the road. The tide was advancing towards the promenade, so that now, when the force of the gale caused a wave to rise up, it crashed down on the shore and sent a shower of shingle towards the road. The storm clouds made the black sky even darker. Only the streetlights cast enough of a glow to enable anyone to see anything. The debris from overturned rubbish bins, broken fences and roof tiles continued to blow from west to east. Then a gust of wind caught a discarded newspaper, sending it up in the air to form a parachute, before the sheets separated and flew in all directions.

'Christina?' Seeing the newspaper, jerked Giuseppe's thoughts away from the dark replay of the back garden of the lodging house, the moments when he had held Edward's hand, listened for his voice.

'She stayed with Stevie.' Anne said. 'She does that sometimes, settles him down and ends up curling in beside him.'

'He must have been frightened by what he saw?'

'I don't think he realised what it was, not really.' Mario

said. 'And all the comings and goings, the thunder and lightning, well, it's the stuff of boyish adventures, isn't it?'

'You must get out of those wet things, Giuseppe.' Anne adopted a motherly tone, despite her husband's cousin being more than ten years older than her.

There was no sleep to be had that night, not for Mario, Giuseppe or Anne. Only Christina and Stevie enjoyed the sweet innocence of closing their eyes and drifting off, undisturbed by a storm that Christina would be reporting on come the morning.

The sensible thing for Giuseppe to do was to change into a clean, dry set of pyjamas and slide into bed. If he closed his eyes, it would block out the light, but not his thoughts, or the images that were on a repeat loop in his mind. He retired to his bedroom, but he had no plans to retire to his bed. Instead, he spent a brief time in the bathroom, washing his face and hands. He had knelt beside Edward and then pushed on the muddy grass to stand again. His hands were stained. He used a nail brush to scrub the worst of the green dirt away. He removed all his wet, dirty clothes and left them in a pile on the floor beside the basin, wrapping a bath towel around him for modesty. He would never wear the jacket again, even dry cleaning could not restore it to its former state. No matter. He would visit the gentleman's outfitters again to buy another jacket – perhaps a heavier one, more suited to the English autumn. Easy to replace to an item of clothing, but impossible to replace a man's life.

He returned to his bedroom and pulled open a drawer in the tallboy, taking out a clean vest, shirt and jumper, then trousers from the wardrobe. Once he was dressed, he felt calmer. The bedroom was sparsely furnished. He often settled into the old armchair that was tucked into the alcove beside the bay window. But this wasn't a time for comfort. The firm seat of the wooden chair beside the bedhead, that doubled as a bedside table would help him feel grounded, rooted in the here and now. He lifted the alarm clock from the chair, setting it on top of the tallboy, and shifted the chair to the window and stared out into the night. The draught whistled through the badly fitted sash windows, so Giuseppe took the top blanket from the bed and wrapped it around his back and shoulders. The storm hadn't eased, but the thunder and lightning had abated, only the rain and wind continuing.

He let the replay roll over in his mind. He had looked out from Stevie's bedroom window, seen the broken building, the uprooted tree, then grabbed his jacket and shoes, running, banging on the door of the lodging house until Lorna Warrington answered. The images were fresh in his mind, the torchlight had dispelled some of the shadows, while creating others. Edward's broken body.

Then, as he stared out into the night, the images were interrupted. It was as if he was at the cinema, anticipating one film, when the projectionist suddenly decided to switch the reel part way through. Now a different set of pictures flicked across his mind.

January. He was at home in his flat in Rome. He had been listening to opera – *La Boheme* – one of his favourites. It was mid-afternoon, much of the city enjoying a siesta. The traffic wouldn't start again until four or five, when shopkeepers returned to open their shops, and families considered a stroll for an ice-cream or a slice of pizza. Occasionally the throaty sound of a Vespa could be heard, a youngster too fidgety to rest, enjoying the opportunity to speed along an empty road.

At a certain point in the opera - towards the end of the

first act, the lovers sang their rapturous duet. As he listened Giuseppe was convinced he heard the beat of a bass drum. But he knew every bar of *La Bohème*, he had heard this opera before, many times. There was no bass drum at this point in the music.

It was a warm afternoon. The doors to his balcony were open, the delicate voile curtains swishing slightly in the pretence of a breeze. He drew them to one side and stepped out onto the balcony. He'd replayed the moment many times since, but still he couldn't pinpoint what it was that made him look across first at his neighbour's balcony, before looking down to the street below. Carlo's stance was a mirror image of his own. They faced each other, each standing with one hand resting on the stone wall of the balcony. What was the expression in Carlo's eyes? Giuseppe had asked himself countless times. Shock? Fear? Guilt?

That day and many days since then, Giuseppe wondered if it wasn't only his stance that mirrored Carlo's. but his expression too. Shock. Fear. Guilt.

It was only when Giuseppe pulled his gaze away from Carlo and looked down at the street that he saw Emanuele's young body, stretched out on the ground. A five-year-old child who would never see his sixth year.

The sound of the toilet chain being pulled, then water running from the taps, broke Giuseppe from his reverie. He glanced at the alarm clock. 4.30am. Still a while before the residents of Bexhill woke to get on with their day. Many wouldn't have slept, many would find their day ahead changed by the events of the night. So much was broken and only some of it could be mended.

CHAPTER 5

At some point during the early hours of Sunday night, Christina had left Stevie sleeping soundly and returned to her own bed. When her dad's alarm went off early the next morning, she slipped into her parents' bedroom and was given a brief update as to the night's events.

'Poor Giuseppe. I've never seen him looking so defeated,' Anne said.

'And he just sat there in his wet clothes?' Christina was attempting to reconcile the Giuseppe she thought she knew with the man Anne was describing. 'I'll talk to him. Try to find out what happened.'

'Go easy on him, darling. I think he was genuinely fond of Mr Swain. The two of them had formed a camaraderie of sorts.'

'He's seen loads of dead bodies, though. He was a detective for God knows how many years.'

'It's not the same when it's someone you know. Trust me.'

Something in her mum's tone made Christina pause. It was true. She had never witnessed the death of a friend, not even a close relative. Finding George Leigh's body on the day Giuseppe arrived from Roma was a trauma that still crept into her dreams. When she and Giuseppe had investigated George Leigh's death, Giuseppe had taken the lead, confident in his abilities to solve a case. Perhaps on this occasion she would need to be the first to ask the questions. That's if there were any questions to ask.

So when Christina heard Giuseppe open his bedroom door, she made sure she walked onto the landing at the same moment, to contrive a 'chance' encounter.

'How did Mr Swain come to be there? And why was he just in his pyjamas?' Christina had perfected her journalistic technique of using open questions that usually led to a fuller report. It had become almost automatic and yet in this instance, surely inappropriate. Giuseppe was her uncle, in fact not her uncle, although she thought of him that way. Her dad's cousin. What did that make him? No matter. Since he arrived in July to stay with the family they had developed a rapport, not least as a result of their joint investigation into the tragic death of George Leigh.

Giuseppe had told Christina that she reminded him of his younger self. He praised her enthusiasm, her tenacity and resilience, faced with a boss who had a different approach to journalism from her own. Charles wanted the shock headline, the front-page article that would sell his newspapers. Something else inspired Christina's route into journalism. It wasn't about giving readers sensational stories to read over their breakfast cereal, before discarding the newspaper to form tomorrow's chip wrapper. For Christina, journalism provided an opportunity to tell the hidden stories, to shine a light on all forms of social injustice, to give a voice to people desperate to be heard. But she was a young female reporter trying to make her mark. Charles relied on her to write about the everyday events of the local area, although - despite his bluster - just occasionally he would print one of her articles focusing on the subjects she was passionate about.

'Are you going to work?' Giuseppe said, seemingly dismissing Christina's original questions.

'Eventually. Charles will expect me to do a bit of a recce, see what damage the storm's inflicted on our little community.'

She noticed Giuseppe visibly flinch. Her offhand

remark had been thoughtless.

'Sorry, that was thoughtless of me. You've had a rough time of it. Did you get any sleep?'

He shook his head and then, 'Stevie?'

'Oh, he's fine. Everything is an adventure when you're six years old.'

'Do you think the school will open?'

'Provided there's no damage and all the teachers can get in. I'm not sure about the roads though, if the seafront is anything to go by. Looks like all routes will involve negotiating our way through and over an eclectic mix of rubble and rubbish. Anyway, Mum will see to Stevie. Tell you what, hang on while I get dressed and we can take Max out together. I'm in no rush to get to the office.'

Giuseppe stood, his arms hanging by his side, his face expressionless. Christina almost wanted to give him a hug. Instead, she put a hand on his shoulder.

'Hey, come on. How about I make us both an espresso? We can have it before we leave.'

'You are going to make coffee?'

'Don't you trust me?'

Giuseppe shrugged his shoulders.

'I've watched you do it often enough. I think I've got the hang of it.'

Since Giuseppe had bought the Italian coffee percolator on his first trip to London back in July, he had been the only one permitted to use it. Christina had overheard numerous conversations between Giuseppe and his cousin.

'You do remember that I am also Italian,' Mario had said, not disguising the irritation in his voice.

'Do *you* remember that you are Italian?' was the general thrust of Giuseppe's replies.

It was more than friendly banter, more even than a niggle between them. Christina was certain it stemmed from past events, something that happened when her dad was young. She had quizzed Anne about it, but to date had yet to receive a satisfactory answer.

'They grew up together, didn't they? Played together. Their mothers were sisters, weren't they?' Christina has asked her mother. 'And now it's as though they can barely stand to be in each other's company. So what happened, Mum? Something must have happened.'

Her mother's replies were little more than platitudes. Something along the lines of 'people change', or 'your Dad's never been a talker'. So Christina continued to watch the cousins' relationship from the sidelines, hoping one day she'd overhear something that would provide a clue. Failing that, she might just ask Giuseppe outright. But not today. Certainly not today.

Espresso made, swiftly downed in one, Christina followed Giuseppe out of the café onto the pavement, with Max dawdling behind at first, seemingly more interested in the splash his paws made each time they connected with the paving stones. The rain and wind hadn't calmed, if anything the gusts when they came seemed stronger. It was the first time Christina had felt the full force of the storm. A particularly ferocious gust made her grab at Giuseppe's arm, fearing she would lose her balance.

'You are too thin,' he said, raising his voice so that it could be heard above the wind, causing his words to sound like a reprimand.

'Yes, well, a girl's got to look after her figure, you know.' She turned, hoping her attempt at humour might have momentarily lifted Giuseppe's mood.

Max was now pulling ahead, energised by the wind,

oblivious to the rain which had taken just minutes to soak his head and back. Even his white-tipped tail, usually carried high and proud, was drooping under the persistent downpour.

They crossed onto the seafront, walking into the wind, which unhelpfully lifted Christina's hood from her rain mac, blowing it from her face, leaving her hair uncovered. There was no point in tugging it back into place as her hair was already soaked, as was Giuseppe's. Umbrellas were clearly not an option.

It was still early, a little after 7.30am. No one else had ventured onto the seafront, either deterred by the weather, or loath to begin the salvage operation.

'Let's just walk to the other side of the De La Warr, then head back,' Christina shouted into the wind.

As they pressed forward Christina made a mental note of all she saw that would help to enrich an article for her editor. She played around with headlines, imagining bullet points she could flesh out later. The main story would be about the unfortunate death of Edward Swain.

Sussex storm results in tragic death

Local man dies in brutal storm

Was he local? She knew nothing about him, although she'd seen him in the café now and then. Of course, Charles would want the piece widened to refer to the rest of it – the Victorian seafront shelter that had its glass shattered by flying debris; the small fishing boats that had broken free of their anchor, lifted by the waves and dumped upside down on the shingle.

Mario had already checked their cars, confirming they'd had a lucky escape as some of the other cars parked further along the street had been badly dented, like as not by rolling metal dustbin lids, or flying roof tiles.

But there had been a death. And if there'd been one death, there may have been others. Later that morning Christina would need to knock on doors, speak to neighbours, contact the hospital and the police. Charles would get the official line from the authorities, he had contacts in all the right places. Christina's responsibility was to get the human interest angle. It was a part of her job that made her uneasy, as though she was taking advantage of people's suffering for her own gain. But she was a reporter and she was good at it, she knew that. Trouble was, on this occasion, the first person she needed to interview was Giuseppe and from the moment she saw him that morning she realised it was likely to be the hardest interview she had undertaken in her career so far.

They returned to the café via the side alley, which led straight into the back garden and from there into the back kitchen. They rarely used that entrance, although most of the supplies were delivered that way. First job was to get Max towelled down, but not until he had shaken his wet fur, showering water over the kitchen floor and most of the kitchen cupboards.

'Did Dad's mac keep you dry? Or your clothes at least. Maybe I should towel you dry when I've finished with Max,' Christina said. Now they were indoors it was easier to talk, but only if she could find a way to break Giuseppe's silence. She was used to his silences, which were usually accompanied by closed eyes – his thinking time, he had told her often enough. But this silence felt different.

'I'll wait until nine, then I'll ring around. The hospital first, then maybe the police. Although Charles has a direct line to them, so he'll know more than me. Let's pray there haven't been too many injuries.'

'Or deaths.'

She filled the kettle, just for something to do, then set it on the gas. 'Do you want to talk about it? It must have been dreadful. You and Mr Swain got on well, didn't you. You'll miss his company on your early morning walks.'

Giuseppe sat, brushing one hand over his hair, the rain acting like a perm, sending his usual waves into tight curls. Then he looked at his wet hand and smoothed it on his trousers to dry it.

'I suppose it will be tricky now for his lodgers,' Christina continued. 'You said he had two.'

'Daniel Forrest and *Signora* Lorna Warrington.'

'And it was Mrs Warrington who opened the door to you last night?'

'*Si.*'

'And Daniel Forrest? Did he make an appearance at any point?'

Giuseppe shook his head.

'So Lorna Warrington was there when Mr Swain died? That must have been really distressing for her.'

'It was distressing for everyone.'

Giuseppe stood and took a step towards the small window that faced the back garden. Although dawn had broken hours earlier, the storm clouds created the appearance of early evening, with shadows moving as branches were caught up in the wind. There was a small shed at the far end of the garden that had remained intact, although a piece of the roofing felt had come loose on one side and was flapping fiercely, like a fish trying to escape capture.

'I'd do not want to go back today,' Giuseppe said, as if finally coming to a decision.

'To the lodgings?'

'*Si.*'

'I'm happy to go. I could make sure Mrs Warrington is alright.'

'You have work to do.'

'Well, that would be work. Although I promise to go easy.'

'No interrogation?'

'Definitely no interrogation.'

Giuseppe turned to face Christina, the beginning of a smile around the edges of his mouth.

'We will speak later then,' he said. 'And now your kettle is whistling, so it must be time for your cup of tea.'

CHAPTER 6

An hour or so later, Christina knocked on the front door of Claremont Lodge, wondering if it was still too early. But, scarcely a few minutes after Christina knocked on the door, a young man opened it. He was wearing shorts and a grubby white tee-shirt.

'Yes?'

'Hello. You must be Daniel Forrest.'

'People call me Danny and if you're hoping to speak to Mr Swain, you can't.'

He paused as though he was going to continue, but thought better of it.

'I know. Sorry, I should introduce myself. Christina Rossi.' She held her hand out and he seemed confused as to whether he should shake it. 'I'm a reporter with the *Eastbourne Herald.*' She went to fish her press pass from her pocket. 'Do you mind if I step inside? I'm getting kind of soaked standing here.'

He stood back, holding the door wide open, allowing her to step into the hallway, as a spray of rain blew in, making him stand even further back.

'What a storm,' he said. He spoke with enthusiasm, reminding Christina of her nephew, despite the difference in age, which must have been fifteen years, maybe less.

Danny's tee-shirt hung off his slight, bony frame, giving his body a forlorn look, while his expression was one of eagerness. She could smell the Brylcreem that he had applied liberally to his hair.

'I'm not really here in my capacity as a journalist, more a concerned neighbour.' She paused, waiting for him to respond before realising she hadn't asked a question. 'My uncle was here last night. He and Mr Swain, they were friends and he came to see if he could help. But by the time he arrived, well, it was too late.'

'It's a real mess, that's for sure.' Hearing Danny's strong Sussex accent made her wonder briefly if he came from a family of farmers, or fishermen. He was certainly local, which made her question why he was staying in lodgings.

'You'll need help with the clear up. But I guess you'll want to wait until the storm's over. Or at least until the wind and rain have eased. I could ask around, get a few sturdy pairs of hands. Once the timbers have dried out you could have a bonfire.' She realised she was waffling, focusing on the least important part of the night's events.

'That's not the mess I mean.' Daniel's forehead creased into a frown, making him look even more vulnerable. 'Mr Swain was our landlord. Now he's gone, what happens to us? Are we allowed to stay here, or what? 'Cos I really need to stay, at least for a while. I've only just got this job and if I mess them about, I'll like as not lose it.'

'What is it you do?'

'I sell typewriters. Well, that's the plan. I get paid commission, the more I sell, the more I make.' His enthusiasm was returning as he spoke of his work. 'Ask me anything you like about the latest Olivetti models and you'll not catch me out. I've done all the reading. Go on, ask me a question.'

There was something surreal about the exchange. Just hours ago a man had died and yet his young lodger wanted to talk about typewriters.

'You weren't here last night?'

'No.'

'You must have had a shock when you got back.'

'Yep.'

Now Danny was no longer the chatty salesman. He had closed down, become guarded.

'And Mrs Warrington? I expect she's still sleeping?'

'I guess so.'

'You haven't seen her since you got back?'

'No.'

There was little more that Christina could do or say. It was doubtful she would get anything from Danny that would help to flesh out her press article. She needed to find an angle for the story that made no mention of Giuseppe. He would be furious with her if his name appeared in print. He'd never said as much, but she could tell he was grateful that the article she had written up after their investigation into the death of George Leigh made no mention of Giuseppe Bianchi.

'Do you want to see it?' Danny interrupted her thoughts.

'Sorry?'

'The summer house. At least what's left of it.'

Danny didn't wait for her response, but proceeded down the hallway, leaving her to follow. Watching him walking ahead of her she found herself studying his gait. It wasn't a limp, but there was an unevenness in his step, as though one leg was slightly longer than the other.

Still looking down, strangely intrigued by Danny's way of walking, she noticed the tattered edges of the carpet that ran centrally along the hallway. The carpet itself was so worn it was difficult to guess what colour it might have been when it was first laid. There was a staleness to the air, clumps of dust sat beside the skirting, the paintwork yellowed and cracked.

The hallway led into a small breakfast room and then onto a large kitchen. The breakfast room appeared to be doubling up as another kitchen, with a small sink in the corner and a countertop two-ring burner on the sideboard. It was the type of cooker she imagined people used when they went camping. Not that she or her family had ever been camping. The requirements of café customers - day in, day out - ensured there was no time for family holidays. At least that's what she and Flavia had been told as soon as they were old enough to ask the question. Flavia was the first to ask it, but then Flavia was the first to do most things.

'Why can't we just close the café? Can't people make their own breakfasts? We have to.' Flavia's relentless questioning of all the rules and routines that governed the Rossi family's life usually went unanswered.

It was true enough that the girls had learned to fend for themselves by the time they were six or seven; tall enough to reach the tap to fill the kettle and steady enough to clamber onto a chair to pull the box of cornflakes from the shelf. Anne walked the girls to school, but before that there were constant distractions. A delivery of cake-making ingredients, the butcher arriving with bacon and sausages. Weekly visits from local traders inevitably meant Anne ended up chatting with them. *Has little Johnny recovered from his whooping cough? Was Maisie settling into her first term in the infants?* While their mother concerned herself with the details of other people's lives, Christina and Flavia would have polished off their cornflakes, tossed their empty dishes into the sink and trotted upstairs to brush their teeth. No reminder needed.

Temporarily distracted with thoughts of her sister, Christina hadn't realised they had moved through to the kitchen. She guessed the musty smell that had followed her since she first walked into the lodging house was coming from the damp patches of plasterwork around the back door and on the chimney breast. In the grate was a large plant pot, the leafy plant it was housing looking as though it was on its last legs, the yellowed leaves drooping and brown at the edges.

Danny pushed open the back door, lingering just inside the kitchen.

'I reckon you'll not want to get too close. Anyway, it's still raining,' he said. 'But you can see well enough from here. Must have been a hell of a wind to bring that tree down.'

Christina looked out across the garden at the pile of timbers and the fallen tree and found herself imagining the horror of it. What must it have been like in those last few seconds, as Edward Swain watched the tree falling towards him, knowing there was no escape. What thoughts flashed through his mind? She gave an involuntary shiver.

'Poor man,' she said, as much to herself as to Danny.

'Pretty stupid to go out there, wasn't he?' Danny's nonchalant tone took her aback. He was younger than Christina, yet he seemed to have the hardened attitude to death one might encounter in a man twice his age; someone who had fought in the war, perhaps. Someone who had seen people blown apart; tragic events her dad must have experienced yet never talked about.

'And you say you weren't here last night?' Christina asked.

'That's right.'

'Like I said, I'm sure there will be plenty of offers of help to get it all cleared up. People are pretty good like that around here, we're all happy to help each other. You've just moved to the town, have you?'

'What kind of reporter are you?'

'How do you mean? I work for the *Eastbourne Herald*, so I cover local news. Bexhill isn't really my patch, but a story like this…'

'A death?'

'The storm generally. There'll be all kinds of damage, but hopefully no other fatalities.'

'Well, you've seen it now. So won't you want to take a photo or something? Reporters usually have photographers with them, don't they?'

'On the nationals maybe.'

Danny's whole demeanour reminded her again of Stevie. It was as if the night's events were nothing more than a *Boys' Own* adventure.

'I'd better go,' she said. 'But thanks for your time. I'll maybe catch Mrs Warrington next time.'

Christina felt an inexplicable sense of relief when she stepped out onto the front doorstep. Nothing about her visit to Claremont Lodge was what she'd expected. Although in truth she hadn't known what to expect. Nevertheless, there was something unsettling about her encounter with Danny Forrest.

CHAPTER 7

Before Christina could return to Claremont Lodge to meet Lorna Warrington, there was reporting work to do, getting in touch with local contacts, gaining more information about the night's events. Parts of Eastbourne had lost power when a telegraph pole came down, crashing onto a butcher's van and almost squashing it flat. Most of the beach huts along the whole length of seafront, from Eastbourne through to Hastings Old Town, had been wrecked in one way or another. At best, roofing had become loose or ripped off altogether, doors swinging off their hinges. At worst, the whole beach hut had collapsed, or been thrown in the air, or tossed towards the waves.

All across the town people were busy mopping up water. Furniture and furnishings were ruined from water pouring in through gaps in roofs where one or more roof tiles had flown off. In the short term, Taylor's Hardware store would benefit from a frantic trade in buckets, and later all the small local builders would have plenty of work to see them through to Christmas and beyond.

Christina had enough stories to fill a double-page spread. Some of the older locals she chatted to chose to recount their memories of storms gone by.

'You won't remember the great storm of 1953,' one chap told her. 'More than three hundred people died.'

Christina did a quick mental calculation. She would have been twelve, but try as she might, she couldn't recall the news reports from back then. No surprise, she told herself, because at twelve years old she was more interested in her mum's promise that as soon as sweets came off rationing Christina and Flavia could spend all their pocket money on sherbet dabs and liquorice.

'All those people died round here?' Christina had her pencil and notebook ready, taking shelter in the front lobby of the man's house.

'Oh no, luvvy, not here. Came down from the north it did. I was living in Skegness at the time. Course it's flat there, isn't it? Nothing to stop the sea flooding in. And that's just what it did. One old couple were going to be swept clean away from their home and some brave policeman saved them. Got a George Medal for his trouble and quite right too, in my opinion.'

She thanked him, made her way down the path, through the gate and up the path leading to his neighbour. After several conversations with people who seemed more interested in speaking about the past than the present, she decided to call back into the café to see how Giuseppe was faring, only to discover he'd gone to lie down.

'He had no sleep at all last night, poor man,' Anne said. 'Leave him a while, I'm sure he'll emerge when he's ready.'

Christina pocketed a couple of digestive biscuits, downed half a glass of milk and headed back out into the weather. This time when she knocked on the front door of Claremont Lodge, a woman answered.

'Mrs Warrington?'

At first glance Lorna Warrington was a contradiction. Her face was young, at a guess around Christina's age. But her floral dress and hairstyle was that of a middle-aged woman. Her hair was crimped in waves, looking as though she had only just removed a set of curlers. A generous description of her figure would be to describe her as buxom. The flowery design of her Crimplene dress reminded Christina of curtain fabric. The fact that she wasn't much more than five foot tall didn't help, giving her the impression of being slightly top heavy. Christina looked down at Lorna's feet, noticing she was wearing the same pattern and style of slippers that Anne wore. Pink quilted uppers with a flat rubber sole.

'Can I help you?' Lorna said, looking Christina up and down.

'Christina Rossi. My family has Bella Café, around the corner. My uncle was here last night when Mr Swain…'

'Oh.' She made no attempt to invite Christina in out of the rain, which although lighter now was still steady.

The rain mac that Christina had worn all morning was proving more than adequate at keeping her dry, except for one area near the top of the zip fastener. The rain had begun to creep in during the walk from the café to the lodgings and, although it was only a few minutes' walk, Christina's blouse was feeling distinctly damp.

'Do you mind if I step inside? It's still raining heavily.' It might be stating the obvious, but if it had the desired effect, she was past caring.

Lorna stepped back and opened the door wide, just as Danny had done earlier in the day. But while Danny had been like an enthusiastic terrier, keen to explore all possibilities, Lorna was more like a cautious Collie, watchful, prepared to react given the need.

And then, no sooner had Christina begun to form one opinion of Lorna Warrington, than that opinion had to be turned on its head.

'What am I thinking,' Lorna said, her face broadening into a smile. 'You must think me very rude. I must still be in shock. Come on in and I'll make us both a drink. It'll be good to have someone to talk to.'

Christina followed Lorna through to the kitchen, where just a few hours earlier she had stood with Danny and peered out onto the site of Mr Swain's death.

'I'll put the kettle on, then we can go through to the sitting room,' Lorna said. 'I don't like being in here to be honest with you. I keep trying not to look outside, but I find I can't help myself. My eyes keep being drawn to it.'

Lorna had a way of speaking that reminded Christina of a friend at school, who had a slight lisp, which Christina found endearing - Philippa Bartlett her name was. Philippa's parents had insisted she take elocution lessons so she could speak 'correctly'. She'd had weekly lessons for a year, at the end of which she no longer had the lisp, but it was as if all her charm had vanished alongside it. After leaving school they'd lost touch. Now and then Christina wondered how her friend had fared and what difference those elocution lessons had made to her life.

'Why don't you go and sit down and I'll bring through a tray,' Lorna said. 'Second door on the left down the hall.'

Having found the sitting room, Christina wasn't sure whether to sit. It was as if she was waiting for Mr Swain to give her permission. After all, this was his house.

The damp chill in the room made her wonder how long ago there had been a fire in the grate. The embers suggested it had been used at some point (unlike the fire in the kitchen). An empty coal scuttle stood to one side of the hearth.

She crossed to the bay window, feeling the draught blowing through the poorly fitting sashes, and stared out onto the front garden, a small patch of lawn, with overgrown hydrangea bushes covering most of the grass. Several pieces of litter were scattered over the grass, with more tangled up in the bushes. She hadn't noticed the shrubs when she'd arrived at the lodgings earlier, but then she was hardly taking in her surroundings, being more intent on avoiding the rain dripping down inside her mac.

She'd never really spoken to Edward Swain, other than to offer a simple greeting when he was in the café. But she'd noticed that he was always smartly dressed; shirt, tie, jacket, a sharp crease down his gabardine trousers. It was hard to reconcile that neat and tidy man with the dishevelled garden. Then she remembered the storm. The wind had blown in the rubbish, up and over the small front wall, and Edward Swain was no longer able to do a single thing about it.

'There you are,' Lorna set a tray down on the coffee table. 'I'll pour, shall I? You can sit down you know.'

Christina hesitated, waiting to see which seat Lorna would choose. The furniture was spread out around the edges of the room - two three-seater settees, a cavernous armchair, a sideboard and glass cabinet - with a faded Persian rug in the centre. Wherever Christina chose to sit, she felt as though she would need to raise her voice to be heard across the room.

'Milk? Sugar?' Lorna said.

'Milk, thanks. No sugar.'

Christina took the cup and saucer, balancing it on her lap for a moment until Lorna slid over the smallest from a nest of tables.

'I haven't put any biscuits out. I'm sure there are some, but I didn't like to go through the cupboards. We usually keep to our own food you see.'

'You and Daniel?'

'Danny. He likes to be called Danny.'

For a moment Christina felt as though she was being reprimanded.

'I met Danny this morning. I bet you wish he'd been here last night. It might have helped. Having another pair of hands, I mean.'

Lorna narrowed her eyes in such a way to suggest she hadn't quite got Christina's meaning. Then she shook her head. 'I'm pretty sure he wouldn't have been much help.'

'Of course. I suppose there was nothing anyone could do. Giuseppe said that by the time he arrived, it was too late.'

'Giuseppe?'

'My uncle. You met him last night.'

'I didn't know his name. At least, he might have told me. It's all a bit of a blur, to be honest. A name like that. He must be Italian.'

'Yes. He's my dad's cousin. My dad is Italian too.'

'I'm hoping to be there soon.'

'Italy?'

'Yes.' Lorna sipped her tea in such a precise, well-mannered way, again making Christina imagine someone much older than the young woman who sat in front of her.

'Are you planning a holiday?'

'No, nothing like that. I'll be working as a nanny, in a family.'

'And you're off soon, are you?'

'I'm just waiting for my start date. My stay here, well, it's just a sort of stopgap.'

The conversation was drifting and Christina had to keep reminding herself that just hours ago a man had lost his life, yards from where she was sitting. She took a moment to glance around the room, while struggling to determine how best to change the subject. The decor of the room could best be described as sombre. Dark brown wood pannelling around the lower half of the walls, and above the dado rail a Regency striped wallpaper. A large, framed painting hung over the fireplace, not an artist

Christina recognised. But then she knew next to nothing about art. A display of china dogs covered most of the mantelpiece, making Christina wonder if Edward had ever been married. Somehow a collection of china dogs seemed more like a woman's choice of ornament.

'I suppose we'll have to look after things for now. Until someone tells us we've got to move out.' Lorna said.

'I really don't know what the protocol is. I suppose the authorities will try to find Mr Swain's next of kin and then decisions will need to be made.'

'Danny might know.'

'Why would Danny know?'

'When I heard them talking yesterday, it sounded as if it wasn't just a conversation between landlord and lodger, if you get my drift.' Lorna dropped her voice to a whisper as if sharing a secret. But with the distance between them Christina wasn't sure if she had heard correctly. She watched Lorna lift the teapot as if she was about to refill their cups.

'Not for me, thanks,' Christina said.

Lorna poured herself another cup of tea, then set the china teapot down on the tray and stood, walking across the room and perching on the end of the sofa beside Christina.

'They had the most almighty row,' Lorna said, her voice still very quiet, but her words crisp and definite, as if she was giving a news report.

'Danny and Mr Swain?'

Lorna nodded, her eyes narrowing again, as if she was struggling to decide how much to divulge.

'It was late afternoon. I'd decided to have a bath. There's just the one bathroom, so we usually check with one another before running the hot water. I'd been in my bedroom, painting my nails.' She paused, looking down at her fingernails, as if reminding herself of the colour varnish she had chosen. 'It was around six o'clock. Mr Swain usually has the wireless on about then, down here in the sitting room.' She nodded towards the wireless that rested in the centre of the sideboard. 'He listens to a lot of classical music. I can't say I'm much for that myself. Most of the time it sounds like whining. Especially violins. I can't bear them.' She stopped speaking for a moment, giving a little shiver. Then she continued. 'Danny said he'd be going out to meet some friends. He's out a lot of the time, so that was nothing unusual. But when I went out onto the landing, I heard loud voices.'

She stopped speaking again. This time she stood and retrieved her cup and saucer, which she had left on the tray, bringing it with her as she sat beside Christina once more.

'Both of them were shouting, almost as if they were trying to outdo each other. And neither one was waiting for the other one to finish a sentence, before launching into another tirade.'

'What was the argument about?'

'I haven't got a clue. It was such a jumble of words, with them talking over each other like that. Besides, I didn't want to get involved. So, I went back into my bedroom, closed the door tight and put my wireless on. I never did get my bath.'

Lorna brought the cup to her lips as if signalling that was the end of the conversation.

'Danny seemed a pretty amendable chap when I met him this morning,' Christina said. 'I wonder what the argument was all about?'

'I really can't say.'

CHAPTER 8

By the time Christina returned to the café late that afternoon, Giuseppe had dozed for a while before freshening up in the bathroom, then changing his clothes. It was as if by putting on a fresh shirt, jumper and trousers he was also taking on a new mental attitude.

Anne had just turned the sign to *Closed* and headed upstairs to see to Stevie. She'd taken Max on her walk to the school to collect her grandson and now the Beagle was settled on his favourite bed in the back kitchen. With the café to himself Giuseppe fixed a fresh percolator of coffee and settled at one of the corner tables.

His friend was dead. There was no point in thinking any more about it. And yet it was all he could think about. The anger he had felt earlier had settled into irritation. He was a retired detective, and yet he had failed in the most basic aspect of information gathering. In all the time he'd spent with Edward he knew so little about him. Yes, he knew about his school geography master, the conversations that young schoolboy Edward had had about bees and the weather. They had discussed Edward's musical likes and dislikes.

'I suppose they call it *pop* because they have decided it's popular,' Edward had said to Giuseppe on one of their walks.

'Well, it is popular. Across the world, or at least America and Britain. Young people can't get enough of it. Screaming and shouting at young boys in tight trousers, with their strange hairstyles.'

'It was all ragtime and jazz when I was a lad. That was popular alright, but we didn't choose to call it *pop*.'

'I do not know ragtime. Jazz, yes, of course. But for me, it was always opera. You have heard of Caruso, of course. And what about one of our greatest tenors, Beniamino Gigli. Sadly dead now, but what a voice he had.'

All conversations that were pleasant, but none that helped him to grasp enough about Edward Swain to understand the meaning of those last words. Who was Josephine? And what was Edward blaming himself for?

Giuseppe was grateful to see Christina come through the door into the café at that moment.

'What a day,' Christina said, flopping down onto one of the chairs. 'Dad not around?'

Giuseppe shrugged. He hadn't seen his cousin at all that afternoon.

'You have been to the office?'

'I typed up the main article, left it with Charles to tinker with. He's bound to tinker. I think he does it to remind me who's in charge.'

'You spoke to people about the storm?'

'Most people were too busy to talk, to be honest. Not that I can blame them. There's so much clearing to do and there's little sign of the rain letting up. Those who wanted to chat seemed more interested in telling me about storms far worse than this one, saying we should think ourselves lucky.'

'Edward is not lucky.'

'God, no. Sorry.' She lifted one of the plastic covers from a plate of fairy cakes and put a couple onto a paper serviette. 'I'm starving. I've not really eaten all day. Do you want one?'

Giuseppe shook his head. 'A cake is not a meal. Your *mamma* is making us lasagne tonight. I think she is hoping to cheer me up.'

'Poor you. You must be feeling pretty rotten. Did you manage to sleep at all?'

'A little. Tell me about your visit to Claremont Lodge. You have spoken to the guests?' Giuseppe was ready to gather information.

'They're both a bit odd in my opinion. No, that's not right, I'm not being fair. I don't know what I think about them.'

Giuseppe couldn't get a tune out of his head. It was one of his favourites. *La Donna e Mobile*, from Verdi's *Rigoletto*. He'd enjoyed many versions of it over the years, but Caruso's rendition was one of his favourites. He started tapping out the rhythm on the edge of the table and then humming it quietly. He found himself thinking that he would hum it to Edward the next time he saw him.

'You're not okay, are you? It's not surprising. Look, why don't we watch television for a while until supper's ready. We might get to see a news bulletin, see what's happening in other parts of the country. If we're lucky, we might even get a weather forecast with an idea of how long this blessed storm is going to be with us.'

There was to be no escaping memories associated with Edward. The all-important shipping forecast that Edward had introduced him to had warned of the storm, but no-one could foresee its tragic results.

'I'd like to hear about Edward's guests. Was *Signora* Warrington still very distressed?'

'Come into the back kitchen. It's so gloomy in here, looking out at all that grey sea. I'll see if I can't find us some little savoury snack to keep us going. How about Twiglets?'

Giuseppe followed her into the back kitchen and as Christina opened cupboards and rifled through storage canisters and tins, Max's interest was piqued sufficiently to encourage him to get off his bed and sniff at imaginary crumbs on the floor. She buttered some cream crackers, and put them onto a plate, pushing them towards Giuseppe. He picked one up and nibbled gingerly at the edges.

'I will have one without butter,' he said, putting down the half-eaten one and taking a fresh one from the tin.

'I met Danny Forrest this morning,' Christina said. 'Nice lad, maybe twenty or twenty-one. But somehow he seems younger. He kept reminding me of Stevie.' She smiled and then continued. 'He wanted to show me the garden where it happened…' She paused, frowning, as if she had ventured into a subject area that was taboo.

'He wasn't at the lodgings yesterday evening.'

'No, that's right. He said he was out, but didn't really say where. Not that it's relevant, I suppose.'

'His presence would have made no difference.' Giuseppe was forming a picture of the young man, preparing a list of questions in his mind. 'And *Signora* Warrington?'

'She made us a pot of tea and we sat in the sitting room together. It was the weirdest thing, but I felt like I was trespassing. Did Mr Swain say much about his guests? Did he say how he knew them?'

'I don't think he did know them. I imagine they answered an advertisement for a vacancy. Isn't that how these things happen?'

'Yes. It's just that Lorna - Mrs Warrington - said she'd overheard Danny and Mr Swain having a dreadful argument.'

Giuseppe's forehead creased, as if he was concentrating, and once again he began tapping out a rhythm on the table.

'You do that when you want a cigarette, don't you?'

'I think you know your *zio* too well. There are times when I am certain that only a cigarette will resolve a problem I am wrestling with.'

'How long since you stopped smoking?'

'Would you like me to tell you in months, weeks, days or hours?'

'Or minutes?'

They both laughed. Giuseppe grateful for the distraction.

'Lorna said she didn't know what the argument was about. Just that there was one. What do you know about Mr Swain? How about his family? Someone will have to let them know what's happened to him. Who does that? Do you know?'

'I can tell you about Edward's likes when it comes to music. I can even tell you the name of his geography master at grammar school. But I know little else about him. I do not know if he is married, if he has children, what he did for a living before retiring. Nothing.' The irritation was still there. Giuseppe had been a detective for many years. He had developed an all-consuming interest in people, their past, their motivations. And yet, for all the hours he had spent in the company of Edward, the only knowledge he had of the man could be written on one small sheet of his pocketbook.

He'd closed his eyes as he was thinking, and when he opened them Christina was looking at him, as if waiting for a reply.

'You asked me a question?'

'I was just wondering how long Mr Swain has been there at Claremont Lodge. Maybe Dad will know?'

It wasn't until later, over supper, that Mario was around

to answer Christina's question. Anne laid the table in the upstairs dining room, a space that was more regularly used for paperwork and updating the accounts for the café. With the curtains closed and the paraffin stove offering a gentle if smoky warmth, the room took on a cosiness, enhanced by the warming smells coming from the oven. Since Giuseppe's arrival back in July, Anne had trialled a whole range of suppers to tempt him to try English food. Sausages were a definite no-no. 'Nothing like Italian sausages' was the pronouncement. She learned that anything with gravy would be rejected before it reached the plate, as were any of her previous 'easy' suppers, such as macaroni cheese, or fish fingers and chips. After worrying that Giuseppe wouldn't last long on biscuits, cakes and ice-cream, with the occasional plate of cheese and apple, she asked for his help.

'What you would make for your own supper, if you were back at home?' she suggested one day.

The ingredients were a problem, he explained. Fresh basil, good quality olive oil, *Parmigiano*, buffalo mozzarella and *pasta fresca*. The list went on. 'Even the water does not taste the same', he announced.

'I often cooked Italian meals for the family when we were first married. Mario would stand over me and tell me, *More olive oil*, or *Let it cook more slowly*.' Anne laughed. 'But then once we moved to England we lapsed into English ways. It was easier I suppose. But I'm sure I can remember it all well enough. And at the very least, it will be better than you starving yourself and wasting away.'

Giuseppe hovered beside her in the upstairs kitchen while she made the sugo for the lasagne.

'Mario is right. Slow cooking, that is the important thing. The flavours need time to blend together,' he told her.

This evening she had made the lasagne on her own and as she placed the dish in the centre of the table with a flourish, Giuseppe gave a small nod of his head, by way of appreciation. Anne's patience with his likes and dislikes didn't go unnoticed. He would buy her some flowers. A gift of flowers was something he could rely on to bring a smile to Rosalia's face in the early days of his marriage. He would stop at the flower stall on his way home from work. The flower seller was an artist, gathering the blooms together into a shaped bouquet, circling them with tissue paper, binding them together with matching coloured ribbon. Rosalia would take them from him, select the perfect vase, set it on the sideboard and stop to breathe in the scent every time she passed by. He had stayed on in Bexhill much longer than he had intended. But without Rosalia his flat in Rome could never be truly home. And each time he thought of returning the reason he had left re-imposed itself, like a vicious reminder, as if someone was waggling a stick at him, saying 'Oh, no you don't.'

And so, he had let the weeks and months drag on, becoming used to Christina's company, Anne's cosseting, young Stevie's excitable chatter, and Max's generous welcome whenever he stepped inside the back kitchen. It was only Mario who kept him at arm's length.

Muted conversation around the dinner table mingled with 'Pass the water,' or 'More cheese?'. Stevie's voice was missing this evening as he had gone to bed early. His school day had been more eventful than usual with children having to weave around the buckets strategically placed to catch the drips coming through the bare patches in the school's roof. It seemed that few buildings in the town had escaped damage of one sort or another.

'How did the meeting go with Councillor Rogers?' Anne asked Mario.

'It wasn't a meeting.'

'Well, your chat with him if that's how you want to describe it.' Anne continued eating, not raising her eyes to look at her husband.

'They won't know the extent of the damage across the town until the storm has passed. But there are bound to be cost implications.'

'And what does that mean?'

'The council will have to find the money to fix the school, the seafront shelters, and all the rest of it.'

'Well, at least they've got money. What about the families who have to do their own fixing?' Christina said.

'Insurance should pay out,' Mario said, in a matter-of-fact tone.

'What about if they can't afford insurance?'

'And if the person responsible for buying the insurance is dead. What then?' Giuseppe said, keeping his gaze on his plate.

'I'm sorry about your friend,' Mario said. 'It was a tragic accident, so unlucky. He was just in the wrong place at the wrong time.'

Tragic accident. The last time Giuseppe heard those words they were spoken by the coroner in Rome, pronouncing the verdict on the death of Carlo's grandson.

'Turns out Councillor Rogers knew Mr Swain,' Mario continued, instantly gaining the attention of everyone around the table.

'They were friends?' Giuseppe asked.

'No. At least I don't think so. I'm guessing it was more to do with business. Mr Swain would have had to get a licence from the council to operate his lodging house. I expect it was to do with that. From what Rogers said, it seems as though Swain had a bit of a disagreement with one of the councillors. Some argument over improvements that were needed.'

'I must admit the place did seem a bit run down,' Christina said, 'I was there today talking to Mr Swain's lodgers.'

'You talk of Edward having arguments with officials,' Giuseppe said, directing his comment at Mario. 'And you, Christina, tell me about an argument he had with one of his young lodgers. This Edward you speak of is not the same Edward I knew.'

'You hadn't known him that long though,' Anne said.

'We never truly understand a person, even when we have known them for years, for more than half a lifetime,' Mario said, holding Giuseppe's gaze.

'What does it matter, who argued or who didn't argue,' Christina said, dropping her knife and fork down noisily onto her plate, making everyone turn to look at her. 'The poor man is dead and all we can do now is to respect his memory and try to find out more about his life, his family, his friends…'

'You are right, Christina. Tomorrow I will visit Claremont Lodge.' Giuseppe pushed his plate away and stood. 'Thank you, Anne, for an excellent supper. Your lasagne was almost perfect, perhaps a touch more salt, but otherwise…'

'What about some fruit salad? I'll just clear the plates and bring it through,' Anne collected the empty dishes and Christina moved to help her.

'You do know that there's no crime this time, nothing for you to investigate, no questions to ask,' Mario said, holding Giuseppe's gaze. 'It's very sad, but that's all it is.

Mr Swain stepped out into the garden at the wrong moment, and that's it.'

'You are wrong, Mario. There are always questions to ask,' Giuseppe said, nodding to Christina and Anne before leaving the room.

CHAPTER 9

Bexhill-on-Sea was one of the more tranquil seaside resorts along the south coast. The neighbouring towns of Hastings and Eastbourne attracted throngs of holidaymakers during the season, but Bexhill was more usually favoured by older folk, who were looking for nothing more than a gentle stroll along the promenade, without the noise and clamour of amusement arcades or funfairs.

Bexhill had benefitted during the Victorian era of house building so that many streets were lined with grand three-storey properties with large rooms, high ceilings and bay windows. Claremont Lodge was one such property. Built at a time when it was usual for wealthy families to live in large houses. One family would occupy all three floors, perhaps with a live-in nanny, or governess who slept in the attic bedroom. Some may have had a housemaid to clean and cook, to lay fires in each of the fireplaces and tend to the family's needs.

But when Giuseppe knocked on the green painted front door of Claremont Lodge, he wasn't thinking of those wealthy families. He was grateful only that he had regained his focus. Edward's death had left him distracted by anger and frustration. Yes, there was sadness, but also irritation for other matters in his own life that were unresolved. It was as if the storm had stirred up the debris of his past, blown it into the air and left it to land all around him. On waking this morning, after a reasonable night's sleep, he went first to the window, pulling back the curtains to see that it was no longer raining. He could tell from the movement in the trees that the wind had eased a little. At least for now, the storm had passed.

Max was eager for his walk as soon as Giuseppe stepped into the back kitchen. But first the coffee percolator needed to work its magic, providing not just the taste but also the smell of his favourite drink. Having downed his espresso, he even managed the beginnings of a smile. Vermouth would rank highly in his list of preferred drinks, Italian wines too, but caffeine was his drug of choice, provided it was not of the instant variety.

When he and Edward had walked Max each morning over the past few weeks, they had taken the same route. Edward met him outside the café, then they would cross onto the seafront and head west to the far end of the promenade, then back on themselves to walk east as far as Galley Hill. The whole return journey was a little over four miles. It didn't matter how long it took, neither of them had critical tasks to return to, so when it took their fancy they had a short break, resting in one of the seafront shelters, or sitting on one of the benches, looking out to sea.

Now that Edward was no longer able to share the walk, Giuseppe couldn't decide whether to repeat the same route, or to change it completely. Whichever he chose felt wrong somehow. In the end he settled on a mix of the two. He went directly east from the café, forgoing the western part of the seafront entirely and heading up over Galley Hill and down the other side to Glyne Gap. Sandstone cliffs created a backdrop to the shingle beach, which had been shifted by the powerful waves, creating huge piles of pebbles that were uncomfortable to walk across. He released Max from his lead, watching him run in among the pebbles, sniffing at the various sea creatures that had been thrown up by the tide.

'*Basta.* Enough now, Max. We will go home.' Giuseppe

still stumbled over his use of the word 'home'. Bexhill was not his home, but right now, it felt as though Rome wasn't either. For a moment he wished Edward was beside him so that he could pose a question. 'What makes a place home?' He wouldn't have expected an answer, sometimes it helped just to ask the question.

A second espresso later, plus a change of trousers and shirt, and Giuseppe was ready to speak to Edward's lodgers, ready with questions he hoped would be answered.

'*Buongiorno.*' When Lorna Warrington opened the front door, Giuseppe's simple greeting said so much more than *Good morning.* He intended the inflexion in his tone to infer, *the last time we met the circumstances were quite different.* Whether Lorna picked up on his meaning was impossible to tell, as her expression was blank, almost as if she had no memory of having met Giuseppe, or of the dreadful circumstances of their previous encounter.

'May I come in?'

She had yet to speak and was holding the door partly open, as if undecided about whether to open it fully, or to close it without a response. Then she stood back and waved him in.

'Of course. Come through.'

She led him to the front sitting room and gestured for him to take a seat.

'Your niece visited yesterday. At least, she's your cousin's daughter, that's right, isn't it? She was very kind. There's such a lot to sort out, I'm honestly not sure where to start.'

He noticed her precise way of speaking, as if she was selecting each word, weighing it up just before saying it.

'I would like to help, if I can. Although I know very

little about *Signor* Swain.'

'You were friends, weren't you?'

'We liked to walk together.'

'Well, there's nothing I can tell you. I'm just his lodger.' She appeared to be momentarily flustered, then smoothed her hands down her skirt and took a breath. 'Although I won't be for much longer.'

'Christina tells me you are going to work in Italy.'

'That's right.'

'Do you know when you will start?'

'No, I'm waiting to hear from the family. Mr and Mrs Ingram, you might know them, you're from Rome, aren't you? Although I guess it's a pretty big place.' Her face broadened into a smile. 'Perhaps you can give me some tips.'

'Tips?'

'Places to visit, where to get the best ice-cream.'

'All of Rome is a place to visit, every street, every building. There is much beauty, much history. And for ice-cream, well, all Italian ice-cream is wonderful.' He gave a polite smile. Giving tourist advice was not what he had expected to be doing today.

'Well, I can't wait. The sooner I get a couple of thousand miles between me and this country, the better.'

'You do not like England?'

'I couldn't care less about England, it's the people I want to get away from.' She was speaking faster now, no longer placing her words in a careful sequence.

Giuseppe was silent, watching Lorna as she gazed down at her hands, which were resting neatly on her lap.

'Of course, not all people,' she said, looking up at him. She gave a little laugh. 'It's my husband I'm talking about. Actually, he's my ex. He decided to make a new life for himself with his floozy of a secretary, so I decided to make a new life for myself too. Two days after he walked out I threw every piece of clothing he owned out of the front window, then sat myself down and answered an advert in *The Lady* magazine.' She rubbed her hands together, as if remembering both events with some pleasure.

'And you moved here?'

'That's right.'

'Where were you living before?'

'You're asking an awful lot of questions. But, like I say, if it's Mr Swain you want to know about, well I really can't help you. You should ask Danny.'

'Ah, yes.'

Giuseppe eased himself out of the armchair, which seemed to have almost swallowed him up. The seat cushions were thick, but the webbing beneath the seat provided little or no support, allowing him to sink right down into it. He pushed himself up on the arms, which he noticed were also well worn.

'Is *Signor* Forrest at home this morning?' He stood beside the mantelpiece and picked up one of the china ornaments, studying it, then setting it down again with care. The dust that had collected around the ornament created a clear guide as to its position.

Lorna was still sitting and Giuseppe could sense she was watching him as he took a step towards the bay window.

'He's a typewriter salesman. Off out early this morning, I think. I didn't see him, but I heard the front door go.'

'*Signor* Forrest and *Signor* Swain. They knew each other?'

'You'll have to ask Danny about the ins and outs of it all.' She rose, moving to the door, as if she had decided the conversation was over.

'You told Christina you overhead an argument between

them?'

'That's right, I did.'

'And this led you to believe that they knew each other?'

'Unless it was because Danny hadn't paid his rent. Or maybe he kept his room in a mess, or pinched food from Edward's larder. How should I know? But, if you don't mind, I've got things to see to, so I'll show you out.'

She held the door open and waited. Giuseppe remained beside the bay window, facing the front garden, keeping his back to her.

'Do you mind if I go into the back garden before I leave?'

'Why would you want to do that? I can't bear to look at the place.'

Giuseppe sidled past Lorna into the hallway. 'You don't need to come. I remember the way.'

He walked slowly into the breakfast room, then through to the main kitchen. On his previous visit to the lodgings he had been running, unaware of his surroundings, anxious to reach the fallen building that he'd seen from Stevie's bedroom. This time he noticed the broken lino beneath his feet, the scuffed paintwork on the skirting boards and door frames, the greasy film coating on the kitchen cupboards and work surfaces. He was reminded once again of how little he knew about Edward. He had clearly allowed the lodging house to sink into disrepair. *Was it through disinterest or lack of money?*

Once out in the garden, he stepped carefully towards the pile of timbers and the fallen tree, keen not to disturb the scene. A moment later he realised what he was doing. He was treating the visit to the lodgings, to the garden, as he would when visiting the scene of a crime. But this event might be described in any insurance policy as 'an Act of

God'. Nevertheless, the challenge was there for Giuseppe to understand his friend's last moments. *What had prompted him to venture out into the garden that night? And what had led him to step into the summer house?*

'Looking for something, are you?'

Lorna had followed Giuseppe into the garden and was now standing behind him, her gaze following his gaze, like a novice following an expert tracker.

'It is best you do not come too close. There is glass from the broken windows.' As he spoke he realised how lucky he had been not to have cut himself when he knelt down beside Edward.

'It's a right mess,' Lorna said. 'Someone will have to clear it all up. God knows who though.'

'It is safer to leave it all for now.'

'Don't worry, I'm not planning to touch it.'

'Did you hear *Signor* Swain go out that night?'

'I didn't hear anything until you came banging on the door.'

'*Signor* Swain sleeps in the attic room, is that correct?'

Lorna nodded and turned to go back into the house.

'You'll want to get off now, I expect?' she said, throwing the question casually back to him.

A little while later Giuseppe had made his way back down Sea Road and crossed over to the promenade. The wind was building again, but the rain had passed northwards. It was too cold to sit, but a brisk walk towards Cooden, this time without Max and without Edward, would give him time to think.

CHAPTER 10

When Christina got into work the next morning she was greeted with a scribbled note from Charles.

Make sure you are here at 10am.

It was strategically placed on top of the pile of papers that permanently covered her desk. She shoved the pile to one side, and picked up the note, then put it down again. When she swivelled around in her chair, she was facing the door to Charles's office, which was closed. It was always closed. He would be leaning back in his chair, probably with his feet up on his desk. That was his usual pose; one she always thought looked so uncomfortable, and for a man of just five feet, five inches, not easy either. Her theory was he did it to make him appear relaxed, even though Charles was the least relaxed person she knew. Maybe it came with the territory; being a newspaper editor was synonymous with pressure - at least that's what he was always telling her. Pressure to get the story, to get it fast before some other paper beat him to it. A year or so after she got the job Charles revealed that he used to work on one of the dailies, but the Fleet Street pressure had left him with an ulcer.

She knew it wasn't the only thing it had left him with. Everyone knew he kept a half bottle of whisky in his left-hand desk drawer and that he spent most of his evenings in the Crown and Anchor *'gathering information'*. The surprise to Christina was that he could remember anything he'd been told after several pints of beer and a few whisky chasers. But despite the drink and his fractious manner, he was a good boss and an excellent editor. She'd learned a lot from him since she'd taken the job.

How she got the job in the first place still amazed her. She'd seen the advert for a 'junior reporter' and turned up impromptu at the newspaper offices, hoping she could make a better impression in person. Her tactic didn't quite work out. She saw one of the other reporters who told her that Mr Charles Ainsworth would be singularly unimpressed by anyone who tried to cut corners. Just as likely to be Charles's words, paraphrased. So she wrote a long letter by way of an application, and hand delivered it. On her second visit, Charles asked her into his office, took the letter from her hand, but never opened it. She didn't know to this day if he'd ever read it.

'Tell me about yourself then,' he said.

'My dad is Italian,' she blurted out, wanting to kick herself.

'And why does that matter to me?'

She knew what he wanted, but faced with his impatient expression, his constant fidgeting and the way he kept looking beyond her as though hoping that someone more interesting might come in to take her place, she couldn't think of what to say next.

'Lived here long, has he?'

Even now, when she thought about that interview, she was so grateful for his prompting. That one question helped her to launch into a relaxed explanation about her parents, how they had run their popular seafront café for years. She explained how growing up in a café meant she had developed a fascination about people's lives, how resilient people were when faced with difficulties.

'So you're interested in people?'

'The hardest thing is when we're not in control. And that means pretty much all the time, doesn't it? Take

77

housing as an example.' She was in a flow now. 'There are families living in damp, cramped basement flats that should have been condemned years ago.'

'Bit of a hobby horse of yours, is it?'

'I guess it is, yes. But jobs too, people who don't get paid a fair wage for the work they do, who work all hours and don't earn enough to feed their children.'

'Maybe you should think of running for the council, rather than applying to be a reporter?'

She paused, checking his expression. Was he laughing at her?

'Journalism gives the voiceless a voice,' she said.

'Read that somewhere, did you?'

Now she could see the beginnings of a smile around his mouth, making his angular features look much softer.

'And you type? Good speeds? What about shorthand?'

'I don't want to be a secretary, I want to be a reporter.' Once she said the words, she wished she hadn't. If either of her parents were here, they would tell her she was being cheeky. 'Um, yes. My speeds aren't bad, thirty words a minute on a good day. I've studied Pitman's, but never mastered it that well. But I can write really fast.'

He didn't even give her a test, or make her wait for his answer. He told her there and then that she had the job and she could start on the following Monday.

'But if your comment about fair wages for a fair day's work was a hint you expect to be paid more than the advert says, you'll be disappointed. And it's a three-month probation. Let's see what you're made of and we'll take it from there.'

Three years on and she'd managed to impress him, not that he would ever admit it. He'd taken on two other reporters since then - Trevor and Joan. They were as keen as she'd been, as she still was. But Christina had a sense that Charles could see a spark in her - or maybe in her articles - that he was happy to let flourish. So she continued to write in her own time, following her own passions. She'd fine-tune an article, drop it onto Charles's desk and now and then it would appear in the paper, with hardly a word changed.

So this morning his cryptic note, which sounded a bit like a summons, had her intrigued. Trevor and Joan were both out gathering more background on the storm damage, so she couldn't check with them. She didn't think she'd done anything that warranted a telling off, but then with Charles one could never be sure.

A little before ten o'clock the main door to the offices opened and in walked Danny Forrest, carrying a sizeable black case in one hand and a slim attaché case in the other. His suit jacket hung off his shoulders and was too long in the sleeves and he'd made a bit of a mess of tying his tie, catching one edge of his shirt collar so that it turned up instead of down. Once again he reminded her of Stevie.

'Mr Forrest,' she said, standing and extending her hand out to greet him.

It was impossible to read his expression. Perhaps he was surprised to see Christina so soon after having met her at Claremont Lodge. But it could just as easily have been a look of apprehension, for it was evident that he was here in the role of salesman. *Selling anything to Charles would have been a challenge for the most experienced, so good luck with that*, were Christina's thoughts, which may well have shown on her face as she smiled at Danny.

'I am here for a meeting with Mr Ainsworth,' he said, shifting his voice from its usual high pitch to something in a lower octave. *More professional, perhaps.*

'Of course. I'll let him know you're here.'

She left Daniel hovering beside her desk, noticing that he was studying the battered old typewriter that she had used since her first day. It was usually shoved to one side, only pulled towards her when she needed to bash out her copy.

A tap on Charles's door, a moment's wait for him to say 'Enter' before she pushed the door open, revealed her boss standing at the window with his back to her.

'Right mess out there, isn't it?' Charles said.

'The storm?'

'All the rubbish. I had to wade through it this morning on my way in.'

'It'll take a while to clean up, that's for sure. But Charles, there's a Mr Forrest here to see you.'

He muttered something under his breath and sat, pushing his chair away from his desk. 'You see him.'

'What?'

'I don't know why I agreed to see him. He caught me at a bad moment. He's selling typewriters. I ask you. Like he thinks we've got money to burn, forking out for some new-fangled thing when what we've got is perfectly fine.'

'He won't want to see me, he'll want to see the person in charge of the money. And that's you.'

'Yeah, well, I'm not interested. Tell him I've changed my mind, and close the door on your way out.'

Christina had held the door open during the brief conversation with her boss, meaning Danny Forrest would have heard it all. She turned now to see him tapping gently on some of the keys of her typewriter, pressing each one down and letting it go again.

'This is very old. I'm surprised you manage to get it to work at all. Let me explain.' Daniel beckoned to Christina.

'Stand just here and I'll show you. You see, your standard typewriter works like this, you might be whizzing along, tap, tap, tap, so fast the keys can barely keep up. Then one key gets stuck to another key and there is no more tapping, quite simply everything is jammed. But I am going to present you with something new and beautiful.'

He shifted Christina's pile of papers out of the way and set the large metal case down on her desk. Then he unzipped his attaché case and took out a glossy brochure, which he spread flat, pointing to a picture that covered the centre spread. 'Olivetti. Look at this - the newest model straight from the Italian factory - here - do you see? There's a small ball that rotates. We call it a golf ball. It's a shame your boss doesn't want to see it. Perhaps he plays golf?'

Danny had hardly drawn a breath. Now she was standing close to him she noticed how smooth his skin was, it looked as if it had never seen the edge of a razor.

'I don't think my boss is in the market for a new typewriter. And, no, I don't think he plays golf. Although I must admit, it's not something I've ever asked him.'

Danny started up again, his words had a rhythm not unlike the thundering repetition of the typewriter itself. There was too much at stake for Danny to stop now. Christina could guess what he was thinking. This could be his first sale, a chance for him to make his mark, prove that he was worthy of his job title. Typewriter salesman. If he didn't sell, then he couldn't call himself a salesman, could he?

'I'll just show you, shall I?' He didn't wait for an answer. He opened the metal case. 'They gave me this my first day in the job. *It's only on loan.* That's what Mr Whippet said. *Your responsibility. Lose it and you'll have to pay for the case and its contents. It'll come out of your earnings. And if you haven't earned anything, then you'll still have to pay.'*

Christina watched Danny running his fingers across the keys of the golf ball typewriter, and all she could think of was that Mr Whippet had presented Danny with a lose-lose situation. She almost felt guilty knowing that soon he would walk out of the newspaper office no closer to achieving a sale.

'Let's run it through its paces, shall we?' He shuffled through the papers on Christina's desk. Even the papers with no writing on were crumpled.

'Hang on a second, try this,' she pulled a ream of paper down from one of the nearby shelves, peeled back the outer wrapping and fished a sheet out.

He took it with care, feeding it into the typewriter roller, clicking the guard down to keep it in place, and then sat on Christina's chair, rolling it close into the desk. The way his hands hovered over the keys reminded her of a concert pianist preparing to perform the most important recital of his life.

'Danny.' She could wait a few more minutes to ask him the question that had been pinching at her ever since he walked into the office. She could let him show off the typewriter he was so proud of, maybe the typing skills that he was proud of too. Instead, she launched straight in. 'Lorna Warrington said that you and Mr Swain had an argument. The day he died, just hours earlier. How well did you know Mr Swain? Someone will need to track down his family, so anything you know about him is bound to be useful.'

Danny lifted his fingers from the keys. He hadn't typed a single word.

'You made out you wanted to help when you called into the lodgings the other day,' Danny said. 'But really you just wanted to stick your nose in, find out something that would make a good story.' Suddenly the young man brimming with enthusiasm and vitality had become someone else. His sharp angular features were now matched by his sharp tone, his eyes narrowing as he stood and glared at Christina. He ripped the empty sheet of paper from the machine, crumpling it and throwing into the wastepaper basket.

'Tell your boss he's missed a golden opportunity to be ahead of the game,' was Danny's closing remark as he clipped the case closed, the shiny new Olivetti golf ball typewriter inside.

Moments later Danny Forrest had left the building.

CHAPTER 11

Along the full stretch of the south coast of England there was clearing to do. Council workers were offered overtime when it became clear there weren't sufficient pairs of hands or hours of daylight to return each town to some kind of order. Men looking after the parks and gardens could forget grass cutting and weeding. It was tree surgery that was needed to bring down branches that were partly hanging, torn from the trunk and creating a danger for anyone walking nearby. Most of the roads close to the seafront had piles of shingle that needed to be swept away before cars could travel safely.

For the last couple of years Bexhill Council had been focused on clearing of a different kind. There were still areas of the town where properties that had suffered bomb damage during the war had yet to be demolished. These part-derelict buildings butted up against houses where damp seeped in through rotten window frames, with roofs that had been patched too many times. In nearby Hollington there had been talk of brand new high-rise buildings that would house hundreds of families. The word was that they'd done the same thing in Ramsgate, but that the Hollington flats would be bigger and better. Many of the families who had no money to keep the coal fires lit, to make the endless repairs that were needed to their homes, dreamed of the chance to move into one of the shiny new flats. But now the storm damage would cause further delay as builders were pulled away from preparing new properties to focus on repairing old ones.

At the end of Wycombe Avenue the scaffolding that had been put in place to complete a row of new council houses had partly collapsed. There would be an investigation into who was responsible, but for now the main concern was the grocer's smashed shop front where a six-foot scaffolding board had careered through the glass and landed on the counter.

Anyone who was strong and able was called on to help. Once they had repaired their own homes as best they could, there was plenty more work that was needed. Mario didn't need to be asked. Anne could manage the café on her own, especially as the only customers venturing in were looking for nothing more than a hot drink and a kind word to revive them, before ploughing on with the next task on the list.

'I will come with you,' Giuseppe said to his cousin, not waiting for a reply as he followed him outside.

'I'm not sure what you'll be able to do.'

'I will do what I can. The same as you.'

Mario nodded in the direction of the De La Warr Pavilion. 'There's bound to be plenty to sort out along the beach. Most of the beach huts won't have been able to withstand those winds.'

They crossed over onto the seafront and down some iron steps that led onto the beach. The tide was out, splintered pieces of timber and tattered pieces of roofing felt in amongst the shingle.

'Where should we put it?' Giuseppe asked, gathering up an armful of debris.

'Let's create piles, it'll make it easier for the council to gather it up and take it away. They'll be able to burn the wood, but the rest of it will just end up on the tip.'

They worked for a while in silence, occasionally looking along the beach at other groups of men who had already created several piles of wood, stacking the pieces up beside the sets of steps that led onto the promenade.

'Does it happen often?' Giuseppe said, stopping for a rest after helping Mario to heave a heavy piece of timber onto the top of a pile.

'Storm damage?'

'*Sì.*'

'Not like this, no. Thank goodness. But we've been lucky, it could have been much worse.'

'Edward was not lucky.'

'No, of course not. I didn't mean…' Mario stepped away to pick up a few pieces of wet cardboard that had landed in a rock pool and were now floating like miniature life rafts.

When he returned to where Giuseppe was standing, he said. 'You think you'll be able to help?'

'Edward?'

'His family?'

'I don't know if he has a family. I will speak again to his lodgers. There is a Daniel Forrest, it seems that he might know something. But I have yet to speak to him.'

'There will have to be a coroner's inquest, I expect. They'll want to determine exactly what killed him.'

'He was crushed. The building, the tree.'

'Yes, but they'll want to look at the circumstances, speak to the doctor who signed the death certificate. No doubt you'll be called as a witness. That's if you're still here.'

Before Giuseppe could pick Mario up on his pointed remark, he heard a shout.

'Mr Rossi.'

'Councillor Rogers.'

A thick set man approached, his hand raised in greeting.

'It's good of you both to be doing this. I'd have thought

it's work more suited to youngsters.'

'We are not old, *Signor* Rogers.' As if to prove the point, Giuseppe picked up a long piece of timber, balancing it on one hand before throwing it at the growing pile.

The councillor gave a hearty laugh. 'Well, don't overdo it. You'll be feeling it in the morning is my guess.'

He stood for a few minutes, watching the two men work and then, 'I'm pleased I've caught you, Mr Rossi. I wanted to let you know that the planning committee hasn't been able to approve the new playground. At least not on the site you mentioned before. Behind the War Memorial. There were a few objections, you see.'

Councillor Rogers seemed to be unaware of the glare Mario shot in his direction. And before any further discussion could take place, Giuseppe interrupted. '*Signor* Rogers. Perhaps you can help me with an enquiry.'

'I'd be happy to. Provided I know the answer that is.' He gave another hearty laugh. It seemed he enjoyed the idea of his own jokes.

'A man has to obtain a licence to run a lodging house, yes?'

'What's that?'

'Permission to have lodgers?'

'Well, yes. Planning to settle here then, are you? Your cousin said you were just here for a visit, but maybe Sussex has gotten a hold of you and won't let you go. Just like the Bermuda Triangle, eh?' That laugh again, which was already getting on Giuseppe's nerves.

'Mr Edward Swain. My cousin said he had dealings with the authorities?'

'Terrible business. They say it was his summer house that collapsed. It's a miracle we haven't had more tragedies. If the storm had been at its worst later in the morning when folk were heading off to work, well, I hate to think what might have happened.'

'Claremont Lodge. It is in need of repair.'

'That goes for more than half the buildings in the town. Places built years ago, well it's bound to happen. Then all the wartime bombing. Foundations shaken at the very least. Claremont Lodge, you say? That's Mr Swain's place?'

'*Si.*'

'I know the council has issued a few demolition orders, but it's not my department, so I don't know the ins and outs.'

'Who do I need to speak to?'

'What is it you want to know?'

While the councillor and Giuseppe continued their conversation Mario stood apart from them. He had stopped picking up the broken timbers, although there were still plenty of smaller pieces scattered across the shingle. He bent down to sift through some of the pebbles, picking up a couple of rusted nails.

'No one will be able to use this beach until it's been thoroughly checked for debris,' he said, directing his comment at the councillor.

This time it was for Giuseppe to laugh. 'It is October. And an English October. Why would anyone want to visit the beach?'

'Folk still walk their dogs, whatever the weather. Try telling Max he can't have his morning walk. I'm just saying that the council should rope off the steps, put notices up, otherwise the hospitals will be dealing with all sorts, the vets too.'

Councillor Rogers stepped away towards the promenade. 'Look, I'd better be going. I really came to check up on things, but then I spotted the two of you down here and thought I'd stop and say hello. To thank you for what you are doing. And if I can help out with whatever it is you need to know, just come and find me at the Town Hall,' he called out to Giuseppe.

The two cousins continued gathering and sorting through the debris, moving steadily from left to right between two of the groynes, scouring the ground for smaller pieces of timber, as well as other pieces of rubbish that had been blown along the shoreline. They had been working for more than an hour and Giuseppe was starting to feel a strain in his lower back. He stopped for a moment, kneading the tight muscle with the knuckles of one hand.

'What the devil was all that about?' Mario said, taking advantage of the pause. 'Those questions you were firing at Councillor Rogers. Why are you always looking for problems?'

'The problems look for me.'

'You need to remind yourself you're retired.'

'A detective is always a detective. I am no longer paid, but that does not mean I no longer think.'

Later, when Giuseppe had the chance to speak to Christina, he could flesh out his thoughts. For now they were just like a collection of small clouds hovering over him. Perhaps Christina would be the sunshine that would help to clear the haze, or perhaps the clouds would form into something much more definite. Something that would bring another storm to anyone caught beneath it.

CHAPTER 12

'I'm not sure Mr Swain would have been much affected by all the changes,' was Christina's response when Giuseppe explained his concerns. 'It's the B&Bs who are really struggling. Those in the seaside resorts anyhow.'

'B&Bs?'

'Sorry. Bed and breakfast places. Cheap holidays to Spain is what everyone wants nowadays. Suddenly flights are affordable and if you can have wall-to-wall sunshine for two weeks, sandy beaches and sangria, then you'd hardly choose a damp English beach with a tub of whelks and half a shandy. And for anyone who's not keen on flying, there are smart hotels springing up everywhere. Who's going to want a draughty guest house with a shared bathroom on the half-landing?'

They had the sitting room to themselves after supper. Mario was catching up with cleaning downstairs in the café and Anne was waiting for some gingerbread to finish baking.

'Whelks?' Giuseppe said, struggling to pronounce the word.

'It's a kind of shellfish. Disgusting in my opinion.'

'Ah. And you believe that English people do not want to have their holidays in England?'

'Not if they can have guaranteed sunshine somewhere else.'

'Nothing in life is guaranteed.'

'No, but there's more chance of a suntan if you spend the day lying on a beach in the Costa del Sol, than if you spend a week in Margate. It's not the same for you.'

'I have never laid on a beach for a week.'

'I mean for Italians. They're bound to want to holiday in their own country. I've never been there, but I can imagine it's too beautiful to want to go anywhere else. Plus your seasons are organised. Ours are a shambles.'

Christina had been applying nail varnish with absolute precision, and now she held her hands out to admire the finished result. 'Not bad, eh?'

'*Bella*. Very nice.' Giuseppe passed his judgement without even a glance. Instead, he appeared to be focused on the far corner of the sitting room, on a spot between the bookcase and the sideboard. Suddenly he rose and moved across the room, bending down to look more closely. 'A cobweb.' He waved his hand through the tangle of silky threads. 'Perhaps Edward was struggling.'

'Struggling? How?'

'The lodging house is dilapidated. Money needs to be spent on it. Maybe it was money he didn't have.'

'Well, he was getting money from his lodgers, wasn't he? Anyway, I don't think the council would have been bothered, if that's what you're thinking. They can't even sort out some of the council houses that should have been condemned long ago. Places riddled with damp, cockroaches, plumbing that doesn't work, electrics that are nothing but a fire hazard and old gas boilers that are death traps. I could go on, the list is endless.'

'They are building new homes.'

'Yes, but not quickly enough.'

'Write another article, create momentum for change.'

'I've already started one, although it's doubtful it'll ever get into print. It's probably too contentious,' Christina said, slipping the bottle of nail varnish into her make-up bag. 'Anyway, what do you think of that Danny Forrest?'

Earlier in the evening Christina had related the outcome

of her meeting with the typewriter salesman.

'I have yet to meet him.'

'But what do you think from what I've told you? It was weird. One minute he was brimming over with enthusiasm about this new-fangled typewriter mechanism, the next minute he packed up and headed out of the office. He didn't even say goodbye.'

'You asked him about his argument with Edward.'

'It might have been that. I don't know, to be honest. But whatever I said or didn't say must have put him off his sales pitch.'

'Let us call on *Signor* Forrest this evening.'

Giuseppe didn't wait for a response. He left the room, returning a few moments later with his overcoat folded over one arm. 'Are you joining me, or are you worried that your manicure will be spoilt?'

Twenty minutes later Giuseppe and Christina knocked on the door of Claremont Lodge. Lorna Warrington answered the door.

'Come mob handed this time?' she said, holding the door open and beckoning them in.

'We hope it's not too late to call,' Christina said. 'We just thought this evening would be a better time to catch Mr Forrest at home.'

'I was just going to make a hot drink. Can I get you anything?' She led them through to the main kitchen and slid a tray out from a gap between the cooker and one of the kitchen cupboards.

'Nothing for me, thank you, *Signora.*'

'I'm okay too, but thanks anyway,' Christina said. 'Would it be okay if I pop up and knock on Danny's door? If you could tell me which is his room?'

'I'll go.' Lorna turned the gas off under the kettle and

left the kitchen.

A few minutes later she returned.

'He's not in.'

'Did you see him come back from work?'

'I'm not his keeper. I have no idea about his comings and goings.' Her words were slow and precise, negating any irritation that might have otherwise been obvious.

'Perhaps we should go,' Christina said to Giuseppe, heading towards the hallway.

'No, don't go,' Lorna said. 'At least, if you've got the time and if you're interested in Danny, then I can tell you what I know about him.' Lorna looked from Christina to Giuseppe.

'We are not in a rush,' Giuseppe said. 'But we do not want to disturb your evening further.'

'Well, I'm hardly overrun with social engagements just at the moment.' She smiled and gestured to them to follow her through to the sitting room.

Giuseppe and Christina positioned themselves side by side on one of the settees and Lorna stood with her back to the fireplace. The coal fire was lit, the warmth not quite reaching the far side of the room, perhaps because Lorna was blocking the full force of the heat. Giuseppe shifted in his seat, easing forward to compensate for the feeling that he was sinking into a pit. He watched Lorna, who in turn was focused on them both, as if she was giving a speech to a captive audience.

'Danny hasn't been here at Claremont Lodge for that long,' Lorna explained. 'It was just a few days after Mr Swain advertised the room that he turned up with all his typewriter paraphernalia. The most unlikely salesman, if you ask me. But then what do I know. Anyway, the arrangement here is that we each prepare our own meals, buy our own food and, of course, tidy up when we're done. So, after a few evenings when I'd been faced with a sink full of dirty dishes, I thought I'd have words with Danny. Tell him that he wasn't being fair leaving me to clear up his mess.'

'You did not think to mention it to Mr Swain?'

She shook her head. 'I didn't want to bother him.'

'Young men often do not have experience of household chores,' Giuseppe said, causing Christina to take a sideways glance at him.

'I can't see why not. And if they don't, then they should.' Christina said, with emphasis.

'Well, I caught Danny one evening, just as he'd finished eating,' Lorna continued. 'He'd left his dirty plate and cutlery on the draining board and he hadn't even put water in the saucepan. If the food dries it's a devil of a job to scrub clean.'

'Was he annoyed with you?' Christina asked.

'No, not a bit of it. Well, maybe a little at first. But then we ended up doing the dishes together and we got chatting. He told me about his family. They live in Eastbourne. His mum and two brothers, I think. Apparently his dad was killed during the war.'

'Poor woman,' Christina said. 'Bringing up a load of kids on your own, with no help. I don't even have sole charge of Stevie, and he still takes up most of my energy.'

'You have a son?'

'No. He's my nephew. My sister's boy. I…' she paused, her face flushing. 'It's complicated.'

'None of my business.' Lorna waved a hand in front of her, as if to dismiss the subject. 'But from what I could gather from Danny there was someone who helped his mum out.'

'A man?' Giuseppe asked.

'I suppose.'

'*Signora* Warrington. Would you be able to look in *Signor* Forrest's room?'

Giuseppe couldn't read Lorna's expression. It might have been surprise, but equally it could have been she was intrigued by the reason behind his request.

'I don't think it's right for me to go poking around in someone's room. After all, I wouldn't want anyone doing that to me.'

'If you take me to his room, you can open the door and then leave me to go inside. Then you will have no responsibility for the intrusion, and *Signor* Forrest can only be annoyed with me. If he chooses to be annoyed.'

'Alright then,' Lorna said with an energy that suggested she was warming to the idea. 'It's this way.'

Led by Lorna, Christina followed Giuseppe up the two flights of stairs to the first floor landing. 'That's my room,' she pointed to the first door they passed. 'That's the bathroom, and that room's empty.' They were at the far end of the landing now. 'And this is Danny's room.' She stood back, leaving Giuseppe to step in front of her. Christina stood to one side.

Giuseppe knocked firmly on the door, at the same time calling out, '*Signor* Forrest. Mr Daniel Forrest. May I come in?'

The three of them waited in silence. There was no response. Giuseppe turned the doorknob slowly and pushed open the door. As he did so, Christina and Lorna peered over his shoulder to look into the room, which was in darkness.

'The light switch is just to the left,' Lorna said. 'At least it is in my room.'

The single bulb that swung from the ceiling cast little light into the corners of the room, but there was a small lamp with a pink tasselled shade on the bedside table, and when Giuseppe switched it on, some of the shadows disappeared. To onlookers it might have appeared that he was making a cursory glance around the room. In truth, his years as a detective had taught him how to absorb every detail when examining a setting, details that might become relevant during the investigation of a case. Without turning to look at Christina, he guessed what she would be thinking. This is not a case. The time to discuss the ins and outs of his thought processes would come later. For now he noticed the dishevelled bed, both blankets tossed back, their edges touching the floor. The single pillow had been folded in two, probably in an attempt to gain more comfort from something that was old and worn.

The bedside table was empty, except for the lamp. At the foot of the bed was a wooden chest. Giuseppe lifted the lid to reveal a couple of blankets and what looked like a pair of old curtains. Danny's bedroom was at the front of the house, benefitting from a deep bay window. When the curtains were pulled back, there was a clear view of the seafront, the street lights shining brightly into the room. To the left of the bay window was a tall double-fronted wardrobe, the dark wood reminding Giuseppe of a wardrobe of his own back in Rome. When he and Rosalia had furnished their flat, she convinced him to choose mahogany furniture '*in the English style*'. He recalled her vivacious laugh when the wardrobe arrived, when the men who struggled to carry it up the stairs into their flat nearly had a heart attack from the effort required. The irony of it was that the wardrobe had been crafted by an Italian cabinet maker. There was nothing English about it, or about the matching chest of drawers that arrived at the same time.

As Giuseppe pulled open one of the wardrobe doors, it stuck on the bottom edge. He tugged at it. A single pair of trousers hung from a wooden coat hanger, one of the legs patched in two places. Poorly patched, with material of a different shade of grey. On the floor of the wardrobe lay a striped woollen scarf and a soiled handkerchief. Giuseppe's interest was piqued. He slid open each drawer of the tallboy, five narrow drawers with brass handles. Each drawer was empty.

'It would seem *Signor* Forrest has moved on.' He said, turning to face Lorna.

'Just like that? Running off without a word. Looks like he must be feeling guilty about something.'

Christina had been standing in the doorway, but now Giuseppe beckoned to her to come into the room. She looked into each of the drawers, dust and fluff was all that collected in the corners.

'I suppose he thought he'd have to leave now that Mr Swain is…' Christina paused, looking at Giuseppe for confirmation that she was thinking what he was thinking.

'Thank you for your time, *Signora* Warrington. We will leave you in peace now. Come Christina, we should go.'

A while later they were back in their own sitting room, Christina cradling a mug of warm milk, and Giuseppe savouring a glass of vermouth.

'You have a theory, don't you?' Christina said.

'*Sì*. But it is only a theory.'

'Will you share it with me?'

'*Signor* Forrest is angry with *Signor* Swain. I ask myself why. Then I discover his mother has had a difficult life since her husband died. A man provided her with some help. Perhaps this man was Edward. Christina, moments before Edward died he said something. It was hard to understand, his voice was weak, the storm was loud.'

'What did he say? At least what do you think he said?'

'I have been replaying it over and over. First there was a woman's name - *Josephine*. And then, *It was my fault*. But now, when I hear the words in my head again I am starting to have some doubts. It could also have been *It was not my fault*. I cannot be certain. So now I am thinking, if Josephine is *Signor* Forrest's mother and Edward walked away from the Forrest family, leaving them to struggle, then, of course, Daniel will be angry. He gets a job, perhaps hoping to send money to his family. He takes a room in a lodging house and encounters the man who walked out on his mother. They have an argument and hours later Edward is dead. Daniel visits your office to sell his typewriters, but then, you question him about the argument. He becomes nervous and decides to run away. Perhaps he has returned to his family.'

While Giuseppe was speaking he tapped out a rhythm on the arm of his chair. When he stopped speaking he stopped tapping, as if he wasn't aware he was doing it.

'Okay, I can see what you're thinking,' Christina said. 'But there's one part of it I don't really get.'

'And that is?'

'What does any of it matter? So Edward and Danny had a row. I can't see how it's relevant. It's not as though the row ended up with Edward being punched, or worse. Danny wasn't even around the night of the storm. So he can't have had anything to do with Edward's death, can he?'

'Sometimes it is important to look in another direction. We think we know all there is to know about an event and then someone pulls the curtains and a light shines on a place where before there was only darkness.'

'Are you sure you don't just want this to be suspicious? You were a detective for a long time, Giuseppe. But you're retired now. And even though Edward was your friend, maybe this time you just have to accept there was no other reason for his death than that he was in the wrong place at the wrong time.'

'*Preciso*. Precisely.'

CHAPTER 13

Later that evening, Christina and Giuseppe sat through the evening television news in silence. It was as she stood to switch the television off that she spoke.

'You know that there's just a week to go before we need to vote.'

'Not for me. I have no vote in this country. I am not interested in politics, even in Italy.'

'You sound like Charles.'

'I hope not.'

'Everyone should be interested in politics. It affects everything we do. It's at the heart of all that is good and bad about the way we live. I'm joining a march tomorrow, why don't you come along.'

'A march, eh? I think you know I am not one for crowds. But you speak with great passion, Christina. Where does that passion come from? Your mother? Your father?'

'I doubt it. Mum and Dad won't even talk about the election, even though it's going to be one of the most important for years, I can just feel it.'

'All elections are important, but also not important. Life continues.'

'I know, but it's what kind of life that bothers me.'

She returned to the settee, tucking her legs up beneath her.

'Perhaps your parents are too busy to talk about politics. Your father worries about the café, and your mother... well, I think that over the last few weeks she has been the only one to take Stevie to school. In the summer you were taking him every morning.'

'You think I've been neglecting him?'

Giuseppe stood and faced Christina to add more weight to his words.

'Stevie knows he is loved. You have nothing to feel guilty about.'

'I'm really loving my work, even when I'm not in the office or on an assignment that Charles has given me, I'm thinking about the next article. Ideas just keep popping into my head. Look at these headlines.' She tossed the newspaper across to Giuseppe. 'There's the Labour chap, Mr Wilson, who appears to be promising all the things we so desperately need - better housing, better schools, more jobs, I could go on.'

'And the present Prime Minister?'

'Alec Douglas-Home. Well, he's saying pretty much the same thing. But it's results that count, isn't it? And look at that whole scandal over John Profumo. What does that say about the Tories?'

'I know nothing about your British politics, but I do know that there is a level of dishonesty in all political parties. If you study Italian politics, you will see I am right.'

'It seems to me that people stand for Parliament, but as soon as they get voted in it's as if they forget about the electorate altogether. They could be doing so much good once they get into power, but...'

'You have heard the phrase *power corrupts*. There was a reason that the Roman Empire fell in such a dramatic fashion. Corruption from the Emperor down.'

'Oh, I don't know what I believe anymore. Then you have someone like President Kennedy. It seemed as though he was going to do so many great things and then someone went and shot him. It'll be a year next month, you know. 22nd of November 1963, is a date that will go down in history, that's for sure. I wonder what future generations will say about it?'

'It was a terrible day for democracy.'

'Charles always says he doesn't want the paper to cover politics, but something like the election, well it's too big a story. It'll be all hands on deck to come up with a local angle.'

'And what angle will you take?'

'If it was down to me I'd highlight all the issues that need sorting out, support for families being made to move from their homes, improved rights for tenants instead of landlords, equal access to further education for youngsters from deprived backgrounds… I could go on.'

'Christina Rossi, the people's champion.' He pretended to clap his hands together. 'You are interested in all that you see around you. We are living in a time of great social change and you have a wonderful opportunity to report on every aspect of it.'

'Exactly. The power of the pen - or at least the typewriter. There's no way I'd want to go into politics, that's for sure. Politicians think only of their own advancement.'

'You believe any new Government will forget their promises?'

'You can be certain of it. Well, some of them anyway. But I have to remain hopeful, otherwise what's the point.'

'As a reporter you have a voice. One day I believe that your articles will be read by many people, perhaps thousands.'

'Yeah, in ten years' time maybe.'

'Do not hurry through your life. *Aver pazienza.* Have patience. You are lucky to be a position, to make your views known, but remember it is also a great responsibility.'

'You're right. It's not something I think about that often. I just write what I'm passionate about. Families stuck on a waiting list dreaming of a home that doesn't have water running down the walls, or war widows who walk around with newspaper stuffed in their shoes because they can't afford to get them repaired.'

'And when the election is decided some of these matters will be better and others will be worse. That is the way of it.'

'Well, it shouldn't be. Do you know, sometimes I'm tempted to sit outside the council offices with a big placard saying, *Step outside of your comfy office and step into the real world.*'

She jumped out of her seat and held her arms out, as if she was holding the placard, before noticing Giuseppe had his eyes closed.

'You're thinking again, aren't you?' she said.

He didn't reply for a few moments, and then he sat up straight in the armchair, as if he had made a decision.

'Your father takes a great interest in the local community. Perhaps he should consider becoming involved in local politics.'

'Dad, a local councillor?' She was about to laugh, but seeing Giuseppe's expression, she stopped. 'It's an idea, but I can't see him going for it. Besides, you said it yourself, he's always busy with the café. Anyway, enough of this talk of politics. Tell me again what else is bothering you about Mr Swain.'

'It is bothering me that he is dead.'

She sighed and sat down again, leaning forward towards Giuseppe. 'You are certain there is something suspicious about his death, aren't you?'

'*Sì.*'

'We need to find out more then, don't we? Lorna says Danny's family live in Eastbourne. Is it worth a visit to see if he's gone back there?'

'Eastbourne is a large town. We have nothing but a surname. No address. But enough now, it is late and we need to sleep. And tomorrow you are marching?'

'There should be quite a crowd, I'm not the only one who wants their voice to be heard.'

Giuseppe stood, stretching out his frame, as though the position he had been sitting in had made him uncomfortable.

'Giuseppe, before we head off to our beds, there's something else I want to ask you. Although it's not really a question, more an observation. Mr Swain's death. It's bad, of course it is. But I'm guessing it's particularly bad for you because it's reminding you of unfinished business in Rome? Am I right?'

He sat down again, heavily this time, as if he had just returned from a long journey and was desperate for rest.

'It is always there. The child's body, lying on the street. My neighbour's expression. The questions I could never ask.'

'Why don't you ask them?'

'What do you mean?'

'Are you still in touch with your team? The detectives who worked alongside you?'

'Silvio Bruni. He was my sergeant. A good man.'

'Write to him. Ask him to do some investigating. Until you try everything to get the answers you need you will never be free of it. It's like a sore place, that won't heal.'

Giuseppe had a faraway expression, as if he was turning the idea over in his mind.

'Okay, maybe not a letter,' Christina continued. 'That

would take too long. Why not telephone? At least it'll give you a chance to find out if anything has changed since you left.'

'Perhaps I will not be pleased to hear what Silvio has to tell me.'

'What is it you always say? *Un passo alla volta.* One step at a time.'

'Well, the steps I take now are only to my bedroom.'

'Thanks, Giuseppe.'

He paused at the door, sensing that she wanted to say more.

'Thanks for listening.'

'Buonanotte, Christina.'

Before Christina had a chance to make her own way to bed, the sitting room door opened again and Anne came in, followed by Max.

'You're still up,' Anne said.

'I've been talking politics with Giuseppe.'

'That must have been interesting. Budge over. You and I so rarely get the chance to chat nowadays. You can keep me company while I sew on these name tapes. It seems no time at all since we got Stevie's first pair of long trousers and he's already grown out of them.'

Christina shifted along the settee, but before Anne could sit, Max jumped into the space.

'Hey, this is supposed to be a mother-daughter chat. Now we've got a male infiltrator, which is just about typical.' Christina shoved Max along to the end of the settee, receiving a grumble from him in reply.

'Sorry, Mum.'

'What are you apologising for?'

'I've been letting work take over, haven't I? Giuseppe said as much. He also pointed out I've been leaving you to do the lion's share of caring for Stevie, which isn't fair.'

'I'm his grandmother, darling. I'm delighted to do whatever is needed. And Stevie is really no trouble.'

Anne paused and looked down at the sewing basket, which was resting on her lap.

'You miss Flavia, don't you, Mum?'

'I've got two daughters and I love you both equally. But Flavia, well she's always been so prickly. Like a hedgehog who is desperate to be loved, but who shoots out his spines if anyone comes close.' She brushed her hair away from the side of her face and as she did Christina noticed her mum's eyes were shiny with tears.

'Hey, come on. You never know, she may just turn up one of these days. It's about time we heard from her.'

'I want to see her, of course I do. But there's Stevie to think about. Look how long it took to get him settled the last time she was here.'

'Flavia should realise how lucky she is. Most families in our situation would have thrown her out and put the baby up for adoption.'

'Oh, Christina. No, we could never have done that.'

'You and Dad were amazing, coping with everyone looking down their noses, all the gossiping and snide remarks. Two years we coped with it, then Flavia ups and leaves. I know she's my sister and I should love her, but honestly, Mum, when I think of what she's put this family through…'

'Ssh now, let's not talk any more about it. What's past is past. At least you and Tony are getting on well together. You are getting on, aren't you?'

Christina nodded, colouring up a little.

'Don't worry, I'm not going to ask you about the ins and outs, it's not like you're a teenager anymore. And

Tony's a nice boy.'

'Hardly a boy, Mum, and there's a whole lot of unresolved discussions to be had there.'

Anne looked up from her sewing. 'About Tony?'

'Mum, fifty years ago Dad would have been chasing Tony down the road with a shotgun until he *did the right thing*. Some days I think Tony is still expecting to be bawled out for his part in the whole mess.'

'Let's not rake it all up now, we've done the right thing by Stevie, and that's all that really matters, isn't it?'

'I guess so. And what about you Mum?'

'I'm just fine. Although I am worried about Giuseppe. He's taken the death of his friend hard, hasn't he?'

'I think it's all tangled up with the death of that boy in Rome, you remember I told you about it. I think he hoped that by retiring he would leave it all behind him, but we can't escape the things that are in our heads, can we?'

'That's for sure.'

Christina took her mother's hand and clasped it in hers. 'Well, that was said with feeling. Anything you want to talk about?'

Anne patted her daughter's hand and then released her grip. 'Oh, take no notice of me. I'm just feeling bad that I'm behind with my paperwork. You know me, I like to stay on top of things.'

'That's what I told Giuseppe. And without Dad's help there would be even more for you to do.'

Anne turned to face her daughter. 'Why would I be without your Dad's help? What are you and Giuseppe planning now?'

'Nothing.'

'Come on, out with it.'

'No really, it's nothing. Just a silly conversation we had

about Dad becoming a town councillor.'

As Anne stood, Max bounded down from the settee, as if hopeful that a late night walk was in the offing.

'You're right about the word *silly*. There's more chance of you joining the council before your dad does.'

'But he's always talking to that Councillor Rogers, and when you think about it, Dad is more a part of the community than Mr Rogers is. The two of you have been running this place for so long, you know all the locals, they're like family. In fact, the more I think about it, the more I realise what a great idea it is.'

'Your dad isn't interested in politics.'

'Politics isn't just about politicians you know, it's about us, you and me and everyone who wants life to get better and does something about it. It's about influence. And we can all influence, Mum.'

'Sounds to me that you're preparing your rallying call for tomorrow,' Anne said, laughing.

'Come with me.'

'Don't be ridiculous.'

'What's ridiculous about it? It won't only be teenagers waving banners? They'll be all ages. We're going to march along the seafront and up to Hastings Town Hall.'

'What are you hoping to achieve?'

'To remind the councillors that their decisions affect people's lives. When they're shuffling their papers around and sitting in their committees, I think they forget that.'

'Well, I won't be joining you, but I will be voting on the 15th.'

'For Labour? Wilson is promising a *new Britain* and I really think he means it.'

'Don't count your chickens. This country has had a Conservative government for many years. It's not likely that people will want to change.'

'You're wrong, Mum. That's exactly what we need. Change is good, it shines a light on dark places. And on that note, I'm off to bed, which is where you should be headed. Leave the sewing for tonight, it's late and you're tired. I can see it in your eyes.'

Confident of her opinions, Christina drove back from Eastbourne during her lunch break the next day to join the march that started at the eastern end of Hastings seafront and ended in front of the Town Hall. She didn't carry a banner, although a few people at the front of the group carried makeshift placards. Some were made of cardboard, painted with rough black lettering. A couple of people held an old torn sheet between them, the words in bold red paint, declaring *Labour in, Tories out*. When the group reached the Town Hall Christina eased her way closer to the front of the crowd. A temporary podium had been placed on the pavement, suggesting there were to be speeches. Most of Queens Road was blocked with people, the police presence clearly there to maintain order.

When a man stepped onto the podium, people around Christina jostled her, one person digging her elbow into Christina's side, pushing her away.

'Ladies and gentlemen,' the man used a megaphone, which crackled and distorted his voice. 'It's good to see so many of you here today. You've taken time out of your busy day to come and let your opinions be known. That's the great thing about our country, we encourage free speech. And what's more, we promise you prosperity. Prosperity with a purpose.'

As he shouted out the phrase Christina realised she'd heard it before, it was the slogan for the Conservative manifesto. Several people around her started applauding.

'We plan to help the young, the old, the sick, the handicapped,' the man continued. 'Your lives will be richer with a Conservative government.'

'Yeah, right,' a woman standing close to Christina shouted out. 'And who's going to help me feed my kids, eh? Some Lord so and so who's never had to fret about finding sixpence for the gas meter?'

Others echoed their support, until the voices got so loud it was difficult to hear what anyone was saying. Then the man on the podium held his hand up, asking for quiet.

'You all have your own worries, of course you have. And that's why you need to vote Conservative on the 15th, because we are the party of the people.'

'That's what they all say,' one man called out.

For a few minutes Christina couldn't see the podium because a six-foot man had stepped in front of her, completely blocking her view. When he shifted to one side, Christina noticed the thickset man had stepped down and another thin-faced man had taken his place. This second man gave a short speech, announcing himself as the Labour candidate. Once again shouts from the crowd interrupted much of what he had to say.

Christina glanced at her watch. She would need to leave now if she was to avoid a dressing down from Charles. Although attending a political rally could be deemed ideal research for at least a short piece in this week's edition, despite Charles's protestations.

'If we take sides and the side we choose ends up losing, it'll be us who'll lose readers. Best to stay neutral,' he'd told her when she'd first raised the topic with him as soon as the date for the election was announced.

As she made her way back to the café, where she had

left her car, she reflected on Charles's words. She'd started the day firm in her beliefs that there was only one political party who could make changes for the better. Now she'd heard both sides, she really didn't know what she thought any more.

CHAPTER 14

Tony's visit to Bella Café on Saturday morning brought news of a rally of a different kind.

'Tony.' The shrill voice of Stevie rang out as he hurled himself at Tony the moment he came through the door of the café.

'Blimey, watch out. You nearly knocked me over. Looks to me like you're going to be a prize fighter when you grow up.' He pretended to throw a few punches towards Stevie, who in turn grabbed Tony round one leg, clinging tightly to him, stopping him from walking.

'Stevie, calm down and let Tony go.' Anne took Stevie's hand and tugged him towards the counter. 'Sorry, Tony. Is it Christina you've come to see?'

'No, he's come to see me. Haven't you, Tony?' Stevie said, his voice high-pitched with excitement.

'I've come to see both of you. First my best mate, then my best girl.' He picked Stevie up, swung him round and plonked him down on a nearby chair. 'Is your Auntie Christina at home? Or is she out somewhere trying to change the world?' He turned to Anne and winked.

'Go on up,' Anne said. 'You'll find her in the sitting room I expect, working on her latest article. Her boss let her bring one of the typewriters home and there's no space for it in her bedroom, so she's taken over the dining table. Or at least sharing it with my bookwork. It's good you're here. A bit of distraction will do her good. Seems like she's always working.'

'Like mother, like daughter?'

Anne waved Tony through to the back stairs, while holding onto Stevie to stop him from following. The click-clack of typewriter keys confirmed what Anne had surmised, and when Tony pushed open the door to the sitting room, Christina didn't slow the pace of her typing. He stood for a few moments watching her as the typewriter rocked on its base each time she reached the end of a line and slammed the carriage return.

'Blimey, you don't hang about, do you? By the look of it, I'd say you're imagining that typewriter is your arch enemy and you're intent on slapping it about as hard as you can until it surrenders.'

The typing stopped, Christina hovering her hands over the keys, as if ready to continue any second.

'Tony,' she said. 'I thought you were working Saturday mornings now? What happened about your declaration that you were going to do all the overtime on offer? That didn't exactly last long.'

Tony pulled a chair out from the far side of the table and dropped down onto it. 'Give me a minute to recover before you start having a go. For a six-year-old, that nephew of yours has one hell of a grip. I reckon he could start training for the next Olympics. You know it started today, don't you?'

'Tokyo, isn't it?'

'The opening ceremony's on the telly tonight. Aren't you going to watch it?'

'It's not really my thing.'

'Let's have a bet. How many medals do you reckon we'll get?'

'Tony, I have no idea. I'm not into sport, you should know that by now.'

'Well, my money is on a round dozen. And if I'm right, I'll treat you to a fish and chip supper.'

'You really know how to spoil a girl.'

113

Tony got up from his chair to stand behind Christina and she swivelled her chair round to face him. 'Sit down, will you? It makes my neck ache looking up at you. There's such a thing as being too tall.'

'It's not me that's making your neck ache, it's too much typing. Are you going to take a break anytime soon?'

'I can't, not yet. I've got to at least try to finish this article.'

Tony pulled the chair across so that he could sit beside Christina and leaned forward to look at what she was typing. 'I read your piece on the storm damage. It was good, Chrissie. But terrible to hear about that poor man, the chap from Claremont Lodge.'

'I know. It's a real tragedy. And what makes it worse is that he was friends with Giuseppe and it was Giuseppe who found him.'

'Bloody hell. I didn't know. There was no mention of it in the paper.'

'No, well, you know how Giuseppe hates publicity of any kind. And it was Stevie who first saw what happened.'

'Crikey, I had no idea. Is he okay? I would have called round sooner if I'd known. Stevie didn't see the body, surely?'

'God no. But he saw the building collapse, at least he told Dad and Giuseppe about it. Exactly what he saw I'm not too sure.'

'What a mess. The whole town looks as though it's been tipped upside down. That's why I'm not at work. Turns out the car I was due to work on was written off in the storm. If the bloke had parked it in his garage, instead of on the drive, well, it could have all ended quite differently.'

'No one hurt?'

'Only their bank balance. It would never have passed its

MOT anyway. Not without them spending more than they can afford. Which reminds me, you should book your car in, it's ten years old now, isn't it?'

'Have you come here just to upset me? I don't need any reminder about my ancient rust bucket. Maybe if it had been squashed in the storm, it would have been a blessing in disguise.'

'You don't mean that.'

He stood again and as he did, she ripped the paper out from the roller and tore it in two. 'It's rubbish. I know what I want to say, but every time I start it's like the words just won't come.'

'Well, I reckon I have the perfect answer, just the thing to take your mind off all of it.'

She pushed her chair back and stood, letting Tony put his arms around her waist.

'And what is your perfect answer? Let me guess, would it have anything to do with spending time with you, Mr Bighead?'

'Me and the band.'

'The band? What crazy idea do you have up your sleeve?'

'Johnnie on bass guitar, Pete on drums and me on rhythm guitar and vocals. And if we manage to persuade him, Joe will join in as lead guitarist.'

'Don't tell me, and you're going to call yourselves, The Second-hand Beatles, or some such nonsense, are you? Well, sorry to spoil your dream, but if it comes to a contest between you and McCartney, I'm afraid you won't even get a look in.'

'Seriously though, Chrissie. We've started practising in Johnnie's dad's garage. You need to come and listen. We're good. No, we're better than good.'

'And modest too?'

She pulled away from him, forcing him to let his arms release from around her waist.

'Well, maybe I will come and listen some time. But not this morning. This morning I really need to write this article.' She sat back at the typewriter, fed another sheet of paper into the roller, and flicked the carriage return back, pausing a moment before hitting the keys. 'Is that what you've come to tell me? About your pop group?'

'Yes and no. What are you doing tomorrow afternoon?'

'Nothing. Although I might be washing my hair.'

He put his hands on her shoulders until she shrugged them off. 'From where I'm standing your hair looks perfect. Anyway, you've got to come, it's not up for discussion. I'll pick you up outside at midday. Make sure you're well wrapped up, because you'll be going for the ride of your life.'

Christina would never have admitted to Tony that when she was riding pillion on the back of his Lambretta, she liked to close her eyes, cling on with her arms around his waist and pretend she was Cilla and Tony was Paul McCartney. She'd even had her hair cut to match Cilla's chic style, which she kept in place with half a ton of lacquer. And she'd spent too much of her wages to buy a fab mini dress, A line with a kick pleat, that even with her new boxy purple jacket would hardly mean she was 'wrapped up'. She would have been better off wearing a parka, like Tony and the rest of the Mods, with desert boots, instead of her square-toed 'granny' shoes. But she needed to do something to stand out from the crowd. Most of the Mods were more interested in their scooters than the girls who swooned after them.

She'd spent longer than usual doing her make-up, trying to copy the Cathy McGowan look, the trendy woman now presenting *Ready, Steady, Go* - one of Christina's 'must-see' programmes. Anne had learned not to expect her daughter to join them around the tea table on a Friday evening. She dished her plate up and left it on the side for Christina to heat up over a saucepan once the music show was finished. People were calling Cathy McGowan 'Queen of the Mods', so even though Christina would never grow her hair long again like Cathy's, everything else about her, from her love of mini-skirts, to her black eye make-up, made her the perfect role model.

Midday on Sunday, as Christina called out *Bye* to her mum, Tony was revving his Lambretta up outside. She'd seen Giuseppe briefly when he returned from his early morning walk with Max.

'I'm off out with Tony later. Will you be okay?'

'You do not need to worry about me, Christina. I am always okay.'

'I'll ignore that remark, because it's plainly not true. But I'll see you later, providing we don't get arrested before then.'

'Arrested?'

'I think Tony's planning for us to join in a bit of a rally, a whole load of Mods riding from Hastings to Eastbourne. Should be fun, but some of the locals may not be too keen.'

'Please be careful.'

'We'll be fine, as long as the Rockers don't turn up.'

She'd dived into the bathroom to finish doing her make-up before Giuseppe could ask any more questions. In truth, she knew the Rockers were bound to turn up. That was the whole point of it. She'd read the newspaper reports on one of the clashes that took place earlier in the year in Margate. A couple of lads had ended up in hospital, with many more arrested, some even getting prison sentences. Then on another occasion in August the local force had to call in extra police to break up fights. People were calling the bikers, 'thugs' and 'vermin', which Christina knew was unfair. Most of the lads were as gentle as Tony, it was the one or two amongst them who ended up causing all the trouble. But once labels were applied they tended to stick. Charles had shown her some of the letters that had come into the newspaper where people were asking for punishments like the birch or hard labour to be re-introduced. The letter writers argued that young people had lost their sense of morality, but in Christina's opinion, all that was happening was that young people were finally finding their voice.

Sure enough, by the time they arrived at Hastings Pier, there were hundreds of bikes and scooters gathered, taking up every available bit of the road and the promenade. With the noise of the engines revving up, the seagulls screaming in the background and the crash of the waves on the shore, Christina could sense something building. Then, as the bikes at the front of the group sped off, police whistles sounded behind her. Within minutes, they had left Hastings Pier and were heading towards St Leonards and beyond.

When they reached Eastbourne, the police were waiting for them, although at that point there had been no trouble. The leather-jacketed Rockers, riding peacefully beside the smartly dressed Mods, called to each other in jest. 'Call that a bike, you might as well try riding a spin-dryer,' one lad shouted out to Tony as he sped past.

It was when they reached Eastbourne Pier that the trouble started. Christina didn't see who threw the first punch, but within minutes fists were flying and scooters were abandoned as more and more lads joined in with the fight.

'Let's go, Tony.' She shouted into his ear, her voice drowned out by police sirens.

Tony stopped the scooter and pointed to the tumble of bodies that looked more like a rugby scrum. Punches were being thrown without anyone looking where they landed.

Then a shout from Tony, 'Oh God, Phil's down, I need to go to him. Chrissie, stand over there, out of the way.' He pointed across the road to a run of shops set back from the road.

'No, I'm not leaving you,' she said, clinging to his arm as Tony pushed forward towards his friend who was lying on the ground.

The next ten or fifteen minutes were a maelstrom of confusion. Sirens blaring, police piling in, police helmets being knocked off.

Mods and Rockers found themselves grabbed and hurled into one of the police vans, their motorbikes and scooters left, some still upright, others pushed to the ground. A couple of ambulances arrived, adding more noise to the ruckus. Phil was just one of a crowd of Mods and Rockers who were nursing injuries following the brawl. Some with superficial cuts and bruises, others more bloodied yet keen to continue the punch up. The last thing that Tony and Christina saw of Phil was as he was being stretchered away, at the very moment they found themselves grabbed by two burly policemen and pushed into the back of the police van.

CHAPTER 15

When the phone call came into Bella Café on Sunday afternoon, Mario answered. He and Anne were enjoying their rest day, settled in the sitting room with a tray of tea, listening to Stevie reading aloud from his favourite story book. But the phone call meant an end to any further relaxation. The fury on Mario's face told its own story. Minutes later, Giuseppe was in the passenger seat of Mario's Hillman Imp, still trying to clarify exactly what Christina had said to her father.

'To be honest, I didn't take much in beyond the fact that the police have arrested them both - her and Tony,' Mario said. 'As soon as she said she's being held in a police cell, my mind froze.'

'You need to stay calm, Mario. All will be well.'

'That's fine for you to say. She's not your daughter.'

'But I care for her as if she was my daughter.'

A prickly silence rested between them for the rest of the journey to Eastbourne. As they approached the police station Giuseppe was the first to speak.

'Do you remember Detective Sergeant Pearce? You met him in July. The sad case of George Leigh.'

'Not sure I met him, but yes, I know who you mean. And you think he'll help?'

'I am certain of it. Did Christina say why were they arrested?'

'Something about a fight and Tony's friend being hurt. I've told them both over and over. All this riding around in groups it leads to nothing but trouble. Fine, if he wants to take her out on his scooter, but why do they have to get involved with these Rockers with their scruffy hair and scruffy clothes. They all look as if they could do with a good scrub in the bath.'

As soon as Mario had parked, Giuseppe pushed open the car door, tossing out an instruction to his cousin that came out sharper than he had intended. 'Wait here in the car.'

'She's my daughter. I should be the one to fetch her.'

'But I am the detective and this is a police station. I know the rules. English rules perhaps, but they cannot be so different from Italian ones.'

'You were a detective,' was Mario's brusque response as he got out of the car, slamming the door closed and standing beside it as if ready to make a quick getaway.

A few minutes later, a police constable showed Giuseppe into Pearce's office, but not before Giuseppe had noticed the shiny new brass plate on Pearce's door.

'Many congratulations, Detective Inspector. The new name plate on your door tells me you have had a promotion since we last met.'

'Kind of you say so, Mr Bianchi. But I reckon it's got more to do with my loud voice than anything else. I'm a dab hand at rousing the troops.'

Pearce invited Giuseppe to sit and as he did so he recalled the last time he had sat in the same chair. Scanning the room it seemed that little had changed. Back in July everything about the Eastbourne police station merely reminded him of the contrast between life in Rome and life here in England.

'Not returned home yet, I see,' Pearce said. 'Is England suiting you more than you'd expected?'

'I am waiting until there is something to return for.'

Pearce slid open his desk drawer and gestured to Giuseppe to look inside. 'See, still no cigarettes. What about you? Succumbed yet?'

'I have struggled several times, but no. I am staying true to my promise.'

'Good man. So what brings you to Eastbourne? A social visit, is it?'

Giuseppe sat again and tapped out a rhythm on the arm of the chair. 'Christina Rossi. My cousin's daughter. You may remember her from our first meeting. The case of George Leigh.'

'I know who you mean. Young reporter from the *Eastbourne Herald*. What about her?'

'You are holding her in custody.'

'You surprise me. What's she done?'

'She has done nothing.'

'Well, you and I both know that when someone is arrested, it's a pound to a penny they've been up to something.'

'She was in the wrong place, at the wrong time. With her boyfriend, Tony. They were mixed up with the trouble near the Pier. Some fighting.'

'And you want me to let them go, I suppose?'

'They have done nothing wrong. They were trying to help a friend and...'

Pearce picked up the telephone receiver. 'Bryant. Couple in the cell, name of Miss Christina Rossi and Mr Tony...' He looked at Giuseppe.

'Evans.'

'Tony Evans. Someone here to vouch for them, so we can release them. Ask them to wait with the custody sergeant and someone will be there shortly to collect them.' He put the receiver down and looked at Giuseppe. 'That do you?'

'I am very grateful. But there is one more small thing,

before I leave you to continue with your day.'

'There'll be no charges against them, don't worry. Most of these lads are harmless, it's just a few troublemakers that give the rest of them a bad name. But we find that rounding them up and sticking them in the cells for a few hours gives them a chance to cool down.'

On Giuseppe's previous visit to Pearce's office he had been struck by the drabness of the place. The yellowed walls, thick with nicotine, were a reminder of Pearce's habit. A habit that, like Giuseppe, he had tried to break. He remembered the rubber plant that sat in the far corner as looking much healthier. Dust now covered its leaves, the soil at the base was cracked and dry. He glanced at the window, noticing how close the neighbouring building was. There was no chance for any light to filter through and Giuseppe wondered what it must be like to spend every working day in such gloom.

'I would like to ask you about another matter. Do you know of a family named Forrest?'

'Forrest. Name kind of rings a bell, but so many names come across my desk every day, I can't be sure. Why? Trouble, are they?'

Giuseppe stopped tapping and touched his hands together as if in prayer. 'The storm five days ago.'

'Terrible, wasn't it? I don't suppose you see the likes of that where you come from. I had all the men on overtime that night. It's one of the reasons I'm here on a Sunday afternoon. When you're dealing with one crisis, a whole host of others get forgotten. But thankfully the worst of the wind was to buildings, not people.'

Giuseppe bowed his head.

'Oh, of course. A life was lost in Bexhill, wasn't it? I read about it in the paper. Dreadful business. Not someone you knew, I hope?'

'*Signor* Edward Swain. An acquaintance. No, a friend.'

'I'm very sorry to hear that. You have my condolences.'

'I was with him when he died.'

For a few moments they sat in silence, and then Pearce stood and moved over to the bookshelves to the left of his desk. 'What's your tipple? I've only got whisky, I'm afraid.' He took the bottle down from the top shelf, together with a couple of small glasses.

'Not for me.'

'Go on, man. It's no fun drinking alone.'

Giuseppe gave the slightest nod and Pearce part filled the glasses, passing one to Giuseppe before sitting again.

'Crushed under a tree, is that right? Brought on a heart attack, I expect. Old age comes to us all, if we survive that long.'

'He was not old. Sixty-five, I think. Maybe a year or two more.'

'And this family you're asking about. Forrest. How do they fit into things?'

'*Signor* Swain had a lodging house. He had two lodgers. A *Signora* Warrington and a *Signor* Forrest. But now *Signor* Forrest has vanished. Left the lodgings without warning and leaving no information about why he has left or where he has gone to. We understand his family lives in Eastbourne.'

'I can't see that's much of a crime. He probably thought he'd have to leave anyway, now the landlord is no longer, so to speak. But I can see from your expression you think there's more to it, am I right?'

'*Si*. I ask myself why *Signor* Swain went out into his back garden, dressed only in his pyjamas, in the middle of the night, in the middle of a terrible storm.'

'And you suspect this Forrest chap had something to do with it?'

Giuseppe shrugged his shoulders, choosing to remain non committal.

'Well, unless Forrest chopped down the tree, having first pushed Mr Swain under it, I'm not sure you have much of a case.'

Pearce sipped his whisky, while Giuseppe merely ran his finger around the rim of the glass and had yet to taste it.

'I must go,' Giuseppe stood, placing the glass down on the desk, the drink still untouched. 'My cousin is waiting in the car park. He will be worried about his daughter.'

'Look, I'll see what I can find out about the Forrest family. You're staying with your cousin? I can reach you there?'

'Of course. *Grazie.*'

'Us detectives, we've got to stick together.'

The two men shook hands and as Giuseppe turned to leave Pearce picked up the untouched glass of whisky and drank it down in one.

CHAPTER 16

Giuseppe remained silent for the journey from the police station to Eastbourne Pier, leaving Mario to have whatever discussion he felt appropriate with his daughter and her boyfriend. But there was no discussion. The remaining three passengers in the car matched Giuseppe's silence. Sat in the front passenger seat, Giuseppe couldn't see the glances exchanged between Christina and Tony, but he could see the steely expression on his cousin's face and he guessed that Mario's tight grip on the steering wheel was nothing to do with the traffic.

When they reached the Pier, Mario pulled up, and they surveyed the dozens of abandoned motorbikes and scooters left lying on the promenade.

'They should toss the lot of them into a lorry and take them to the scrap yard,' Mario said. 'And I don't mean just the bikes,' he added as an afterthought.

'Dad, you don't mean that,' Christina said.

'Don't I?'

'Mr Rossi, thanks very much for collecting me and I'm really sorry for all the trouble I've caused.' Tony leaned forward, intending to shake Mario's hand. But Mario remained fixed, looking forward. So, Tony opened the car door and stepped out. 'Bye, Chrissy. I'll ring you.'

'Christina will not be riding out with you again,' Mario declared.

'Dad, I think you forget how old I am. I can make my own decisions, you know.'

'Tony has brought nothing but trouble to our family. It's best you don't see him again.'

'I'm not listening to you, Dad. Like I said, I'm old

enough to decide who I see. I'm twenty-three years old, for God's sake.'

'Watch your language, young lady. Yes, I remember exactly how old you are. Which is why I'm ashamed to see you behaving like some teenage hoodlum.'

Giuseppe came close to reminding Mario of their own teenage years, but thought better of it and instead tapped out a rhythm on his leg, until Mario gave him such a steely look he stopped. When they arrived back at Bella Café, Christina barely waited for Mario to park before getting out of the car, slamming the door behind her.

'Don't say a word,' Mario said to Giuseppe.

'I have nothing to say about Christina, or Tony. She is your daughter, as you reminded me.' Giuseppe paused, matching his cousin's glare, holding eye contact until Mario looked away.

'I want to ask you again about Councillor Rogers,' Giuseppe said after a pause.

'What about him?'

'Do you think he would introduce me to his colleague? The one he mentioned who had dealings with *Signor* Swain?'

'I'm pretty furious with Rogers, so this may not be the right time for me to ask him for a favour.'

Mario turned the car engine off, but was making no attempt to move from the driver's seat. He looked across Giuseppe towards the promenade and the sea beyond. Giuseppe followed his gaze, noticing the way the water was reflecting the darkening sky above. It reminded him of liquid mercury, an inky, silvery blue, which had a depth and beauty to it he hadn't noticed before. For a moment he was tempted to say as much to Mario. Instead he said, 'I thought you and the Councillor were on good terms.'

'The council are talking about widespread demolition of some of the buildings close to the seafront.'

'Demolishing derelict buildings? That is a good thing, surely?'

'All depends what they intend to put in their place. And now they've put the play park on hold, what about the children? Don't they need a safe place to play?'

'When I look around Bexhill, I see many safe places for children to play. Perhaps more than in Italy. You must remember how we played in the streets when we were small. But now, with so many cars, it is dangerous.'

'It's the same here. More and more cars…'

'But here the children have the beach. Even on these cold days I see families sitting with their blankets, having a picnic as if it was the middle of summer.'

'Then there's the problem of the buildings that need demolishing that aren't even on the council's list. Take Claremont Lodge, for example,' Mario continued, as if he was running through the argument in his mind, building a case to present to the councillor.

'You think the lodging house needs demolishing?' Giuseppe turned to face his cousin.

'Well, you said yourself it's in desperate need of repair. How is it they allowed Mr Swain to run it as a lodging house? Seems to me the council have got their priorities all wrong.'

'You are angry. But maybe not with the council, or with Councillor Rogers. Not even with Christina. Mario, until you let go of the demons that haunt you, you will never be able to let go of the anger.'

'This isn't the time to talk about the past. My daughter has just been arrested. She spent the last two hours in a police cell, for pity's sake.'

'You are right, this is not the time. But let us agree to speak together soon.'

Mario ran his hands over the steering wheel and Giuseppe waited, but when there was no response, Giuseppe said, 'I was there, remember. The day you received the news about Filomena. I walked up into the hills with you, I wanted to see how I could help.'

'No one could help.'

'You closed down a part of yourself that day, Mario. It's time to let go, to open up the wound, let the air at it. It is the only way it will heal.'

Giuseppe hadn't posed a question, but if he had, he was left in no doubt as to his cousin's silent answer, as Mario flung open the driver's door and stormed out of the car. Giuseppe followed Mario inside, nodded at Anne, who raised an eyebrow by way of enquiry and listened as his cousin went up the back stairs to the flat.

'Not a good day for the Rossi family, is it?' Anne said, gesturing to Giuseppe to follow her through to the back kitchen.

'Your husband is angry.'

'You're not wrong.'

'And Christina? Did you speak to her?'

'Briefly. Enough to get the gist of what went on with Tony, and what her father said to her. They'll sort it out. They usually do. He blows his top, she shouts back, they both sulk for a while and then the sun comes out and life returns to normal. But something like this stirs everything up. All those bitter rows that lasted for days when we found out Flavia was expecting - I never want to live through a time like that again. Although the thought of Christina sitting in a police cell - well, if you'd told me that one of my daughters was going to be arrested, I would have expected it to be Flavia.'

'Life does not always turn out as we expect,' Giuseppe said. 'You must try not to worry. Christina is strong. I expect she will see her arrest as research for her articles.' He cast a smile in Anne's direction. 'Sit and rest and I will make us both an espresso.'

'I'd like that, Giuseppe. Thankfully, the sun was in and out today, so Stevie and Max were able to play out in the garden. My grandson tells me he has taught Max to sit, but I haven't seen it with my own eyes, so I'm reserving judgement.' She smiled, stretching out her legs in front of her and flexing her feet. 'I'm not sure it suits me to relax. It just makes me notice all my aches and pains even more.'

'Age. I was reminded today that it comes to us all, if we are lucky enough to survive.'

'Well, I'm not sure that's a cheery thought.'

Giuseppe prepared the percolator, adding water to the base, filling the little metal basket with coffee, screwing the top and bottom together tightly, and then setting it on the gas. Neither spoke, Giuseppe intent on his task, Anne watching. A few minutes later they could both hear the water bubbling up through the coffee and the rich aroma filled the air. Giuseppe took in a deep breath, then sighed.

'Each time is like the first,' he said.

'I remember the first time I smelled Italian coffee and the first time I tasted it. It was so bitter I could barely swallow. Then someone suggested I add sugar…'

'And you fell in love.'

'Ha. Yes, I did. In more ways than one. But that's another story.'

Giuseppe gave a short stir to the coffee, before pouring each of them a small cup, and then the focus was on drinking it while it was at its best.

'Mario tells me he is angry with Councillor Rogers,' Giuseppe said, as he set his empty cup down on the table.

'He thinks they're on different sides, but they both want the best for the people of this town, and I keep telling him that's all that matters. The trouble is it's not as simple as pulling down buildings that are no longer fit for purpose and replacing them with shiny new tower blocks. Each home is a family, and each family is part of a community. So if you force people out of their homes, even if that home has water running down the walls and rattling windows that let in more of the cold than is kept out - well, then those people lose their community support, their neighbours, their friends.'

'What do you believe is the answer?'

'I have no idea. But that's why I've chosen not to be a politician.'

Anne picked up the empty cups and put them in the sink, running water into them before wiping her hands down her apron and sitting again.

'What about you, Giuseppe? And your friend, Mr Swain?'

'I know that you all think I search for something that is not there.' He started drumming his fingers on the table, studying them as they moved. 'You think I have the need to always investigate, that it is in my blood.'

'If it is, then there's nothing wrong with that. It's just that if you keep looking but find nothing, won't you feel worse? As though you've let your friend down?'

'I have one picture of *Signor* Swain from our walks together, from our conversations, and now that he is gone, another picture is emerging.'

'In what way?'

'He cared about his clothes, his appearance, and yet he

appears not to have cared about the place where he lived. He offers accommodation to others, and yet the standard of that accommodation is very poor. He gets his licence from the council, but they appear not to mind about the holes in the ceiling, the wiring that is hanging from places it should not hang. Then I learn that Edward knows a councillor. What does that mean? Has he received his licence in an underhand way?'

'But surely you don't think…'

'I try not to think, I try only to look for facts. I am told that Edward had a terrible argument with his young lodger, a *Signor* Forrest. And when we try to discover the reason for the argument, *Signor* Forrest disappears.'

'When you say *we*, you mean Christina?'

'*Sì*.'

'When you list all the facts like that, I can see why you think there may be more to his death, than a mere accident. You don't think he tried to take his own life, do you?'

Giuseppe stood and eased out his neck and shoulders, turning away from Anne.

'There are many ways to take your own life that are much easier than waiting in a summer house in a storm, hoping a tree will fall on you.'

Anne stood beside Giuseppe, putting her hand on his back. 'Thank you for what you did for Christina and Tony. Tony's not a bad soul, he's got his heart in the right place and Stevie thinks the world of him.'

'We need to remember some of the things we did when we were their age.' He turned to face Anne.

'I spend most of my time trying to forget.'

'You should be proud, your actions during the war made a difference to many lives.'

'I have mixed feelings. Everything looks quite different

with hindsight. When you are in the moment, decisions come easy.'

'And Mario?'

'You know your cousin. We've been married for over twenty years but sometimes it's as though we're still strangers.'

Before Anne could respond, the back door opened to reveal Tony, no longer in his parka, his expression a mix of hope and embarrassment.

'I've come to apologise to Mr Rossi.'

CHAPTER 17

It appeared that Mario wasn't interested in apologies from Tony, or from anyone else. He stayed in the café, choosing to clean the inside of the windows, which he did with such fervour it was a surprise to anyone watching that the glass wasn't pushed out onto the pavement.

'You'll find Christina upstairs,' Anne told Tony. 'And don't worry about Mr Rossi, he'll come round soon enough.'

'I'm really sorry, Mrs Rossi. I would never have taken Chrissie with me if I'd known how it would turn out. We weren't involved in the fighting, you know.'

'Christina is old enough to make her own decisions and tough enough to accept the consequences. But I'll be honest with you, Tony, the thought of my daughter in that police cell sends a chill right through me. We just have to hope her boss doesn't get to hear about it.'

'From what Chrissie has said about her boss, I'm guessing he'd be impressed to have one of his reporters in the midst of a local rumpus. A chance for a first-hand account. And the police cell wasn't that grim, although I'm not sure I'd have wanted to spend the night there.'

Anne nodded by way of acknowledgement, but before Tony had taken a step towards the staircase, a shout from Stevie, accompanied by a bark from Max, stopped him in his tracks. Stevie hurled himself, throwing his arms around Tony's legs, so that any movement was impossible. Sensing the excitement, Max started dancing around Tony in circles, his tail beating like a metronome in double quick time.

'Hey, you two. Careful, or you'll have me over.' He

freed himself from Stevie's embrace, lifting the boy up, causing Max to start jumping up as well.

'Tony, I've taught Max to sit. Look.'

Released from Tony's arms, Stevie stood in front of the Beagle, lifted his hand just above the dog's head, with his palm facing down. 'Sit,' he said, the word coming out crisply and firmly, and at the same time he moved his hand down in slow motion.

Max looked at Stevie, then at Tony, as if he was unsure whether the excitement was over for the day, or whether there was still more to come.

Then Stevie repeated the command and the hand action, and Max sat.

'Good dog.' Stevie plumped himself down beside Max, throwing an arm around the dog's neck. 'See, Tony, isn't he clever?'

'I reckon you both are. Now why don't you go back into the garden and try teaching Max another trick. How about getting him to lie down? Have you tried that yet?'

'Are you coming?'

'I just want to chat with your Auntie Christina for a bit, then I'll come and find you. Okay?'

'Okay.'

Tony watched Stevie lead Max outside, before taking the stairs two at a time. Christina had a bunch of loose papers spread out on the dining table, and she was moving them around as if they were chess pieces.

'Your dad is blanking me completely. I was hoping to apologise.' Tony said, pulling a chair out from the table and turning it so that he could sit backwards on it, his arms leaning over the chair back, his long legs stretched out.

'You have nothing to apologise for.'

'Well, I got us both arrested, didn't I? If it hadn't been

for your Uncle Giuseppe…'

'We didn't do anything wrong. You were looking out for a friend. Did you find out how he is?'

'By the time I picked up my scooter, everyone else had headed home.'

'Anyone who wasn't arrested, you mean. Did you go to the hospital?'

'Yeah. Phil wasn't there, they'd already discharged him. There were just a couple of the Rockers nursing cuts and bruises. I reckon the worst bruises were to their pride. They couldn't stand it that us Mods were better than them. Better bikes, smarter clothes, prettier girls.' He got up and stood behind Christina, leaning over her. 'Are you going to write about it? Shock headline - *Wrongful arrest of innocent reporter.*'

'It's not funny, Tony. I was quite scared when we were thrown into that police cell, although I'd never admit that to Mum and Dad. You have to promise that next time I ride out with you it'll be just the two of us.'

'I promise. Scout's honour.' Tony held his hand up, making a three-finger salute. 'So what are you working on today?'

'The generation gap.'

'What's that in plain English.'

'Exactly what we came up against today. All the things we believe are important. Not just our music and the length of my skirt, but freedom of speech, our rights as individuals.'

'Blimey, sounds heavy.'

'Yeah, well. If I make it too *heavy*, Charles won't ever print it, so I'm working out ways to tone it down, while still getting the message across that young people have more power than they realise.'

'Except if they get arrested.' Tony pulled Christina up and put his arms around her waist, pulling her towards him. Just as he was about to kiss her they both heard Anne's voice, loud and shrill, almost a scream.

'Mum, are you alright?' Christina called out, while at the same time leaping down the stairs two at a time, followed closely by Tony.

When they reached the back kitchen, Anne was standing stock still, her arms outstretched, and in front of her stood Flavia.

'Well, would you look at that,' Flavia said, directing her gaze at Christina and Tony. 'Don't you two just look cosy together.'

Christina opened her mouth and closed it again, without a sound emerging, while Tony said, 'And so, the wanderer returns.'

'Is anyone going to invite me in then, or do I just stand here on the doorstep of my own home while you gather yourselves?'

'Flavia,' Anne said, going towards her daughter to embrace her. 'It's wonderful to see you, but it's a...'

'Shock? Yeah, well.'

'A surprise, a lovely surprise. Why didn't you let us know you were coming?'

'Well now, that would have spoiled the surprise, wouldn't it?'

'Come in and sit down and I'll put the kettle on. You wait until your dad sees you, he'll be that thrilled.'

'Will he? I'll believe that when I see it.'

Flavia sat, crossing her legs with a flamboyant gesture, and tossing her long platinum blonde hair back over her shoulder. She was wearing an all-in-one trouser suit, made of a patterned, flimsy material, in shades of brown and cream. The long brown suedette jacket she wore over the top was something Christina had only ever seen in magazines, together with the natty matching cap that Flavia had pulled down on one side to create a jaunty look.

Christina and Tony remained standing, with Tony gripping Christina's hand, which he could feel was trembling.

'You've dyed your hair,' Anne said.

'Just as observant as ever, Mum.' Flavia quipped.

'And you're just as sarcastic,' Tony said, gaining a warning look from Christina.

'So, where's my son then? What have you done with him? Packed him off to an orphanage to get him out from under your feet?' Flavia stood and stepped towards the window that looked out onto the garden. 'Got a dog now, eh? I would have thought you'd have enough trouble on your hands without adding a mutt into the mix.'

She rapped on the window several times before Stevie looked up. Everyone else in the kitchen watched to see the lad's response. It had been just over a year since he'd seen his mother and on her last visit her hair was still as black as her sister's, but a change of hair colour hadn't changed her face, a face that Stevie would always recognise. They watched as Stevie pushed open the side gate and a few moments later he ran into the kitchen. But once he arrived, it was as though he didn't know who to run to.

'Hey, no hug for your mum, then?' Flavia said, moving towards Stevie, as he backed away a little, sidling towards Tony.

'It's all a bit overwhelming for him, Flavia. He hasn't seen you for ages, it's bound to feel a bit strange,' Anne said.

Flavia made a huffing sound and turned away from

Stevie, looking instead at Christina and Tony. 'Back together, then? How long's that been?'

'Not really any of your business, is it?' Tony said.

'Look, why don't we all go upstairs to the sitting room and I'll fetch your dad,' Anne said. 'I'm surprised you didn't seem him on your way in. He said he was going to fix one of the shelves that looks ready to collapse, but he must be done by now. And there's someone else for you to meet. Your Uncle Giuseppe is here. He's been with us since July.'

'Well, there's a thing. Giuseppe, the famous detective. What brings him to our cold climes? Still broken-hearted about that wife of his walking out on him?'

'Flavia.' Mario came through from the café and his greeting was both a reprimand and a warning.

'Hi Dad.'

Neither father nor daughter blinked as they held each other's gaze.

Anne shushed everyone upstairs, while pulling Mario back. 'Let's not have a scene. For Stevie's sake.'

'If there's a scene to be had, you can be certain it will be our youngest daughter who will create it. Not me.'

'Help me get a tray of tea together. Let's see if we can't all have a civil conversation for once. And go and knock on Giuseppe's door, will you? He's in his bedroom. At least I think that's where he is.'

The atmosphere was a little less tense by the time everyone had finished their drinks. Tony had taken his leave before Anne had poured the tea, saying he needed to be somewhere. Christina knew it was an excuse, but was grateful all the same. His presence was bound to create more problems than it would solve. Stevie was persuaded to show off his dog training skills, which brought a few chuckles and some easier topics of conversation.

'Flavia,' Giuseppe said. 'It is many years since my last visit. You were just a little girl and I remember your hair was as black as your sister's.'

'I remember you taking us on the train to Eastbourne. You bought us the biggest ice-cream I'd ever seen and then had a bet with me that I wouldn't eat it all.'

'Ah, *si*,' Giuseppe smiled. 'And I lost the bet.'

'Of course. I always win. My sister knows that.' She glared at Christina, then softened the glare into a fixed smile.

'Is this a flying visit?' Anne said, her voice sounding overly cheery.

'Why? Keen to see the back of me already, are you?'

Christina watched as Stevie looked around at the faces of the people in the room. She wondered what he was thinking and was about to lean forward to pick him up for a cuddle, then thought better of it. Instead, she made a gesture of friendship.

'Stevie, would you like your mummy to read your bedtime story to you tonight? Maybe even give you your bath?' Christina could sense Anne's and Mario's eyes on her.

'Yeah, I could do that. What do you say, Steve?' Flavia said, going to take her son's hand to pull him towards her.

'My name is Stevie.' He sidled away from Flavia, so he was no longer within reach. Then he sat cross-legged on the floor clutching Max to him, or at least as much as the dog would allow him to.

'I know, I know. I was teasing you. Steve sounds a bit more grown up, doesn't it? Makes me think of Steve McQueen, such a hunk, especially in that film, *The Great Escape* - have you seen it, Stevie? You'd love it, mind you, a few people do get shot dead, so you might have to close your eyes when it gets to that part.'

Stevie's eyes widened.

'Stevie is too young for the cinema and certainly too young for war films,' Mario announced. 'Come Stevie, Granddad will get you bathed and ready for bed tonight.'

Mario took Stevie's hand, ignoring the reluctant tug in the opposite direction.

'Well, I guess that's told me, hasn't it? I can see nothing much changes around here,' Flavia said. 'But to answer your question, Mum, I was planning on stopping a couple of nights if that's okay?'

'This will always be your home, Flavia, you know that. I'm going to finish getting supper ready,' Anne said.

'And I will help,' Giuseppe said, following her, leaving Christina and Flavia alone, with Max lying at Christina's feet.

'Why do you always make everything so difficult?' Christina said.

'Because easy is boring, I guess.'

'Giuseppe sleeps in the front bedroom, so you'll have to have the folding bed in Stevie's room. Let's go and get it ready while Dad is giving him his bath. And try to think of something nice to say when we sit down to supper later. Do you think you can manage that?'

CHAPTER 18

Later that evening, after a supper that passed off without too much sniping, Christina shushed Anne out of the kitchen.

'Flavia and I will clear up, Mum. Go and relax for a change, put your feet up.'

Anne glanced at Flavia's sour expression. 'I'm not sure your sister is of the same opinion. Washing up was never her favourite chore.'

'Yeah, and trust you to never let me forget it,' Flavia said, turning away.

It was only Christina who saw the look of hurt on her mother's face. She waited until Anne had left the kitchen, then took a tea towel from the hook by the kitchen sink and handed it to her sister. 'I'll wash, you dry.'

'You always were bossy.'

For a while the sisters focused on washing and drying the crockery and cutlery, putting it away in the cupboards and drawers. Supper had been served on the best dinner set, in the upstairs dining room. It was as if a VIP had deigned to visit. Once the kitchen was tidy again, Christina wiped the surfaces, while Flavia pulled out a chair, sitting astride it.

'Has anyone told you that the way you sit on a chair makes you look more like a man.' Christina said.

'Bother you, does it?'

'It's like you want to make a statement with everything you do. Your hair, your clothes, even the way you sit.'

'And you don't? What about all your ranting in the newspaper? That's you making a statement, isn't it?'

Flavia stood, lifting the chair and making a show of

turning it around, then sitting on it again, but this time in a neat pose, with her legs tucked beneath the chair and her hands placed on her lap. She gave a forced smile, which Christina tried to ignore by turning away.

'Why are you really here, Flavia and what have you been doing since we last saw you? It's been over a year, and all you've managed is two phone calls, one birthday card for Stevie and one postcard. Don't you think we deserve more than that?'

'Missed me, have you?'

'Grow up, Flavia. Do you ever stop to think how lucky you are? Most parents would have thrown you out when you announced you were pregnant. Instead, Mum and Dad did all they could to help you, to care for Stevie, and all you've ever done is throw it back in their faces. You don't deserve to have people who care about you.'

'Do you care about me, then?'

'I would if you let me. If you didn't hide behind that smokescreen the whole time. Pretending you don't care about us, about Stevie, about yourself even. I don't buy it.'

'I messed up, okay?'

'You can say that again.'

'I made some bad decisions and now I'm trying to sort myself out. Really. I want to get my life back on track.'

'Yeah, you did make some bad decisions, but it's always other people who suffer.'

'You? Tony?'

'No, for God's sake, I'm talking about your son. He's six years old and he has no real understanding about who his mother is and why she lives at the other end of the country and appears to want nothing to do with him.'

'That's not true. Anyway, I've moved. I'm living in Eastbourne now.'

'When did that happen?'

'I'm working, Chrissie.'

'But if you're living in Eastbourne, how come you haven't visited more often? Or come to see me at the newspaper offices. For God's sake, Flavia, you've been just a stone's throw from us and yet we haven't seen you for more than a year.'

'I've been trying to get myself on an even keel again. I'm renting a flat. It's nice, Stevie will have his own bedroom.'

Christina took a deep breath, conscious her heart was beating fast, creating a throbbing sensation in her neck.

'No, Flavia.'

'Who are you to say no to me? He's my son, remember.'

'You're doing what you always do.'

'And what is that?'

'You're thinking about yourself and not about Stevie.' Shoving her chair to one side, Christina gripped the edge of the kitchen sink, in an attempt to steady her emotions. 'Have you stopped to think what a move like that would do to him? You'd be taking him from his school, his friends, us…'

'Like I said, he's my son, Chrissie.'

'He's your son when you want him to be. He's not a plaything. Something to pick up and put down at will. Anyway, how would you work if he was living with you? What sort of job would let you be around in all the school holidays, or when he's sick? It's madness for you to even think about it.'

Christina took a deep breath, trying to slow her thudding heartbeat. She pressed a hand against the side of her forehead, feeling the fierce pulse of her blood, which was beginning to make her head hurt. She turned her back on Flavia, running the cold tap and splashing a little water over her wrists.

'You get yourself so het up, don't you?' Flavia said.

'Because I care about your son. Funny that, isn't it? I would have thought that was your job.'

'Oh God, lighten up. You take life too seriously. He's just a kid. He'll get over whatever it is you think I've done to him. You wait, by the time he's a teenager he'll be running rings around both of us.'

'Like you did?'

Despite Flavia's outwardly stylish appearance, Christina noticed her sister's nails were rough and bitten almost down to the quick. She watched her picking around the edges of her nails, pulling at the skin tags and rubbing away the small pinpricks of blood that appeared.

'You and Tony an item now, then?' Flavia turned her head a little, giving Christina a look at her expression, which was almost childlike. 'Not that I care either way.' She looked back down at her fingernails.

'No, you don't care. Just like you don't care how much you upset people with your meddling. You know that one day Stevie is going to ask you the question that you're always avoiding answering?'

'And what might that be?'

'Who his dad is, of course.'

'Honestly, Chrissie. If I knew I'd tell you. Tony and I had a one-night stand.'

'You don't need to tell me that part, he's already told me.'

'Do you remember Pete? He used to follow us around all the time.'

'Gawky lad, all teeth and glasses? Bit of a problem with acne, I seem to remember.'

'Yep.'

'You never did.'

'It was more of a challenge really. I just thought I'd see how far I could push it and well it turned out I managed to push it all the way…'

'God, Flavia. Do you have any morals at all? And you think Pete might be Stevie's dad? Do you even know where he is now? Does he still live around here?'

'I have no idea. Hopefully not. Not sure I'd fancy bumping into him now after all this time, although if he's got rid of his acne… he had really dreamy eyes, I seem to remember.'

Flavia was quiet for a few moments, as though lost in a memory.

'Well, you just need to realise that at some point Stevie is going to want to know,' Christina continued. 'And he'll be hoping it's Tony, I can bet you that.'

'What does it matter if there's no biological connection. There's every other connection, isn't there? I could see it the moment Stevie came in from the garden earlier. He ran to Tony first, even before you or Mum.'

'That's another reason you can't take Stevie to live with you.' Christina thumped her fist on the edge of the sink. 'Ow, I didn't mean to do that. At least not with quite such force.' She looked at her hand, which was now throbbing.

'You silly mare. You always were clumsy. Let's change the subject. What's the real reason Giuseppe is here. It's not for a seaside holiday, is it?'

'He arrived back in July, but he's made no mention of how long he's staying. Although the timing was pretty awful. The day he arrived a boy's body was found at the beach near Norman's Bay.'

'Bloody hell.'

'I found the body. It was dreadful, Flavia, not something I ever want to experience again.'

'Who was it? No one we know?'

'A lad called George Leigh. You won't know him. Anyway, Giuseppe believed there was more to the boy's death than first appeared. So he and I dug around a bit to find out the truth of it all.'

'Crikey. Like some kind of detective duo? Who would have thought it, my timid sister a private investigator.'

'It's nothing like that. I just helped out a bit. It was a terrible time, Flavia. People were scared to let their children out of their sight and Stevie had so many nightmares.'

Flavia shook her head. 'Must have been tough on the little man. I'm sorry he had to cope with something like that. But well done to you, seriously.'

'That's not praise you're handing out, is it? Have you had a personality transplant?' Christina pulled a chair out and sat. 'Anyway, things settled down for a while but now something else has happened and Giuseppe is really struggling with it. Trouble is this time I'm not sure there's anything I can do to help.'

'I'll put the kettle on and you can tell me.' Flavia busied herself by filling the kettle and getting out two mugs. Then she took the biscuit barrel down from the worktop and looked inside. 'Rich tea, now there's a surprise. Our mother is so predictable.'

While her sister was making the tea, Christina was reflecting. *Was there really nothing to be done to help Giuseppe?*

'You know there was that dreadful storm the other night,' Christina said. 'You must have been caught up in it too.'

'I slept through the whole thing. First I knew of it was

147

the next morning when the buses weren't running down my road. Turns out a couple of trees had come down and they took the whole of the next day to clear them away. I had to walk to work.' Flavia's tone was indignant as if she had yet to forgive the bus company for being so inconsiderate.

'Well, it was a fallen tree that caused the tragedy here too. But it was a bit more serious than a cancelled bus.'

'Tragedy?'

'Yep. The man who runs Claremont Lodge - the place up Sea Road - his name is Edward Swain. Anyway, he and Giuseppe had become friends. They'd been walking Max together every morning. Well, Mr Swain was killed. He was in his summer house when a tree crashed down and killed him.'

As Christina spoke she felt as if she was reliving the trauma of that night. Her palms were sweaty, her face flushed.

'Oh my God. That's terrible. Poor bloke.'

'Yes. And poor Giuseppe. He was with him when he died.'

Christina sipped her drink, noticing her hands were shaking as she put the mug to her mouth. Flavia watched her, then reached her hand out, placing it on her sister's as if to calm her.

'So, it was a dreadful accident. Nothing you or Giuseppe can do. Did this Mr Swain have a wife and kids?'

Christina shook her head. 'No, at least not as far as we know. But it's not straightforward. Or let's just say Giuseppe thinks it might not be straightforward.'

'Yeah, but he's a detective, isn't he? So he probably thinks everyone is guilty of something. The police are like that. I've been on the receiving end of their suspicions often enough, haven't I?'

'Let's not get into that.' Christina pushed her empty mug away. 'Anyway, Giuseppe isn't a detective anymore. He's retired. And the reason he retired has something to do with an unsolved case in Rome that he won't talk about.'

'Ooh, I love a mystery.'

'This isn't a game, Flavia, it's not some Agatha Christie whodunnit. It's people's lives we're talking about.'

'Or their deaths.' Flavia began a smile, but then forced her mouth into a straight line again.

'Giuseppe has an inkling that one of Mr Swain's lodgers might have had something to do with his death. Don't ask me how or why, but we found out that this chap had a row with Mr Swain just hours before the poor man's death.'

'Who is this lodger? Can't you just ask him straight out?'

'His name is Danny Forrest. And I tried that, but I got nowhere and now he's done a runner.'

'Danny Forrest?'

'Yep.'

'I know him. It was me who suggested he get lodgings in Bexhill.'

CHAPTER 19

The *who, why* and *when* questions were tossed around between Giuseppe, Christina and Flavia for the next few hours. Just a mention that '*Flavia knows something about Danny Forrest'* was enough to persuade Giuseppe from his bedroom. He had been listening to the wireless, soothing his muddled thoughts by tuning in to the BBC Third Programme, and a performance of Beethoven's opera, *Fidelio*. It was all in German, so he couldn't understand a word of it. Nevertheless, he was able to close his eyes and imagine he was sitting in the Royal Opera House in Covent Garden, the music surrounding him. By the end of the first act, he had made a promise to himself that he would try to get tickets and go there in person. It would need to be soon if he was to hold fast to the other promise he'd made himself about returning to Rome. He would ask Christina if she wanted to join him at the opera, although he doubted she would appreciate anything that was not 'pop'. Mario and Anne would love it, he was certain. But convincing his cousin to close the café early in order to make a night of it would require too much persuasive energy. And he knew that Anne hated the frenetic confusion of the city. She had told him as much when he'd stepped in to help with the George Leigh case.

While he was wrestling with these thoughts, there was a knock on his bedroom door.

'Giuseppe, are you still awake?' Christina's voice.

'Come in, come in.'

Although Giuseppe's bedroom was spacious, he had been loath to make it too comfortable in case it gave him another reason to linger in Bexhill. Anne was frequently apologising for the drabness of the room.

'We should hang some pictures, maybe get some new curtains. Make the place look a bit more cosy, otherwise you're just staring at four blank walls,' she had said some weeks earlier.

Giuseppe waved her worries away, reassuring her it was just fine and anyway, he was imposing on them far longer than he had originally planned.

The flat above the café wasn't in the same poor state of repair as Giuseppe had seen in Claremont Lodge, but was best described as 'unloved'. All his cousin's efforts went into the café, ensuring it provided a bright and welcoming space for customers. The flat was just a place to sleep.

Soon after Giuseppe's arrival, Anne tried to convince her husband to let his cousin have their wireless. 'We've got the television set now, we don't have so much need for a wireless.' It was a suggestion, more than an announcement, but a suggestion that was not well received.

'I never watch the television,' was her husband's reply.

So recently Giuseppe had visited the shops and bought his own small wireless, which had its new home on top of the tallboy. It meant he had an easy excuse whenever he wanted to absent himself from the rest of the family, providing everyone with a bit of much-needed space from each other. On more than one occasion Mario had grumbled about the loud music emanating from Giuseppe's room. Perhaps Mario would not enjoy a visit to Covent Garden after all.

Despite the energetic sound of *Fidelio*, Giuseppe had heard Christina's voice. He turned the wireless off and called to her to come in.

'I think you'll want to hear what Flavia has just told me.

It's about Danny Forrest. She knows him.' Christina said.

He slid his feet into his slippers and followed Christina along the landing, and down the four steps that led to the kitchen of the flat.

Flavia was standing by the sink, one hand hovering over the handle of the kettle. 'Hot drink, anyone?'

'Giuseppe only drinks espresso, and he's the only one who's allowed to use the coffee percolator.' Christina nodded towards the silver percolator that sat on a shelf above the worktop, a packet of *Lavazza* coffee beside it.

'It's a bit of an art then, is it? Making proper Italian coffee?'

'Making it, waiting for it to percolate, drinking it - it is all an art,' Giuseppe said.

'Going to show me, then?' Flavia took the percolator from the shelf and handed it to Giuseppe.

'I will show you while you tell me what you know about *Signor* Forrest.'

'Not that much to be honest.' Flavia pulled a chair out from the table and sat, this time sitting the right way round and smirking at Christina as she did so. 'I got chatting to him one day in a café. He looked in a bit of a state to be honest, so I took pity on him.' She paused and glanced again at Christina. 'I know what's it like to be down on your luck.'

'The two of you made friends?' Christina asked.

'Not friends. I bought him a coffee, asked him if he was okay. He told me how his dad had died in the war and his mum had linked up with this bloke. The family all moved into this bloke's flat and at first everything was sweet.'

'Lorna Warrington told us that Danny has two brothers,' Christina said.

'Yeah, both younger than him. Anyway, it was all good

until the bloke threatened to throw them all out on the street.'

'Why would he do that? Had Danny's mother been unfaithful or something?'

'Look, remember, all I'm doing at this point is buying the bloke a coffee. I wasn't up for a counselling session.'

The water in the percolator began to bubble through the ground coffee, capturing everyone's attention. The noise broke the quiet that had settled inside the flat, as well as on the street outside. Giuseppe turned the gas off, leaving the water to continue to filter through into the upper chamber of the percolator without added force. He waited a few moments and then lifted the lid and gave the coffee a single stir. As he took three cups down from the shelf above the worktop Christina shook her head.

'Not for me, thanks.'

'Come on then, let's see what's so special about *your* Italian coffee,' Flavia said, smirking as she held Giuseppe's gaze.

He poured a little coffee into two of the cups, sliding one of them towards Flavia. She took a sip and then pursed her lips together tightly. 'Wow, strong then.'

'*Zucchero*? Some sugar, perhaps?'

'No, let's keep it authentic. You don't take sugar, do you?'

'Ah, but I am Italian.' The beginnings of a smile crept around Giuseppe's mouth.

'And I'm half Italian,' Flavia said with gusto.

'Okay, now that you both have your coffee, can we get back to the conversation we were having about Danny Forrest?' Christina glared at her sister and waited.

'Like I said, I don't know that much about him. Except after that first time when I met him in the café…'

'When you bought him a coffee,' Christina added.

'Yeah. Then it was a bit of a coincidence because a few days later he came into my bookshop.'

'Your bookshop.'

Giuseppe watched the exchange of looks between the sisters that said so much more than the words they were speaking.

'Not my bookshop exactly, but the one I was working in.'

'You've been working in a bookshop?'

'Don't sound so surprised. I told you I got a job and in case you've forgotten, I grew up watching how to offer perfect customer service - it was the only thing I did learn, pretty much.'

'Don't make me laugh. The moment the customers were out of the door you couldn't wait to say something rude about them.'

'Yes, darling sister, but never to their face. That's the important thing to remember.'

Giuseppe rapped on the table, to gain their attention.

'*Signor* Forrest came into the bookshop where you worked.'

'Exactly. I asked him if he was okay, whether things had settled down at home. And that's when he told me he'd got himself a job as a typewriter salesman. *I'll show him*, he said. *I'll make enough money to get my own place and then Mum and Mickey and Fred can move in with me and they'll be safe again.*'

'He was frightened for his family?' Giuseppe had created one image of Danny Forrest, which was not matching the one that Flavia was describing.

'I've met Danny. Giuseppe hasn't,' Christina said. 'And, trust me, he's never going to make a successful salesman.'

'But he is someone with a temper. We know that from

Signora Warrington's account of the argument between *Signor* Forrest and *Signor* Swain.'

'What exactly do you think Danny did?' Flavia pushed her empty cup away. 'I think I could get to like Italian coffee, by the way. So make sure you tip me the wink when you're making your next pot.' She winked at Giuseppe, receiving a frown in return.

'Tip you the wink?'

'Just ignore her, Giuseppe. She's trying to be clever,' Christina said.

'Well, you should know all about that dear sister.'

'*Basta*. Enough. You have asked me what I think *Signor* Forrest did. I try not to think, but to follow facts. Fact. There was an argument between the two men that *Signora* Warrington heard, but she could tell us nothing about the content of that argument. Fact. The argument occurred just hours before I found Edward lying crushed beneath the summer house. Fact. Something or someone led him to leave his bedroom in the middle of the night, in the middle of a storm, wearing only his pyjamas.'

'Didn't have a cat, did he?' Flavia said.

Giuseppe and Christina both looked at Flavia and then at each other.

'A cat,' Christina said. 'What in heaven does a cat have to do with anything?'

'Well, say Mr Swain knew that his cat was trapped in the summer house. Maybe he went out to save it.'

'Edward did not have a cat.' Giuseppe stood, putting his empty cup into the sink, turning his back on Flavia and Christina.

'Just a thought,' Flavia said.

'Flavia, you told me it was your idea that Danny Forrest came here to Bexhill? So, how did that come about?'

Christina asked.

'He came back into the bookshop a few times. It was like he'd found someone to listen to him or something. I don't really know why he kept wanting to tell me things. But each time he took the next step forward he came in to tell me about it, like he was reporting in somehow.' Flavia turned the chair around and sat astride it, as if by doing so she was returning to a more comfortable place in her mind.

'He had found a friend,' Giuseppe said.

'I suppose. Although he's not exactly the kind of bloke I'd hang out with.' Flavia's face coloured a little.

'I wonder how he got the sales job,' Christina said. 'I mean don't you need loads of chat to be a salesman? You'd be good at it, Flavia. I bet you could sell sand in a desert.'

'Very funny. But you're right, I would be good at it. I am good at it, that's why I've just got a pay rise.'

'As the bookshop sales assistant?'

'Deputy manager, I'll have you know.'

'Just remind me - which of us was the bookworm when we were kids?' Christina forced a smile, unseen by Flavia who turned to look in the other direction.

'*Per favore*. Please can we focus on *Signor* Forrest.' Giuseppe struck the edge of the sink with one hand, as if he was calling a meeting to order.

'Yeah, well, it turned out that the first time Danny told me about the sales job he hadn't even had the interview. But he must have made a good impression somehow - chat or no chat - because a few days later he came into the bookshop full of smiles, saying he'd got the job. I asked him where he'd be working and he said he'd been given a choice of territory. He could cover Brighton and the surrounding towns, Worthing, Hove, that kind of thing. Or he could focus on Eastbourne and head east to Bexhill and Hastings. I could tell he was in a bit of a quandary and that more than anything he wanted to get away from this bloke that his mum had teamed up with. He said he'd never even been to Brighton, so he wouldn't know his way around. And that's when I came up with the answer. Clever, eh?'

'You suggested he focus on the area he knew - Eastbourne - but base himself somewhere nearby, as in Bexhill,' Christina said.

'You've got it in one.'

'And did you know about Claremont Lodge?' Giuseppe asked.

'No, of course not. I just told him to head for Bexhill seafront and look for any vacancies for a room, I knew it wouldn't take him long to find one.'

'So he didn't know Edward before he moved in. And if he came to Bexhill to escape his stepfather, then Edward could not be the man he was escaping from.' Giuseppe stepped towards the window and looked out into the darkness.

'Which gets us where?' Christina said.

'Nowhere, Christina. It gets us nowhere.'

CHAPTER 20

The next morning Christina struggled to respond to the alarm when it buzzed at seven o'clock, after a broken night during which she kept being woken by conversations between Stevie and Flavia. Four or five times she woke, swung her legs out of bed, padded out onto the landing and put her ear against their bedroom door, to be met with silence. Either they had stopped speaking or the voices she heard were only in her dreams. She didn't hide her irritability when she elbowed her sister to one side to slide a couple of slices of bread under the grill.

Stevie was slowly pouring milk onto a bowl of Rice Krispies, leaning his face down close to the bowl and then jiggling it around.

'What on earth are you doing?' Christina said.

'Leave him be. He's alright.' Flavia said. 'He's listening out for the snap, crackle and pop, aren't you, Stevie?'

A nod was Stevie's only reply. Then, seemingly having given up on listening, he started to munch his way through the cereal with such speed that most of the milk dribbled down his chin.

'How long do you really plan to stay?' Christina said as quietly as possible, hoping her nephew was too engrossed to notice the subject of the conversation.

'Like I said, a couple of nights. Is that a problem?' Flavia made no attempt to lower her voice, glaring at her sister as if to challenge her.

'We'll talk about it later. Is Mum taking Stevie to school?'

'No, I am. That's okay with you, is it?' She didn't wait for a reply, instead putting Stevie's empty bowl into the sink and taking his hand. 'Come on, let's get you ready, shall we?'

The toast was ready, but Christina had lost her appetite.

When Flavia returned an hour or so later, Christina was up in the sitting room, a large Quality Street tin in front of her.

'Bit early in the day for sweets, isn't it?' Flavia said.

'Look at this.' Christina pulled out a handful of photographs, spreading them out onto the table, pointing to one small black and white one of an eight-year-old Flavia, sitting on the bench in the back garden of the café, holding a box of Kellogg's cornflakes.

'Ha. Maybe I was hoping to be picked for a television advert.' Flavia took the photo, walking over to the window. 'Look at the state of my hair. One of Mum's worse attempts at hairdressing, I'd say. I'd forgotten we kept the photos in that tin. Let's find one of you.' She returned to the table and shuffled through more of the photos, picking one that was inside a cardboard sleeve.

'School photo.' Christina said, opening the sleeve. 'What an innocent pair we were.'

The photo showed Christina and Flavia in their school uniform, sitting side by side at a school desk, both gazing directly at the camera.

'Look at the state of your tie,' Flavia said. 'I reckon you've got gravy on it or something.'

'Tomato ketchup, probably.' Christina laughed, then bundled the photos up and put them all back into the tin.

'What made you get these out, anyway?'

'I've been trying to remember a time when we weren't at each other's throats.'

'And can you?'

'I don't think I'll ever understand you, Flavia.'

'There's not much to understand.'

'It's as if you don't only want to destroy your own life, you want to take everyone else down with you.'

'Now you're just being melodramatic.'

'Am I? You've been living in Eastbourne and you didn't let us know, or come to visit, or ask how Stevie was getting on. It's like you've forgotten he's your son. And then you suddenly turn up and want to take him away from everything he knows. You can't do it, Flavia. I won't let you.' Christina slammed her hand on the table causing the lid of the Quality Street tin to clatter to the floor.

'Hey, calm down, I'm not going to do anything to upset the little chap,' Flavia said, pulling out a chair and sitting astride it, facing Christina.

'Pretty much everything you've done since he was born has upset him.'

'Well, thanks for the vote of confidence. Look, I know I've messed up, but isn't everyone allowed a second chance? I've moved closer now, I've got a job, a nice flat and I was thinking I could just have him over to stay now and then. At a weekend. That wouldn't be so bad, would it?'

'I just don't want him hurt, Flavia.' Christina's voice was croaky now, and it was all she could do to stop herself crying.

'Neither do I.'

Flavia picked up the lid, put it back on the tin and slid it to the other side of the table. 'How are things here, anyway?'

'What do you mean?'

'With Mum and Dad.'

'Same as ever. Why?'

'Dad seems even more grumpy than I remember him.'

'That might have something to do with you turning up.'

'And you wonder why I stay away. When your own family treats you like a pariah…'

'You've brought it all on yourself, Flavia.'

'It's the silences I can't stand. I wish he'd just come out and say what he's thinking, instead of glaring at me every time I walk into the room.'

'You should know Dad well enough to realise he rarely says what's on his mind. And if you want the truth, it's not only you turning up that's causing an atmosphere. I think having Giuseppe here is creating tension as well.'

Flavia raised an eyebrow and waited for Christina to continue.

'I don't know the ins and outs, just that Giuseppe has made the odd oblique reference to something in Dad's past. I'm guessing it could be the reason Dad has never wanted to return to Italy. And I suppose having Giuseppe here is a constant reminder.'

'Have you asked Mum about it?'

'I'm not sure she knows what it's all about, or if she does she's as loath to talk about it as Dad is.'

'Maybe I should do my own digging then. See if I can't get one of them to open up,' Flavia said, rubbing her hands together, as if she had completed a complicated task with great success.

'You can try, but I'm doubtful you'll have much luck. Anyway, I need to get to work or I'll have Charles on my back.' The tiredness that Christina had felt earlier that morning washed over her again. As she stood her limbs felt heavy, as if she had been running uphill, struggling to reach the summit.

'You'll pick Stevie up from school later?' Even her voice sounded tired.

'I know you don't like to question the status quo, but sometimes it's worth it. Anyway, I thought you'd turned into an investigator with all that nosing around you've been doing with Giuseppe. This should be right up your street.'

'We're talking about family, Flavia. That's the difference.'

CHAPTER 21

While Flavia was reflecting on the best way to question her parents about the past, Giuseppe was rethinking his announcement that his investigation was going 'nowhere'. He had left behind much of the sadness he felt about his friend's tragic death and as each day passed he became increasingly energised by the certainty that this was a case that needed investigating.

Listening to Flavia the evening before had raised his hopes regarding Danny Forrest, only to smash them on the rocks again. There was now no reason for Giuseppe to suspect Danny Forrest had anything to do with Edward's death. What would be the motive? And yet... he was certain there was unfinished business regarding the typewriter salesman that Giuseppe needed to resolve before he could unravel the truth.

So when Mario called up to Giuseppe to say that Detective Inspector Pearce was on the telephone, it was as if a small chink of light was appearing in the shadows that had fallen over him since Edward's death.

'*Signor* Pearce. *Buongiorno.*'

Mario hovered close to the phone, having handed over the receiver.

'*Si*. I will come this morning,' Giuseppe said.

'Did you want to take my car?' Mario was intent on wiping down some of the café tables, but had clearly heard the outcome of the conversation between his cousin and the policeman.

'Are you sure?'

'I won't be needing it today, so you might as well use it. It'll give it a run out.' Mario's reply was brusque, leaving

Giuseppe uncertain whether his cousin was content with the idea of loaning out his car or anxious that it might return with a new dent or scratch.

'I will catch the train, I think. It is more relaxing.'

'You mean it will save you from having to negotiate British roundabouts.' Mario's expression softened.

'I will buy a newspaper,' Giuseppe said, as if considering the options. 'No, I will look out of the window and enjoy the English scenery.'

The train journey from Bexhill tracked the coastline through the seaside village of Norman's Bay. It was just yards from this station that back in July, when Giuseppe was nearing the end of his journey from Rome to Bexhill, he had jumped off the train when he heard ambulance sirens. Sadly, the sirens signalled the tragic death of a teenage boy. Now, as the train took the bend, he spotted the railway crossing that reminded him of all the angst of those few weeks, when he had worked with Christina to uncover the truth about who was responsible for George Leigh's death. The weather on that fateful summer day had affected much of what transpired. It was a further reminder that once again the weather - the recent October storm - was what had led to Edward's death. During all the years his cousin had lived in England, Giuseppe had lamented the English weather on Mario's behalf. Any letters that were written, as well as phone calls made between the cousins, would inevitably start with a question from Giuseppe.

'Is it raining again?' Giuseppe would ask, knowing that Mario would ignore the question and the inference. Giuseppe understood the reasons that Mario clung to that caused him to turn his back on Italy, but Giuseppe was ready to challenge them. And with that potential for challenge forever bubbling under the surface, Giuseppe was certain that sooner or later there would have to be a conversation that both were avoiding, one that would either heal the rift between them or split it so far apart that it would be impossible to repair.

Giuseppe turned his focus away from the train window, looking down the carriage. There was no one else sitting in his immediate vision, but he could see the back of someone's head a few seats down from him. He deduced that the man - and he knew it was a man as he was wearing a smart felt hat - must have been at least as tall as Giuseppe, even a little taller. The only movement the man's head made was to occasionally dip forward, as if he was easing out tension from the back of his neck. And then Giuseppe heard a snore, followed by a cough. The man must have been dozing, his head falling forwards as he began to sleep, then each time he snored he woke himself up, coughing to hide any embarrassment he might feel at the thought that others had heard his rumbling noises. Giuseppe was tempted to walk up to the man and reassure him, tell him to relax, to sleep and snore and not to mind what others might think of him.

Instead, his thoughts went to Rosalia. All of their married life her concerns were focused outwards - thinking always about how she appeared to others. She had chosen the furniture in their flat to create an image of fine living, her clothes too. Whenever they entertained she tried several outfits on before selecting the one she felt sure would make a statement to their guests. She paraded each one in front of him, irritated by the shrug of his shoulders, his vague, '*Si, bella*', to each of them. When she waved him away, told him to leave her in peace to choose for herself, he felt only relief, as if he was a child told he no longer had to do his homework. There had been a shallowness to their life together that, with hindsight, he could see more sharply.

The train came to a halt, bringing his attention back to the present. The carriage door banged closed and he saw the felt hatted man strolling along the platform. For a moment Giuseppe felt as though he had made a connection with the man, even though they had never spoken and likely would never speak. The man's shoulders were hunched forward, as if he was carrying a great weight on his back. He had pulled the hat down so that the wide brim shaded his eyes, eyes that Giuseppe felt sure would have sleep still lingering in them. Moments later, the man had walked through the ticket barrier and was out of sight.

The platform sign indicated they were at Pevensey and Westham station, and Giuseppe knew there was just one more stop before arriving in Eastbourne. The track had left the coast now, so that either side of the train his view was of fields, interspersed with residential areas. Although this wasn't his first visit to England, or his first train journey, it still surprised him to see the way that every house had a patch of green in front of it, sometimes behind too. And yet he knew from Christina that while the view gave the impression of easy, spacious living, there were many families struggling with dreadful housing conditions, in properties that might have escaped wartime bombing, but should now be condemned as no longer fit for purpose. But replacing old houses with new tower blocks created a whole host of other problems, not just to do with the absence of grass.

An hour later and Giuseppe was sitting in Pearce's office, having declined a drink - hot or cold - waiting while the detective completed a telephone call.

'Sorry about that,' Pearce said, as he put down the receiver. 'It's a job to get any of my team to make a decision on their own, seems they need to check every step with me. I suppose they think I'll bawl them out if they get it wrong.'

'And do you?' Giuseppe smiled.

'Probably. Didn't you?'

'E vero. It is true. It is often difficult to know when to lead and when to follow.'

'I suppose that's what we get paid for, eh? Being in charge comes at a price, whichever way you look at it.'

'Si, but of course I am no longer paid, because I have retired.'

'Retired from Italian policing, but not from detective work, eh?' Pearce gave a throaty chuckle as if he was pleased at having told a joke.

Giuseppe gave a polite smile and nodded. 'Of course, police work is in our blood, I think. You and I, we will never retire from it.'

'Don't tell my wife that, she's counting the days. Although having me under her feet all day every day will likely end in divorce.'

The smile left Giuseppe's face as he was reminded of his own marriage.

'And you have some information for me? About Signor Forrest?'

'Yes, yes, of course. When you mentioned the name to me the other day, I thought it rang bells. So after you left I did a bit of digging and had a chat with uniform. Turns out the Forrest family is well known to the Eastbourne constabulary.'

'They have committed crimes?'

'Well, let's just say they are often on our radar. Three lads, two of them in and out of trouble. Nothing to warrant borstal, not yet anyway. But the warnings are piling up, so if they continue along the same path, then…'

'And Daniel? He is one of those who have been in trouble with your *uniform*?' Giuseppe allowed himself the briefest of smiles, proud he was understanding more and more of the English language, the phrasing and casual use of words to mean one thing when they sounded as if they should mean another.

'No. There have been no charges against Daniel Forrest. The two boys - his brothers - are Michael and Frederick. Michael Forrest has just turned fifteen and Frederick is two years younger. From what my men have told me and looking at the files, they're not bad lads, but easily led. Wilful damage, shoplifting, that kind of thing. Trouble is Mr Bianchi that all it takes nowadays is for a youngster to get in with a bad crowd and often there's no turning back for them. Years later they end up in prison, where they learn ever more bad ways, and suddenly all they know is how to lead a life of crime. Look at your Miss Rossi and her young man.'

Giuseppe pushed his chair a little further from Pearce's desk, and began tapping his fingers on his leg.

'Don't take it the wrong way. I'm not saying your cousin's daughter is a criminal, or even that she could end up as one. All I'm saying is that it doesn't take much for someone to get caught up in situations that can end up beyond their control. Being in the wrong place at the wrong time, sometimes that's all it takes.'

'*Si*, Detective Inspector. Sadly, I know that.'

It seemed to Giuseppe that all conversations led him back to the reminders of death. Carlo's grandson, and now Edward Swain. There were times when he wished he could have spent his time absorbed by the beauty of life - great music, fine art, inspiring literature - instead of the bleak tragedies of crime.

'I would like to call on the Forrest family. Are you able to give me their address?'

Giuseppe waited. Asking Pearce for personal details about a family who were being watched by the police when Giuseppe had no connection to the Eastbourne Constabulary, or any constabulary, would leave him beholden to Pearce. He was asking Pearce to breach police protocol. It would be a favour offered that Giuseppe would be unable to return.

Pearce opened one of the top drawers of his desk and pulled out a notepad. The top sheet was blank, but as Pearce lifted the page Giuseppe could see there was writing beneath, mostly scribbles and doodles with numbers and letters in a random pattern. Pearce tore the bottom half of the sheet off and wrote down an address, then thrust the slip of paper at Giuseppe.

'You didn't get it from me,' Pearce said.

'Of course, I understand.'

'And if you see either of those boys and you get a chance to give them a bit of friendly advice, remind them that their chances are running out. A cat might have nine lives, but that doesn't necessarily follow with teenage hooligans.' Pearce stood and extended his hand.

'It is very good to see you, Detective Inspector. I hope we will see each other again.'

Giuseppe slipped the piece of paper into his jacket pocket, then watched Pearce take a pencil sharpener from a pot on his desk, sharpen one of the pencils from the same pot and begin scribbling on the notepad.

'You tap, I scribble,' he said, smiling. 'We've got to do something to keep those cigarettes at bay, haven't we?'

CHAPTER 22

On Giuseppe's arrival at Eastbourne railway station he had bought a street map, which he referred to now as he made his way to the address Pearce had given him. Clouds had been hiding the autumn sun since early morning and now they created a blanket of pale grey, with no shades of blue to be seen. Giuseppe had listened to the shipping forecast before he took Max for his early morning walk. He listened to it every day now, the words that seemed so strange the first time he heard them were becoming familiar.

As he listened to the almost poetic rhythm, the all-important warnings to sailors around the British Isles, he replayed his conversations with Edward, the last one in particular. Edward had seemed especially quiet that day. He had asked Giuseppe to call round to Claremont Lodge the next day when he had promised to explain what it was that was worrying him. Of course, the meeting never took place, because by the next morning Edward was dead.

Besides Giuseppe's misgivings about Danny Forrest, there was another thought niggling away at him. He'd mentioned it to Christina, but now he wished he could wipe the thought from his mind, instead it kept resurfacing, like steam from a rumbling volcano. *What if Edward had reached a point of desperation leading him to take his own life? Had he been involved in shady dealings with a council member to gain a licence for premises that were not fit for purpose? Perhaps he had run up debts he feared he could never repay.* And then there were Edward's final words. *Why would he need to apologise and who was Josephine?* Giuseppe reached this point in the silent argument he had with himself several times a day since Edward's death, and then stopped and began asking questions, such as - *Aren't there better ways to kill yourself than to walk out in the night in a storm, in your pyjamas?* There was a more pressing question too, which was chipping away at Giuseppe's confidence in his own abilities as a detective. *Wouldn't I have known if Edward had been brought so low as to want to take his own life?* And then, if all these thoughts were laid out like a flowchart, they brought Giuseppe to the end point.

But that end point was not just the resolution of the truth behind Edward's death. There was another unresolved case - the death of Carlo's grandson. And a question he had punished himself with since the day he saw Emanuele lying on the street below his balcony in Rome. *Did the child fall to his death, or was it something far, far worse?*

He was so engrossed in these thoughts that he stepped off the pavement without realising he was almost in the path of an oncoming car. The driver hooted and as Giuseppe stepped backwards he knocked into an elderly woman who was standing just behind him.

'Careful there, luvvie, you nearly had me down.'

The woman was carrying a wicker basket filled with carrots and onions, which she swapped from one hand to the other as if the weight of it was making her arm ache. She was a little over five foot tall, and with her arm at full stretch the heavy basket was almost touching the ground.

'*Scusi, signora.* I am so sorry. Are you alright?'

'Oh, you're Italian, aren't you?' She placed the wicker basket down by her feet, tucked a stray hair underneath her headscarf and looked up at Giuseppe. 'Of course you are. You don't get a tan like that in England.' Her laugh was more of a giggle. 'Do you know, I'm going to be eighty next week and I've never been abroad. But there's not

172

much I don't know about Italy. It's a passion of mine, you see, and I've read every library book that has even a mention of the country. I suppose you know that it was the Romans who built most of our English roads?' She giggled again, then stooped to pick up her basket. 'But listen to me rattling on, I must let you get on your way. Are you lost? I can see you've got a street map there. I've lived in Eastbourne all my life, so I'll bet I can point you in the right direction.'

'*Grazie*. Yes, I am looking for Tower Street.'

'Well, Tower Street is just around the corner from me. Come on, we'll walk together and I'll show you.'

'You are very kind, and I would like to return your kindness.' He went to take the basket from her, but she seemed reluctant to let it go for a moment, but then passed the basket over. 'Just a few vegetables for soup. It's all I fancy at the moment, don't seem to have much of an appetite for dry food, but a warming bowl of soup, well it slips down a treat.'

She carried on chatting as they walked, with Giuseppe content to listen. He slowed his stride and stayed a pace or two behind her, letting her lead the way. They passed a row of small shops and what looked like an entrance to a builder's yard. Then she pointed towards a narrow alleyway.

'This is me,' she said, stopping and reaching her hand out to take the basket.

'Would you like me to carry it to your door?'

'Well now, I wouldn't usually let a stranger walk me home, but you've got such a trustworthy face.'

'And I am Italian.' Giuseppe smiled down at the woman, reminded for a moment of one of his elderly aunts who was ferociously independent. Zia Maria would visit the fruit and vegetable market every morning, walking home laden with produce and then spend the rest of the day cooking. Whenever he visited she would press two lire into his hand, put her finger to her lips, making him promise to keep the gift a secret from his cousins. But they all knew that Zia Maria did the same for all of them. The money was never spent, but put in a terracotta pot and when the much loved aunt passed away, the cousins paid for a beautiful floral tribute to grace her coffin. It was something he could remind Mario about. A time when the cousins shared everything.

'Visiting friends in Tower Street, are you?'

They had arrived at a narrow gateway about halfway down the alley. Giuseppe looked beyond the rusty metal gate that led onto a brick path, up to a row of narrow terraced houses.

'Mrs Forrest,' Giuseppe said. 'I am an acquaintance of her son.' It was a truth of sorts.

'That poor woman. Seems as though she's destined to have trouble follow her all her life.'

'You know her?'

'Like I said, luvvie, I've lived here for years. There aren't many families round here who don't know the Forrests. And you know her son, you say? Which one would that be?'

'Daniel Forrest.'

'Ah, Danny, the eldest. He's had to grow up quickly, that's for sure. Having to watch out for those two ragamuffins…'

Giuseppe could have asked for an explanation, but guessed he had the gist of what the woman was saying.

'Have you seen Danny recently?' he asked.

'I can't say I have. But then there are so many comings

and goings from that house, it's a job to keep track. Well, I'll let you get on your way. Just go up to the end of the alley, turn left and you'll see No 22 on your right. They're on the first floor, but how they all squeeze into that place is a mystery to me.'

'It's been a pleasure meeting you, *Signora*...'

'Mrs Amy Farnham, that's me.'

'I am Giuseppe Bianchi.' He extended his hand, the basket now on the ground beside her. 'And enjoy your soup.'

He tucked his scarf more firmly into the collar of his jacket and headed down the alleyway, turning just once to see Mrs Farnham pick up her basket and walk slowly towards her front door.

The entrance to No 22 Tower Street was a reminder to Giuseppe that a town could be many things. On a previous visit to Eastbourne he had ambled along the promenade, taken note of the grand hotels that overlooked the seafront, the Carpet Gardens with their well-tended flower borders, all combining to offer a welcome to the holidaymakers who spent their summers in the south coast resort. But here, he was looking at a different side to the town. Hidden away from the eyes of tourists, the drab frontages suggested an even more bleak interior. Some of the windows either side of No 22 were boarded up and Giuseppe wondered if this was an area of housing listed for demolition.

There was no need for Giuseppe to knock on the door of No 22, as it was already ajar and a firm shove enabled him to step into a dingy hallway, with a staircase ahead of him. A broken bicycle lay at the foot of the stairs, together with a couple of empty hessian sacks and a stack of old newspapers. He stepped over the bicycle and climbed the stairs slowly, noticing the creaks each time he placed his foot down.

'Hello, I am looking for Mrs Forrest.' He called up ahead of him.

A door was slammed shut, followed by the sound of thudding footsteps on the floorboards above. And then a man's voice, calling out, 'And don't bother coming back this time.'

Giuseppe had reached halfway up the first flight of stairs. He hesitated a moment and then a young lad appeared, brushing past him and running out of the front door. According to Pearce, Danny's younger brothers were Michael, aged fifteen and Frederick, two years younger. The brief glimpse of the boy who had pushed past him led him to guess it was Michael Forrest.

Continuing to climb the stairs, he reached a half landing, spotting a doorway he presumed was to a toilet, then up the second flight of stairs until he stood face to face with a man.

The man was thickset, a few inches shorter than Giuseppe, almost bald and wearing a string vest with braces over the top holding his trousers up over a fat belly.

'And who the hell are you?' The man's face was flushed, and as he spoke Giuseppe could smell alcohol on his breath.

'Good morning, sir. I am Mr Giuseppe Bianchi.'

'What the hell are you doing in my flat? Lost your way home, have you?' The man stood, legs astride, with his hands on his hips, as though ready for a fight.

'I am looking for Mrs Forrest, but perhaps I am in the wrong place.'

'You're in the wrong place alright. Clear off, go on, push off back to wherever you've come from.' He gave

176

Giuseppe a shove, but instead of moving back and away from the man, Giuseppe stepped closer to him.

'I am looking for Mrs Forrest,' he repeated. 'I have been told this is where she lives.'

'And what's it to you if she does, eh? Who are you - her new fancy man?'

A judgement had to be made. If Giuseppe pursued his request to meet with Danny's mother he could create difficulties for her, given that the bully blocking his way could misinterpret the reason for his visit. Alternatively, he could turn and walk away, perhaps catch up with the young boy who had dashed past him on the stairs. He chose the latter route of action, holding his hands up in a gesture of surrender.

'I am sorry to have disturbed you, sir. Good day to you.' He turned to walk back down the stairs, aware that the man was watching him.

When Giuseppe reached the half landing, the man called out. 'Don't bother coming back.'

It seemed that it was the man's favourite phrase that day.

CHAPTER 23

Giuseppe didn't have to go far to find Michael Forrest. As soon as he stepped back out into the alleyway, he saw the lad crouching down, his back pushed up against the brick wall, his head hanging down.

Calling out, even walking up to him too suddenly, might frighten the lad and cause him to run. Instead, Giuseppe stayed fifty yards away, keeping him within his peripheral vision. If Giuseppe had been ten years younger, he might have mirrored the lad's position, sitting on his haunches, but he knew that if he tried it now, he would struggle to get up again easily. The years had stiffened his joints, which was a persistent annoyance to him.

There was nothing old or withered about Giuseppe's mind though, as he delved into his memories of similar situations where he had to use tact and diplomacy to get a witness talking, or a suspect to admit the truth.

'I was hoping to see Danny,' Giuseppe said, almost as though he was talking to himself, not looking across at Michael. 'He promised to show me the new typewriter he keeps in that special suitcase. It is not for me because I can't type. It is for my niece.' He paused, noticing that Michael hadn't altered his position, and so he continued. 'Have you seen it? I expect he has let you see it as you are his brother.'

This might have been a step too far. Michael stood and spun on one heel, as if intending to walk away from Giuseppe. Then he stopped and spoke, without turning around. 'How do you know he's my brother?'

'It was a good guess,' Giuseppe said, forcing a little chuckle as if he was proud of having made the connection.

'You look like him.' Again, he was treading on dangerous ground. Christina had described Daniel Forrest to him, but Giuseppe had never seen the man, so there may have been no likeness between the brothers.

'Yeah, well, I'm the good-looking one.'

Michael approached Giuseppe, his shoulders hunched forwards, his head bowed slightly so that his long fringe fell in front of his eyes. He had a way of looking up through his fringe, as if he had found it offered him some protection. 'Who are you, anyway? And how do you know my brother?'

'As I said, I am just an interested customer.'

Michael kicked at the ground beneath his feet, digging one heel into the earth and then scuffing away the loose gravel. As he did so Giuseppe noticed the sole of one shoe was flapping loose. He was wearing no socks and his trousers were stained and patched at the knee.

'I'm off to meet Danny now. You can come with me, if you like.'

Michael began to walk away, not waiting for Giuseppe's response. Then he stopped and pushed back his fringe, looking more directly at Giuseppe. 'You're not police, are you?'

'You don't like the police?'

'Who does?'

'I am sure there are good policemen.'

'Yeah, well, I'm not bothered if they're good or bad, so long as they keep out of my way.'

'It is just the typewriter salesman I am interested in.'

Michael gave a slight nod, then continued ambling along the alleyway with Giuseppe a few steps behind him.

No words passed between them as they walked back towards the town centre. Giuseppe sensed they were getting closer to the seafront, then Michael turned a corner which led into an open area, with gardens on one side and an imposing building opposite.

'New theatre,' Michael said, focused on the pavement, rather than the building he was referring to. 'They knock one theatre down and build another, all that money, just so that folk can sit and watch a load of people pretending to be someone they're not. Ever been to the theatre, have you?'

For a moment Giuseppe wished he could share his own thoughts about stage performances, which were not so different from Michael Forrest's. Comedies and dramas were not for him. But opera was something else entirely. It transported him to another place, one of great emotion and intensity. Shaking away these thoughts, Giuseppe searched for a topic that might generate some trust between him and the lad.

'I expect you like football.'

'Me and my brother, Fred, we're always having a kickabout over the back of the park.'

'There is a football field there?'

'Nah. We just put our jumpers down as goalposts. Trouble is, we don't have a decent ball. We were using one we found in a ditch, turned out it had a hole in it, so now it's good for nothing. A bit like my attempts at a header.' There was a lightness in Michael's tone that Giuseppe hadn't heard until now. 'My brother is useless at footie.'

'Fred?'

'Nah, Danny. Mostly on account of his leg.' As he said the words, it was as if a shutter had come down. His head hung low again, his fringe falling forward and his steps became a shuffle, the loose sole of his shoe catching at the uneven paving.

Giuseppe remembered Christina mentioning that Danny Forrest had an uneven gait, as though one leg was longer than the other. Leaving the subject alone seemed to be the safest thing.

They were approaching the seafront now, the Pier ahead of them. Despite the cloudy sky, people had chosen to venture out. By looking at the lightweight jackets and coats many were wearing, Giuseppe guessed they considered it a mild autumn day. He hadn't donned his overcoat today, but still had his woollen scarf wrapped tight inside the neckline of his jacket, grateful for the warmth it offered.

Continuing to follow Michael, Giuseppe found himself momentarily distracted as they stepped onto the Pier. He had been intrigued by the imposing structure whenever he had seen it from a distance, but now walking down the length of it - several hundred metres - he could see at close quarters the grandeur of its individual structures. A large theatre, a café and two saloon bars, with cupolas of various sizes adorning their roofs. To Giuseppe's mind it was an odd mix - rooftops that reminded him of some of the great cathedrals of his beloved country, decorating places that typified the most secular of pastimes - entertainment.

'Come on, he'll be down here.' Michael turned to beckon him forward.

As they reached close to the end of the Pier there were fewer people milling about. They passed two fishermen, perched on small wooden stools, at quite a distance from each other. Each man was intent on his rod and line, seemingly oblivious to anything else happening around him. Giuseppe had never fished, but he could understand the pleasure in it, the solitude, the chance to focus on one thing alone, that sudden movement at the end of the line, the tug on the rod, suggesting a successful catch. He remembered the conversation he'd had with Edward about fishing and a sadness washed over him, making him wish for a cigarette, or failing that a generous glass of vermouth.

They were past the fishermen now and had arrived at the furthest point, where the only structures to separate them from the gunmetal grey water were the railings, their colour so similar they almost blended into the foreground. Giuseppe looked past Michael, who had now come to a halt. Then, the wind suddenly whipped up, catching the end of his scarf, causing him to turn so he had his back to the sea.

'Mickey, who's this? What he's doing here?'

Danny Forrest was sitting alone in the corner of a wooden shelter sited at the end of the Pier, facing out to sea, facing into the wind, and now facing Giuseppe who extended his hand towards him.

'*Signor* Forrest. I am very pleased to meet you.'

'Mickey?' Danny's focus was on his brother only.

'It is my fault,' Giuseppe said. 'I asked your brother to bring me to meet you.'

'Why? Who are you?'

'My name is Giuseppe Bianchi, and I was a friend of *Signor* Swain, the man who owned Claremont Lodge in Bexhill. You were staying there until recently, yes?'

'Hang on a minute,' Michael said. 'You didn't say anything about that to me, you just said you wanted to buy a typewriter. Honest, Danny. If I thought he was anything to do with that Swain bloke, I'd never have brought him here.'

Michael stepped over to the railings, kicking at a pile of shingle that had gathered and shoving it over the edge of the Pier and into the sea.

'It is true, *Signor* Forrest. You must not blame your brother. I persuaded him to bring me here to meet you, because I think you can help me.'

'I don't have anything to say to you.'

'But I have not yet asked you a question.'

'You can ask what you like, there's nothing to tell.'

'I visited your home, but your stepfather would not allow me into the flat.'

'You've been to the flat? Is Mum alright? Mickey, what's happened to Mum, he hasn't hurt her again, has he?' Danny stood beside his brother, putting a hand on his shoulder, encouraging him to turn towards him.

'It's a mess, Danny. You've got to get Mum out of there. Fred too. You promised.'

Danny ran a hand through his hair and then slumped down to the ground, kicking his legs out in front of him.

'Look, I don't know who you are, or what you're doing here, but if you think I had anything to do with Mr Swain's death, you can forget it,' Danny said. 'And if you poking your nose into our family means trouble for Mum, then there'll be another death before long.'

It was fighting talk. The death that Daniel Forrest tossed into his curt response could have been his mother's, or it could have been his stepfather's. It could even have been Giuseppe's.

'Let us all be calm,' Giuseppe said. 'The shelter is a better place to sit than on the wet ground and it is a private place to talk. I know you and your brothers have been having a difficult time. There has been trouble with the police, yes?'

'What do you know about that?' Michael stood right in front of Giuseppe, putting his face so close that Giuseppe could smell his sour breath.

'You and your *friend*, you're both the same,' Danny said, standing beside his brother now, and confronting Giuseppe. 'Sure, my brothers have nicked a few things, mostly because Mum barely has enough food in the house to give them a proper meal. And, yeah, they've smashed up a couple of telephone boxes, but imagine how you might feel if you lived with someone who likes to use you as a punchbag. Go on, Mickey, show him.'

Michael looked at his brother, hesitating before taking his jumper off. The shirt he had on underneath was ripped under one arm. He rolled one sleeve up, revealing several bruises that merged together, reddish-purple in the centre, fading to yellow and blue on the outer edges.

'I am so sorry,' Giuseppe said, the words doing little to reflect the sickening he felt in the pit of his stomach. 'And you are trying to save enough money to help your mother and your brothers to get away from this man?'

'I'm trying, yeah. So, I get a good job, someone helps me out by suggesting where I can get cheap lodgings and then that Mr Swain starts accusing me.'

'Accusing you?'

'Look, Mr Bianchi. I know my brothers aren't perfect. I've done some bad things too, when I was a kid. But I believe in being honest. So when I moved into Claremont Lodge, I told Mr Swain everything. I explained how I needed to earn enough money to help my family. I told him that my brothers had had a bit of trouble with the police, but that I was keeping an eye on them. So, that was all good. Then one day - the day he died as it turned out - he stops me when I was on my way out, starts having a go at me.'

'You had an argument?'

'It ended up as an argument, yeah. Mostly because he

was accusing me of going into his bedroom, rifling through his things. And that's the trouble with people, they make assumptions. Just because my brothers have been in a bit of trouble here and there, well he just assumed I was the same.'

'He thought you were a thief? That you had been in his bedroom and stolen something? Did he say what was missing?'

'I don't even know if something was missing. I told him he'd got it wrong. Yeah, I shouted at him. You would have too if someone had accused you of being a thief.'

'And that night you stayed away?'

'I came over here. There's no way I'd go to the flat. This is where Mickey and I meet most evenings and that evening I was going to kip here in the shelter. But then the storm started up. Well, this is pretty much the worst place to be in the middle of a storm.'

Giuseppe muttered something to himself. He was thinking of another place that was far more dangerous on that fateful night.

'Were you able to find a safe place to sleep?'

'There's a little outside café kind of place in Devonshire Gardens. It's a shelter of sorts, not that I really slept, but it kept me dry at least until the morning.'

'And when you returned to Claremont Lodge the next day, you learned about *Signor* Swain's death.'

'Yep.'

'*Signor* Forrest - Danny - did your stepfather cause an injury to your leg?'

The brothers exchanged a look and Danny put his hand on his left leg, as though he was remembering a time that he had since tried to forget.

'Seen those steps up to the flat, have you? Well, he

185

thought it would be fun to see how well I bounced down them.' Danny flinched as he spoke.

'Danny, I can only imagine what you and your family have suffered,' Giuseppe said. 'I promise to do all I can to help you - all of you. But first you need to return to Claremont Lodge.'

CHAPTER 24

For much of the train journey back to Bexhill, Giuseppe kept his eyes closed. Everything he had seen over the previous few hours added to the rest of the painful images that had accumulated in his mental photograph album during his years as a detective. He would never get used to seeing the pain that one human being could inflict on another, physical pain as well as mental anguish, the results of which fanned out and multiplied. Just as the threads of human kindness offered support, so the opposite was true - acts of violence, greed, hatred, could remove every foundation, leaving the victim as fragile as poor Danny Forrest, with his damaged leg.

As Giuseppe walked into Bella Café that afternoon, he could sense all his muscles relax, tension in his back and shoulders that he hadn't even realised was there, now vanished. Cheerful faces of customers and Anne's welcome greeted him.

'There you are,' Anne said, coming towards him and taking his arm. 'You look as though you need a strong coffee.'

He chose a seat near to the counter, nodding at a couple of the regulars who lifted their hand in greeting. He unwound his scarf, draping it over the back of his chair and then Anne was beside him, smiling.

'Well, you won't want me to make your coffee, will you?'

'Ah, *si*. I will come.'

He went out to the back kitchen and spent a few moments preparing the percolator. Mario was checking off a grocery delivery, intent on ticking items off a list and counting boxes. Max was enjoying the new smells that had arrived with the delivery, even though none of it would end up in his food bowl.

'Is there anything I can do to help?' Giuseppe asked his cousin once the percolator was on the stove.

There was only one box left to be checked, which Mario now opened, taking out two large boxes of tea and several bags of sugar. 'I'm done now.' He put the list and pen down on the kitchen table, pulling out one of the chairs and sitting. 'A good time for coffee, I think.'

Giuseppe nodded, taking another cup from the shelf, as well as the sugar bowl. 'You always liked an extra spoon of sugar, even as a boy,' he said.

'And you always liked the *biscotti* that your *Zia* Silvana made.'

'Your mamma's biscuits were the very best, although I never said so in front of my mamma.'

The coffee was ready. Mario watched as Giuseppe gave it a single stir and then filled both cups, careful to leave any coffee dregs in the bottom of the percolator.

'I saw something today that reminded me of the importance of family,' Giuseppe said, his eyes clouding at the memory.

'I have never forgotten its importance.'

'And yet I think you would prefer me to return home. Perhaps I have stayed too long.'

They both drunk their espresso in one, setting the cups down on the table at the same moment. Mario ran his finger around the lip of the cup and gave out a heavy sigh.

'You are welcome to stay.' It was a curt invitation that seemed to leave much unsaid.

'But we remain apart?'

'All the time you want me to return to the past, then, *sì*, we remain apart.'

'And Anne?'

'Giuseppe, you are my cousin, you know something of the dark times in my past. When I am here, those events remain in the past. That is why I cannot return.'

'Even though all that happened was many years ago, another life? Filomena was your friend, you spent day after day sitting beside her bed, her family welcomed you as if you were their son. She was ill, Mario. She had tuberculosis. There was nothing you could do to change that.'

'You know nothing about it, Giuseppe. Please just leave it.' Mario lit a cigarette, moving to fetch the ashtray from the worktop.

'Have you ever spoken to Anne about that time? She may not be your blood, Mario, but she is your family. Please don't let the past continue to overshadow your future.'

'And you have looked at your past, have you? Is that not the very reason you are still here, hiding in Bexhill? Because you don't want to face up to your part in the breakdown of your marriage? Because you know there was more you could have done to discover the truth about the death of Carlo's grandson?' As he spat the words out, Mario blew the smoke from his cigarette directly at Giuseppe.

Before Giuseppe could respond, the door that led from the café opened and Anne came in.

'Oh, that's nice to see the two of you chatting together. About time.' She glanced from one to the other and as she did both men looked away as if they were mischievous schoolboys caught out by the headmistress. 'I can't stop,' Anne continued. 'It's just that Christina mentioned you might like to phone Rome. I'm sure there will be people wondering how you are. Is someone looking after your flat for you?'

'Thank you, Anne. You are very kind. A neighbour has the key to my flat, they are keeping the post for me. But, yes, Christina is right. She is reminding me to ring my sergeant, Silvio Bruni.'

'Well, just ring whenever you like. You don't have to ask, you must treat our home as your home. And now I must go or our customers will be feeling neglected.'

As Anne shut the door behind her, Mario stubbed his cigarette out in the ashtray and stood. 'I'm sorry. I spoke harshly just now. I know you mean well, but remember that we both choose to keep things hidden. You are no different from me.'

Giuseppe stood as well. 'You are wrong. At least on this occasion. Because the phone call I am going to make to Silvio will be the first step forward.'

'Or backward? You're going to ask him about Carlo? The verdict was accidental death, Giuseppe. You might just have to accept it, like I need to accept the past mistakes I made. I'm trying to look to the future, to making sure Bella Café continues to thrive. Who knows, perhaps one day I can hand over the reins to Stevie, or Christina's child, if she ever has one.' Mario picked up the clipboard and stepped towards the door. 'I'll leave you to your phone call.'

'Let us talk again soon. Don't shut me out, Mario.'

All the time the cousins had been chatting, Max was lying beneath the kitchen table, precisely positioned between the two of them, occasionally opening one eye before closing it again. Now he stretched long, kicking his back legs out behind him, and coming to standing. He sidled over to Giuseppe, resting his head against Giuseppe's legs, looking up at him.

'Another walk, eh?' Giuseppe leaned forward, tousling the dog's fur and stroking his ears. 'Well, perhaps in a while. Maybe we can persuade Mario to come with us, eh, Max?'

Mario muttered something under his breath, then stood. 'I must take over from Anne, it's time she had a break. But this evening maybe? If it's not raining.' He winked at Giuseppe and walked to the door. 'Good luck with your phone call.'

CHAPTER 25

After supper that evening Giuseppe and Christina settled in the sitting room, leaving Mario and Anne in the downstairs kitchen to prepare their food order for the coming week. Stevie had come in from school full of excitement, telling them in great detail about the school's plans for the Christmas nativity play. His class teacher had promised them all a part and Stevie had already convinced himself that he would play Joseph, despite Anne and Christina reminding him that there were plenty of other parts that were just as important.

'I'm not going to be a donkey,' Stevie announced with gusto. 'Or a chicken.'

'A chicken?' Mario was only partly listening to the conversation and the look of confusion on his face confirmed he had already lost the main thread of it.

All through Stevie's early tea of cheese on toast, his bath, and bedtime story, he continued to reinforce his plea to whoever would listen.

'But I'll be the best at remembering my lines. Miss Scott told me the other day what a good memory I had. She said my description of the night of the storm was the best of the whole class.'

'Why were you talking about the storm, Stevie?' Anne asked.

'We had to stand up and speak for five minutes about something that was really important to us and I chose the storm.' His matter-of-fact tone made Anne smile.

It wasn't until Stevie was ushered into the sitting room to say goodnight that Giuseppe heard the child's proud account.

'Eh, Stevie. You told the class about the storm? You were very brave that night, weren't you?'

'I didn't need to be brave because I was inside. Mr Swain was brave though, wasn't he?'

Before Christina or Giuseppe could say anymore, Anne came in, and gently led Stevie away to bed.

'What do you think Stevie meant, Christina?' Giuseppe said.

'I don't think he meant anything at all. We have to remember that Stevie's imagination is second to none. He'll end up a brilliant novelist, you see. Now tell me about the Forrest family. How did you get on? Did you get to meet Danny?'

Giuseppe gave her a brief summary of all he had seen and heard during his visit to Eastbourne. 'They are a family living in fear,' he explained.

Christina listened without interruption, although he noticed her face becoming paler the further into the report he got. When he reached the end of his story, she stood and began to pace around the room.

'Dear God. This is exactly the kind of thing that is going on all over. Not just here in Sussex, but across the country. People are scared to speak out about it and there's little or no help for them when they do. It's not right, Giuseppe.' She stamped her foot, making one of the framed photographs on the mantelpiece shudder slightly and then fall over. 'Oh, Lord. It's Mum's favourite photo too, lucky it hasn't broken the glass.' She stood the photo frame up again, moving it a little further back from the edge of the mantelpiece. The photo was of Anne and Mario, standing in front of Bella Café with a six-year-old Christina holding her dad's hand and Flavia leaning against her mum's leg, with her thumb in her mouth.

'See that?' Christina pointed to the photo. 'I should remind Flavia about it. She was four years old and still sucking her thumb. Right mummy's girl she was. You'd never believe it to look at her now.'

'Where is she tonight?'

'Out *revisiting old haunts*, apparently.'

'We all have special memories, but memories are about the past. It is the loyalty we have to each other that makes us act in the present, to look to the future.'

'How do you mean?'

'Think about Daniel Forrest. He had to leave his mother and brothers, knowing that they could experience further harm, because he has a plan for the future. But he can only make that plan work by leaving them in great danger.'

'I suppose we all make trade-offs, compromises. So, from what you know now about Danny Forrest, have you changed your mind about him having any involvement in Mr Swain's death?'

'I think it unlikely he would want to inflict harm on someone, having been a victim himself.'

'That doesn't always follow though, does it? Maybe the trouble that Danny's brothers got mixed up in was their way of venting their anger - so the bullied becomes the bully.'

'*Forse*. Perhaps.' Giuseppe began tapping his fingers on the arm of the chair, humming a tune very quietly so that Christina could barely hear it. 'I will go to my room and listen to the wireless. I have found it calms me, helps me to think.'

'Aren't you going to wait with me to watch the late-night news? I want to see if I can get a better idea of the election manifestos. The more I read and hear, the more confused I am.'

'Ah, *si*, the election. You have decided how you will vote?'

'That's the problem. It's the single most important thing each of us can do to help make a better world and I need to make sure I get it right.'

Giuseppe smiled. 'You are hoping your politicians will make a big impact then?'

'I'm not daft enough to believe that things will change overnight, whoever wins. But we have to start somewhere, don't we? Otherwise the same inequalities will persist, the same injustices.'

'When I was a young boy, I read a lot. I read about the history of Italy, the history of the Roman Empire, and I tried to see patterns.'

'How do you mean?'

'So much is repeated - successes, failures… For many years I believed the human race learned from its mistakes. It is only now I am reminded more and more that we do not learn. We tread the same paths, fall into the same traps.'

'Your view of the world seems pretty dismal to me. I need to believe that we can learn and we can make things better.'

'And whoever your new Government might be, they will lead your country to a bright future?' He stood, easing his back out by stretching tall. 'Well, I will leave you to watch your television and I will retire and listen to the wireless and in the morning we will compare notes to see which of us enjoyed the most restful night.' He smiled and turned to leave. '*Buonanotte*, Christina. *Dormi bene*. Sleep well.'

CHAPTER 26

The next morning Christina forced herself out of bed earlier than usual, allowing herself a brief smile at the memory of Giuseppe's words of warning about late nights and early mornings. Grabbing her dressing gown she pulled her bedroom chair towards the dressing table, positioning it such that she could see her face in the mirror. For most of the night she had been rehearsing the conversation she intended to have with her sister. Not just the words that Christina wanted to say, but the inevitable response she anticipated from Flavia.

Her sister had done what she always did, or at least what she had done for the last four years since she first walked out on Stevie. It seemed as though Flavia sensed just the right moment to turn up to create the maximum impact. Her last visit coincided with Stevie's first week at school. His mother suddenly blew into his life and then just as suddenly blew out again. For weeks following Flavia's visit Christina struggled to settle her nephew, not knowing whether the change in his behaviour was due to Stevie suddenly being at school full time, or whether at five years old he was beginning to grasp the truth about his relationship with his mother - or rather the lack of it. Now she had turned up again, suggesting she wanted to be more involved in Stevie's life, having him to stay with her for weekends.

And it wasn't only Stevie that Christina was worried about. This time around it was her own relationship with Tony that felt under threat. For years Christina had kept Tony at arm's length. They had been teenage sweethearts until Flavia decided to intervene, setting her sights on

Tony, resulting in the breakup not just of their relationship, but of their friendship too. Six years on and Christina was learning to trust Tony again. They'd been going out for a few months now - ever since the events that followed the death of George Leigh. Christina loved the time she spent with Tony, but her sister's arrival left her feeling unsettled all over again.

It was as if everything that previously had been neatly stacked on a shelf had been swept off by a random hand, to land in a heap of confusion on the floor. Except it wasn't a random hand. Flavia was living just half an hour away, she could turn up at any moment, assert her maternal right to get involved in Stevie's life. It was impossible for Christina to pinpoint how that made her feel. Did she dread the inevitable change to the relationship she had with her young nephew? Or would she feel only relief in the knowledge she no longer carried the responsibility she had chosen to take on? That thought led on to feelings of guilt. Was it self-interest that was really eating away at her? Something she had always accused her sister of.

It was a mess.

And had she detected anything in Tony's expression suggesting he still held a torch for Flavia? He'd deny it if she asked him outright, but even in the asking she was giving in to emotions she didn't want to feel. Doubt. Jealousy.

The only person she would consider talking it all through with was Giuseppe, but she sensed his focus had changed. He'd made the decision to return to Italy, she was certain of it. Even though he hadn't said as much. The clock was ticking. He'd want to reach a resolution over Edward's death to free him up to go back to resolve another death. The young boy who had fallen from the balcony in Rome. Certainly a tragedy, but she knew Giuseppe believed there was a truth to uncover, something he had allowed to fester by resigning from the police force and travelling to England.

By the time Flavia returned from taking Stevie to school Christina was dressed and down in the back kitchen. When she heard Flavia's footsteps come up the side path she ran more hot water into the sink and added a little too much washing up liquid. She kept her back to Flavia, aware that her sister had pushed open the back door and was stamping her wet shoes on the doormat.

'God, it's disgusting out there. Make us a cuppa, Chrissie, will you?'

The words that Christina had carefully rehearsed seem to have floated away into another universe, lost to her completely. It was as if she had written the words down on a sheet of paper without realising she had used invisible ink. She focused on the billowy suds that covered the washing up, willing her mind to settle.

'Okay, don't bother then, I'll make my own tea,' Flavia said, pushing Christina to one side as she put the kettle under the cold tap, waiting for it to fill. 'Going in late again today, are you? Or have you waited to bid me a fond farewell?' She spooned tea leaves into the teapot, then pulled a chair out from the table and sat astride it.

Christina continued washing and rinsing the dishes, wishing for once she'd gone to work early. Anything to avoid the discussion with her sister that was now inevitable.

'Are you ignoring me?' Flavia stood, put her arms on her sister's back, attempting to get her to turn around. Instead Christina shook Flavia away, then emptied the water from the sink before slowly drying her hands. Only then did she turn and look directly at her sister.

'I need you to promise me something,' Christina said at last.

'What?'

'You have to promise that you won't do anything more to upset Stevie.'

Flavia's laugh was raucous. 'Anything more? What are you talking about? I've never purposely upset my son.'

'Except for walking out on him when he was just two years old and pretty much staying out of his life since then?'

'Chrissie, you should listen to yourself. You want me to stay out of his life, but when I do you accuse me of abandoning him. Make up your mind.'

For the next few minutes Christina watched as Flavia poured the boiling water into the teapot, then took the milk jug from the fridge and two mugs down from the worktop.

'Do you want to know what I think?' Flavia said, taking the tea strainer from the draining board.

'You're going to tell me whether I want to hear it or not.'

'It's not Stevie you're really worried about at all. It's your precious Tony. You're scared I'm going to ruin your relationship with him again - just like I did seven years ago. Well, you'll be pleased to know, dear sister, that I'm not interested in your boyfriend. I never was, not really.'

'It's the power you like, isn't it?'

Flavia lifted the teapot, pouring the tea from such a height that it splashed over the side of the mug as she poured.

'Knowing that you can affect our lives. Makes you feel good, does it?' Christina continued.

'Isn't that what families are all about? Do you think you

haven't affected me then? Or Mum? Or Dad? It hasn't been easy for me, you know. Growing up in your shadow, knowing that you were the favourite.'

'What are you talking about?'

'Don't tell me you're blind to it. You've always been their favourite. Christina, the saint, the girl who can do no wrong.' Flavia poured milk into the mug, stirring the tea slowly, with great precision, as if the conversation that was unravelling was about nothing more than inane niceties.

'If you stopped for just one moment to reflect on your behaviour, you might understand why Dad gets so riled with you. And Mum. If you really can't tell how much she misses you, how she's wanted nothing more than for the two of us to be closer, to act like we actually like each other…' Christina paused, pushing the fingers of one hand against the side of her forehead, trying to settle the thudding ache that was building at her temples. 'Do you know what, Flavia. Why don't you just go back to Eastbourne and leave us in peace.'

Flavia lifted the mug to her lips, taking the smallest sip, then putting it back onto the table. For a few moments neither sister spoke. Then Flavia stood, pushing the chair away and tipping the rest of her tea into the sink. 'Well, I'd better go and gather my bits and pieces and head on out of here, then, hadn't I? If I don't see you again before I leave, good luck with everything, Chrissie. I really hope it works out for you and Tony. Oh, and I hope you and Giuseppe manage to get to the bottom of the whole Edward Swain mystery. I'll look forward to reading about it.'

'So, you're going, just like that.'

'That's what you want, isn't it? I always said I was only here for two nights. I've got a job to get back to, remember.'

'What did you tell Stevie? Did you explain you wouldn't be here when he gets home from school this afternoon?'

Flavia nodded, then brushed past Christina. 'I promised him I'd see him soon. Definitely before Christmas.'

'And you'll see Mum and Dad before you go?'

'Of course. What do you take me for? I'm not completely heartless, despite what you clearly think of me. I'm really not that different from you, you know, but I don't expect you to see it that way.'

Christina studied her sister's face and as she did much of the anger she had been feeling melted away, leaving sadness in its wake. 'Mum isn't the only person who misses you, Flavia.'

'Stevie has all of you to fuss over him, he doesn't need me complicating things.'

'I'm not talking about Stevie. I miss you. At least I miss the person you used to be.'

'Well, I live in Eastbourne now, remember? And most days you'll find me at Taylor's Books in Station Road. I guess we could meet up now and then, in your lunch hour - if you get one. But you'll have to accept me as I am, Chrissie, not the person you want me to be.'

When the door closed behind Flavia, Christina's greatest wish was that Giuseppe was on hand to make the strongest pot of Italian coffee. Nothing less would do.

CHAPTER 27

Giuseppe was barely aware of Flavia's departure. He had only one thought in his mind that morning and that was to make a return visit to Claremont Lodge. He was hoping that Danny Forrest had returned to the lodgings. Giuseppe wanted to speak to him to make sure no further harm had occurred to any member of the Forrest family. If Danny's stepfather believed that Mrs Forrest had had any dealings with another man, he guessed the poor woman would suffer for it.

Giuseppe also wanted to take another look around Edward's home, perhaps easier to do if Christina accompanied him. But first there was a telephone call to make. Despite Max pestering him for his morning walk, Giuseppe waited until he heard Christina come downstairs, her coat in her hand.

'You are late for work this morning?' he said, noticing she was avoiding his gaze. 'Are you alright?'

'Difficult start to the day, that's all. And now I need to get my skates on.'

'Would you like to talk about it?' He turned away from her, sensing she might open up if she was given some space.

'Maybe. But not now.'

'I understand.' He would take another tack. 'Your mother says she is happy for me to telephone Italy. I am taking your advice.'

He smiled at Christina and waited while the international operator confirmed the connection, and within just a couple of rings Silvio picked up the phone. Giuseppe could picture his sergeant, lying back in his chair, feet on the desk, with half an eye on whatever was going on outside the police station. Silvio had been a good sergeant, but easily distracted, with a tendency to put good food, beautiful women and football before the demands of his job. They had worked together for ten years, and over that time Giuseppe had perfected the exact expression that would bring his sergeant into line. A raised eyebrow, a tightening of the jaw. No words were needed, but Silvio soon learned. Of course, since Giuseppe's retirement it was highly likely the sergeant had fallen back into his old ways, unless the new detective in charge had grasped the measure of the man. If there was ever a need for a character reference Giuseppe would write: *Silvio Bruni - a well-intentioned officer, whose performance is enhanced by firm supervision*. Not that a reference would ever be needed. Silvio would never seek promotion, he would be a sergeant until the day he retired.

Perhaps there was something in Giuseppe's stance, in the tone of his voice, that made Christina delay her departure. The telephone conversation was all in Italian, of course, but as Giuseppe was saying little more than, *si*, and *no*, she had no trouble understanding him. After a few minutes, he ended the call with *Grazie e buongiorno*. He put the receiver down, his hand not moving, as if being motionless was helping him to replay the conversation and assess its implications. Then he turned to Christina.

'How did that go?' she asked.

'He wants to know when I will return.'

'Have you thought about it?'

'I think about it all the time. I promise myself it will be this week, next week, but I have not yet booked the ticket.' He paused, before continuing. 'It seems Silvio is excited about the new *autostrada* they have opened between Milan and Naples.'

'You're kidding. He's excited about a road?'

'It is a big event. They have been building it for many years and at last it is finished. The Prime Minister has officially opened it. Silvio says it will be the perfect road for me and my Lancia.' Giuseppe gave a little chuckle. 'I miss my Lancia. It is a beautiful car, Christina. And a little bigger than your Morris Minor, eh?'

'Well I really can't imagine anyone getting excited about a road. Or driving for that matter. The only thing I hope for when I get into my car is that it will get me to my destination without breaking down. But didn't you ask him about the death of the boy?'

'Carlo's grandson? *Si*, he tells me to leave it alone. He says the family need time to grieve and that asking questions now would only disturb their grief.'

'Don't they want answers? If it was me, I would want answers.'

'They think they have the answers.' Giuseppe closed his eyes for a moment, then opened them again as if forcing himself to shift from an unpleasant thought to one that might provide some distraction. 'But I also spoke to him about *Signora* Warrington.'

'Lorna? Why did you mention her?'

'She tells us she is to work as a nanny in a family in Rome. I asked Silvio if he could find out anything about the family. I thought it may help to reassure *Signora* Warrington. It is a big move for a young woman to go from one country to another, to live and work with strangers.'

'I'm guessing Rome is a big place,' Christina said, the beginnings of a smile creeping over her face. 'Silvio isn't likely to know everyone, is he?'

'When you are a policeman it is your job to know

everyone and everything,' Giuseppe said, matching Christina's expression. 'And on this occasion Silvio has proved more useful than I had hoped. He tells me his son receives English lessons from a *Signor* Ingram. He is going to speak to him this morning and telephone me later with some information.'

'That's quite a result.'

'But first I would like your help.'

'Sure. What do you need me to do?'

'Will you come with me to Claremont Lodge? I think *Signora* Warrington is more ready to talk when you are there.'

Giuseppe had turned back to face Christina and noticed her questioning look.

'Okay. But it'll have to wait until lunch time. I'll meet you back here at midday?'

As soon as Christina left, Max could no longer be ignored. Giuseppe clipped the lead on and headed off along the seafront. The heavy rain that had soaked Flavia earlier that morning had eased a little. Nevertheless, an umbrella would have been welcome, but wasn't practical when walking a lively Beagle who persisted on pulling on his lead each time he spotted anything of interest ahead of him. Instead Giuseppe had bought a hat. It wasn't something he was used to wearing in Italy, but he had got so used to it in recent days that he was starting to think it might become a permanent addition to his wardrobe, even once he was home.

An hour or so later and he was back at the café, looking forward to an espresso and some of Anne's shortbread. Max needed drying down, so he went down the side alley and in through the back door. Moments later Anne came into the kitchen.

'Ah, I thought I heard you come in. Your friend has telephoned,' she said.

'My friend?'

'Mr Bruni. We had a nice chat in Italian, I was quite pleased with myself, I remembered more than I thought. Mario and I barely speak Italian to each other now, which is a real shame. I should push him, shouldn't I? Otherwise he'll end up forgetting his own language.'

Giuseppe removed his coat and hat and lifted Max's water bowl to refill it.

'Did Silvio leave a message?'

'Oh, yes, of course. Sorry. I'm all in a muddle this morning.'

'Are you alright, Anne? Why don't you sit for a moment.'

'Take no notice of me. I'm just a bit out of sorts. It was so nice to see Flavia, but her visit was over so quickly. She left this morning. She did say goodbye to you, didn't she?'

'She will return soon?'

'Yes. At least, I hope so. And now she's closer, well, it will be easier, won't it?' Anne plumped down on one of the kitchen chairs, sighing as she did so. 'Anyway, the reason I came through was to tell you that Mr Bruni telephoned and he would like you to phone him back. He says he has some news for you. Something to do with an English family?'

'Ah, *sì. Grazie*. I will just make some coffee and then I will telephone. Would you like an espresso, Anne?'

'I should be getting back to the café, but thank you. Maybe later.'

When Christina met Giuseppe outside the café later that morning he had some news for her, but first a question.

'Christina, when *Signora* Warrington spoke to you about

the position she was planning to take in Rome, what did she say exactly?'

Christina narrowed her eyes, as if focusing hard on the exact words that Lorna had said to her. 'All she said was that her marriage had ended and she wanted to make a new start.'

'This is not all that ended for her.' Giuseppe said. 'Silvio has already spoken to *Signor* Ingram.'

'So soon?'

'Perhaps it is a quiet day for the Rome police today,' Giuseppe said, smiling. 'Or perhaps Silvio is more efficient that I remember him. No matter. He confirms what Lorna told us, that the Ingram family knew *Signora* Warrington's family. He also says that there was a great sadness several years ago. *Signora* Warrington's father committed suicide. She was just fifteen when it happened and she was the person who found her father's body.'

'Goodness. How dreadful. It's weird that she chose not to mention that to either of us. I mean there's no reason she should have, but it must have been such a traumatic event and it must have all been stirred up again when she witnessed a second death - Mr Swain's.'

'I am thinking the same as you. It is another piece of the puzzle, another fact to consider.'

'You think it might be relevant in some way?'

'Some things we know and some things we can only guess. Something or someone must have drawn Edward into the garden that night. I do not like to say it aloud, but I have been thinking that one possibility is that he had decided to end his life.'

'That's a horrible thought. You don't really think that, do you?'

'We know that Claremont Lodge is very dilapidated.

Perhaps Edward was facing money problems, or wrangles with the council over the licence for his lodgings.'

'You always say we should only consider the facts. So, I think we should discount that supposition.' Christina said, waving his words away with a sweep of her hand.

'You are right. There was something that Edward wanted to share with me, something that was worrying him. There was the strange, but apparently heated conversation between Edward and *Signor* Forrest and then we have the mystery of Josephine, a name that was so important that it was among the last words Edward spoke.'

They had left the café and walked slowly to reach the corner of Sea Road. They stood, facing the seafront. The early morning rain had now completely cleared. Grey skies had been replaced with patches of the palest blue, interspersed with creamy white clouds, colours that were reflected in the sea. A strong wind was at its worst on this corner as the seafront opened up into a wide road, creating a funnel. But this morning there was only warmth from the autumn sun. If Giuseppe was at home in Rome, he would choose such a moment to sit at a pavement café, enjoy a glass of vermouth and ponder. Christina was right to remind him that he needed to focus on the facts. The trouble was that each of the facts they had just discussed were like random musical notes, jarring against each other. Giuseppe would need to be a talented composer to work through the music, choosing which notes to discard and which to keep. The remaining sounds could then be strung together to create the perfect harmonies, a musical composition that made sense. The reasons for the sudden end to a man's life resolved.

An investigation of Edward's room could help Giuseppe to understand more about his friend. Danny

Forrest told Giuseppe that Edward had made an accusation. Someone had been rifling through his personal possessions, and he had wrongly assumed it was Danny. Of course, Giuseppe only had Danny's word that he hadn't been in Edward's room that day - or any other day. Did Edward have something to hide? Is that why he was so angry with Danny?

'Come, Christina. Let us call on *Signora* Warrington and see if she can help us with our facts.'

Lorna seemed pleased to see them both, inviting them into the sitting room and offering to make tea.

'I almost didn't recognise you,' Christina said, as they followed Lorna along the hallway. Lorna had exchanged her Crimplene frock for a scarlet woollen shift dress, as modern and chic as her new hairstyle. 'Did you get your hair done locally?'

Previously, Lorna's pinned back waves made her appear almost middle-aged. Now her thick dark hair was styled into a cute bob, the fringe sitting just above her eyebrows, the sides curling around the edges of her face, giving her an almost angelic look.

As they transferred from the hallway into the sitting room Lorna stood in front of the mirror that hung over the fireplace, inspecting her new hairstyle, as if reminding herself of it, moving her head this way and that.

'Do you like it?' Lorna said.

'It's gorgeous,' Christina said. 'You remind me of that American actress, Doris Day. Only she's blonde, of course.'

'I cannot share your conversation as I fear my hair is no different now to the day I first wore long trousers,' Giuseppe said. 'Although some grey here and there.' He ran his fingers through his hair, giving the barest of smiles.

'And so, I will take my leave for a moment and visit *Signor* Swain's bedroom.'

Lorna turned to face Giuseppe. 'What do you want to go into his room for? Looking for something, are you?'

'I have often found that it is the times when we are looking for nothing in particular that we find the most important thing.'

'Sounds like a riddle to me.' Lorna turned to Christina. 'Do you know what he's on about?'

'My uncle used to be a detective, in Rome. He's retired now, but he still thinks like a detective.'

'Good at poking his nose into things, is he?' Lorna's tone was suddenly sharp, almost sarcastic. 'They're like that, the police. Sniffing around and coming up with nothing, except anything that helps them close a case as quick as they can. They're not interested in the truth.'

'I can assure you, *Signora* Warrington, that I am only interested in the truth.'

Lorna seemed able to shake off one attitude to replace it immediately with another. She had a way of rearranging her expression, even her stance, changing her from a sharp, irritated accuser, to a welcoming hostess as she now smiled at them and said, 'Why don't you sit down and I'll make us all a nice cup of tea.'

No words were spoken while Lorna was out of the room, but the exchange of looks between Giuseppe and Christina suggested they both had misgivings about Lorna's strange reaction. She returned carrying a tray with teapot, milk jug and sugar bowl, and matching cups and saucers. She placed the tray down on the mahogany table that was to one side of the room and turned to face them both.

'I was a bit sharp just then, sorry about that. It's been a

difficult time for me. I'm sure you can appreciate how difficult. What with Mr Swain's death and then all that trouble with Danny. He's back here now, you know, and well, it makes me kind of nervy.'

'Why does he make you nervous, *Signora* Warrington?'

'I heard that argument, didn't I? And if Danny had been poking around in Mr Swain's room, well, maybe he was looking to pinch something. The old man didn't have much worth stealing, but I've got some personal bits that are treasures to me and if he gets his hands on those…'

The pause was accompanied by a look of discomfort, as if Lorna had said more than she intended to say.

'I am confused, *Signora* Warrington. When we spoke before you said you did not know the subject of the argument between *Signor* Swain and *Signor* Forrest, only that you heard raised voices. But now you tell us something different. Which is it, *Signora*?'

Lorna had been standing beside the table, her hand poised over the lid of the teapot. She turned her back on Giuseppe, lifted the lid and gave the tea a stir. Then she replaced the lid, her movements precise and considered.

'You're just the same as every other policeman I've spoken to. They like to take people's words and twist them all about.' She stepped across the room and sat on one of the upright armchairs, placing her hands in her lap, spreading out her fingers, making a point of studying them.

'I don't think we have done any twisting, *Signora*. Either you heard the words that were spoken or you didn't, which is it?'

Christina was sitting beside Giuseppe on the settee. Now she shifted a little, as if indicating she planned to take another tack.

'You must be looking forward to your new job, Lorna?

A whole new adventure, in another country.'

'Yeah, I am. New hairstyle, new clothes, new life.'

'And the people you are going to work for. They're family friends, you said?'

'That's it, yes. What of it?' A sharpness had crept back into Lorna's voice, but she was still looking down at her hands, so neither Christina nor Giuseppe could see her expression.

'We understand you've had to deal with a great sadness in your life.' Christina selected each word with care.

Lorna lifted her head, her gaze flicking from Christina to Giuseppe, and then she stood and stepped towards them, her eyes glistening with anger. 'Just because you used to be a detective doesn't mean you can go traipsing through my private life. Have you been speaking to the Ingrams?'

'I have not spoken to them. A friend spoke to them on my behalf.' Giuseppe's tone was conciliatory, as if he was offering an apology. 'I thought I might help by finding out a little of the family you are going to work for. It can be difficult starting life in a new country, leaving behind all you know. Instead, I discovered that your decision to move to Rome was driven by your need to leave behind painful memories.' Now it was Giuseppe who was choosing his words carefully.

'You have no idea,' Lorna said, returning to her seat. She plumped down as if the anger she had felt earlier had left her feeling wrung out, all her energy gone.

'Would you like to talk about it?' Christina said, her tone gentle.

'Where would you like me to start?' She spat the words out. 'I could tell you about the day I came home from school to find my dad slumped on the settee, empty pill bottles beside him, the remains of a bottle of brandy in his hand. Or I could tell you about the hours that Mum and I sat in the hospital corridor outside the ward, waiting for the doctor to tell us there was nothing they could do to save him. If I'd found him earlier, if Mum hadn't been out that afternoon… plenty of ifs… but the fact of it was that he had chosen his moment.'

She stopped speaking suddenly, as if she had run out of words.

'I'm so sorry,' Christina said. 'It must have been a dreadful shock. And you were still at school? So you were…?'

'Fifteen. Seven years ago.' She gave a hollow laugh, which did nothing to alleviate the tension in the room.

'Your father must have been very unhappy,' Giuseppe said. 'Did you or your mother know what led him to end his life?'

'Oh, I know alright.' Lorna swept her hair away from one side of her face, tucking it behind her ear. Her face was flushed, the carefully applied makeup now tinged with a vibrant pink, making her look like a doll whose face had been highly coloured to attract the attention of a potential customer. 'Even back then I had my suspicions, but at that age, well what could I do about it?'

'What did you suspect?'

'Dad knew too, I'm certain of it. But instead of blaming the person who caused it all, he blamed himself.'

Lorna looked into the distance, beyond Christina and Giuseppe, as if she was returning to a place where her assumptions were logical, where they made sense.

'So then it was just Mum and me,' she continued. 'Then I lost her too.' Her voice was now barely a whisper. 'She couldn't bear it, you see. The shame, the loneliness.

Working at three jobs, scrimping money together to get food on our plates. It destroyed her in the end. She died on the 20th July, same day as Dad, six years apart. It was her heart that gave way in the end, which is kind of perfect. She died of a broken heart.'

Christina stood beside Lorna, putting one hand on her shoulder, but Lorna pushed her away and moved to the window, looking out onto the front garden.

'Both your parents gone, that is very sad,' Giuseppe said.

'Sad? Yeah, it's sad. But the saddest thing of all is that the person who caused it all was able to walk away scot free.'

'You blame someone for your father's decision to take his own life?'

'Oh, I blame him alright. Dad trusted him, he was his accountant, for God's sake. In the perfect place to siphon off money behind Dad's back, so in the end there was nothing. The business folded, Dad had to declare himself bankrupt. But that wasn't all of it. Dad suspected him of having a thing about my mum. So he destroys my dad's business and his marriage, takes his ill-gotten gains, moves to another county and buys himself a nice property that he turns into a lodging house, so he can make even more money out of folk like me.'

'You are not saying this man was *Signor* Swain?' Giuseppe said.

'Yeah, old man Swain. He wasn't just my Dad's accountant. He was supposed to be his friend. Instead he was just waiting for his chance - not only to steal all his money, but to steal his wife as well. And now he's dead. And do you know what? I'm pleased. There, I've said it. At last he's got what he deserves.'

CHAPTER 28

There was a chill in the sitting room at Claremont Lodge that had nothing to do with the unlit fire, or the draught that blew through the ill-fitting bay window.

After Lorna's admission that she blamed Edward Swain for her father's death, Giuseppe had a whole host of questions he wanted to fire at her. But this wasn't the time. Her outburst merely suggested she knew Edward, that on her own admission she was pleased he was dead. Nothing more. There was another conversation that Giuseppe needed to have with the youngest member of the Rossi family before he could pursue the matter to its conclusion.

The tray of tea had been forgotten. Lorna moved over to the table, putting one hand on the side of the teapot. 'It's gone cold. Shall I make a fresh pot?' Her question was posed in such an offhand manner, as though all that had been said over the last half hour remained undisclosed.

'We have taken up enough of your time,' Giuseppe said, receiving a quizzical look from Christina. 'We will go now, but perhaps we may return later? I would still like to have another word with Signor Forrest, so perhaps when he has returned from work?'

He didn't wait for a response, but stepped towards the door, gesturing to Christina to follow him. For a few moments Lorna remained by the table, as if she was surprised by the sudden departure of her guests.

'Danny, yes,' she said with emphasis, as if she had just reached a decision. 'He's the one you need to speak to alright.' She glared at Giuseppe. 'I reckon he had something to do with the old man's death. But you're the detective, so I'll leave you to figure it out.'

'*Grazie, Signora.* That is just what I hope to do.'

Once they were outside, Christina gave a huge sigh. 'Crikey, that was all a bit of a turn up. Had you guessed that she knew Mr Swain? She sounded so vindictive when she spoke about him, calling him an *old man* like that. She seems to switch her personality as quickly as our famous British weather goes from sunshine to rain. One minute she's the demure woman, polite and gentile, next she's a harridan, all bitter and twisted.'

Giuseppe fell into step beside Christina but said nothing.

'I'm not saying she doesn't have just cause,' she continued. 'I mean losing both her parents like that, well it would affect you forever, wouldn't it? But can you believe what she said about Mr Swain? Can you imagine he was the sort to have an affair with a married woman? Not only that, but the wife of his employer. And then he steals from him too? You're a good judge of character, wouldn't you have sensed if he was capable of being so underhand and deceitful?'

When there was still no response from Giuseppe, Christina stopped walking, putting her hand on his arm. 'You're wondering about Josephine, aren't you? Do you think she might be Lorna's mother?'

'Christina, you need to return to work. I will take Max for a long walk. Then this afternoon, when you come home we can both speak to Stevie.'

'Stevie?'

Giuseppe had started walking again, so Christina had to take a few long strides to catch him up.

'Are you going to tell me any more, or leave me in suspense for the rest of the afternoon?' she said.

'Go to work. Finish your article about the coming

election, impress your editor with your understanding of the plight of local families. On your return we will talk with your nephew and then perhaps we will have the answer to many questions we have not yet dared to ask.'

Bella Café was busy when Giuseppe returned from Claremont Lodge, with Anne and Mario both serving customers. He chose not to stop and chat with them, instead clipping Max's lead on and taking him out through the back kitchen door, down the alleyway and onto the street. The autumn sun had brought a handful of people out onto the seafront to enjoy the bright chilled air.

Crossing onto the promenade, he turned left in the direction of Galley Hill. When he reached the bench where he and Edward had often stopped he sat, Max seemed happy to lie by his feet while keeping an eye out for any other four-legged friends who might happen by.

Even before Lorna's outburst earlier that day, Giuseppe had guessed the woman had been hiding something. Her reaction to Edward's death had been strange, as if she had chosen a role to play and she had to constantly remind herself of it. It was evident now that she had a motive for wanting Edward dead, by way of retribution for her father's suicide and the resultant death of her mother. But there was still confusion in Giuseppe's mind. Whatever the truth, it was clear that the last words Edward spoke suggested he had been at fault. Was it true that he had stolen from his employer? Or was it only Josephine he stole? And if the romantic feelings between Edward and Josephine had been mutual, why had they not made their life together after the death of Lorna's father? Lorna was pleased that her father's accountant was dead, happy even that he had lost his life in such a brutal way. But it was a long way from that to believing that Lorna was capable of murder. Even if she was, how could she have made it happen in the way that it did?

A golden retriever passed by, close to the bench, his owner some paces ahead of him. Max seized the opportunity to greet the other dog, and as they sniffed each other in the only way that dogs like to sniff, Max's lead got tangled around the retriever, causing Giuseppe to stand to unwind the tangle. Then the retriever's owner whistled and the dog ran off, without so much as a backward glance, leaving Max looking a little downhearted.

'Come, Max. Let us walk.'

They headed down the east side of Galley Hill, along the beach towards Glyne Gap. The tide was further out than he had ever seen it, revealing great muddy areas that looked from a distance like a submerged forest. Giuseppe stayed on the shingle, while Max was pulling him towards the mud.

'Mario will not be happy if I return you covered in wet sand. I will not be happy either.' He looked down at his shoes, which until now remained surprisingly clean. Then he heard the tinkling sound of an ice-cream van. *'Senti,* listen. I think it is time for my lunch.'

Several minutes later Giuseppe and Max had returned to the bench, but this time Max was more intent on gazing longingly at Giuseppe's ice-cream cone, than on looking out for friends. It was a frequent occurrence for Giuseppe to miss out on lunch, replacing it instead with a cake or a few biscuits. Since his arrival in July he had discovered that English vanilla ice-cream was not quite a match for his favourite Italian flavours, nevertheless he had developed a taste for it. Although he was sure his cousin would be surprised to see him enjoying an ice-cream today. *Perhaps I am becoming used to the English weather, after all.* He smiled to himself, letting a little dollop of melted ice-cream fall to the floor so that Max could share in his delight.

On their return journey Giuseppe rehearsed the questions he would put to Stevie. It was important to tread carefully. The boy was impressionable, with a vivid imagination. Filtering the facts from the fantasy might prove to be a challenge.

A few hours later, Giuseppe turned his wireless down a little when he heard Stevie's voice. Anne had collected him from school and was persuading him to change out of his uniform before having his tea. For the first hour or so after Stevie had been 'released' from the constraints of being in a classroom, he seemed to have twice as much as energy as usual. In Giuseppe's opinion the child would have benefitted from several runs around the garden, maybe being chased by Max, after which both dog and boy would be happy to fall in a heap and rest. But Giuseppe would never offer his opinion when it came to childcare. He had no experience of being a father. It was a thought that brought back sadness he still tried to suppress.

He turned the wireless off, changed his slippers for shoes and took his jacket from the hook on the back of his bedroom door. It would be another hour or more before Christina got back from work and he wanted her there before he questioned Stevie. But until then, perhaps he could entertain him and give Anne some much-deserved respite.

'Bon gorno. *Zio* Giuseppe.' Stevie's attempt at Italian words were as charming as everything else about him.

'You are learning, Stevie. Well done. *Bravo*. But try again, it is *Buongiorno*. Watch the shape of my mouth as I say the word.' Giuseppe accentuated each syllable, bending down a little so that Stevie could see the way his lips moved. 'Now repeat.'

Stevie giggled and twirled round in a circle, before mirroring Giuseppe's movements as best as he could, the words coming out almost perfectly.

'You see, you are speaking the language just like an Italian. Now, if your nonna says you are allowed to come outside in the garden, we can have a short lesson. I will tell you some Italian words as we walk around and you repeat them. What do you say?'

Stevie clapped his hands in excitement. 'Can I Grandma? Please say I can.'

Anne laughed, patting Stevie gently on his bottom. 'Run upstairs, change out of that uniform and put on an extra jumper. It's already quite chilly and I don't want you catching a cold.'

As Stevie disappeared up to the flat, Anne put her hand on Giuseppe's arm. 'Thank you. It's very good of you. But don't let him tire you out. He's like a whirlwind this afternoon, even more full of energy if that's possible. It's as though it's Friday, with the whole weekend to look forward to.' She smiled, brushing a strand of hair away from her face.

'You look tired, Anne. When will you persuade your husband to take a holiday?'

'Oh, I've given up on that front. I'm alright. Nothing that a couple of hours with my feet up tonight won't sort. And you? You were back over at Claremont Lodge today, weren't you? Is there still something that's worrying you about Mr Swain's death?'

'All deaths worry me,' he said, holding her hand for a moment, then releasing it as Stevie bounced down the stairs and grabbed Max's lead from the hook.

'Can Max come too?'

'To learn Italian?'

Max looked eagerly from one person to another, as if trying to guess what was being said, and what implications it might have for him.

'I think Max should definitely come. He will be our audience.'

Half an hour later, Christina joined them in the garden, explaining she had managed to get off early with the promise to her editor that there was a potential lead she wanted to follow up that could result in a story for the paper.

'Listen, Auntie.' Stevie grabbed Christina's hand, tugging at her to follow him over to the largest of the apple trees at the far end of the garden. '*Albero.*' He said with a flourish. 'That means tree. And see the grass. Well it's *verde,* that means green.'

Christina snatched a sideways smile towards Giuseppe, then turned to focus on Stevie once more. He continued spilling out a few more words until Giuseppe held his finger to his lips.

'*Aspetta.* Wait, Stevie. You do not want to disclose all your new words in one go. Perhaps you could leave some to try out on *Nonno* Mario, eh?'

Stevie did a little hop on the spot, almost tumbling over as Max bounded towards him, sensing the excitement.

'Now Stevie, your Zia Christina and I would like to ask you a question. Shall we sit here on the bench for a minute?'

'Is it to do with my Italian lesson?'

'No, but it is to do with how clever you are,' Giuseppe continued. 'You told us the other day that your teacher was very pleased with you because of how well you had remembered the night of the great storm.'

'*Sì.*' Stevie giggled as he showed off his new foreign language prowess.

'Can you tell your *zia* and me everything you saw that night?'

Stevie wriggled his bottom against the back of the bench, kicking his legs out in front of him, then took a deep breath as if he was about to launch into an important performance.

'Just tell us what you really saw, Stevie,' Christina said. 'Don't add anything in to try to impress Zio Giuseppe. He will be more impressed if you can repeat the facts. That's what detectives like to hear about.'

Stevie jumped down from the bench, turning to face them both. He closed his eyes for a moment, as if he was trying to bring himself back to that night, then he opened them again and spoke clearly and slowly.

'There was a huge bang of thunder. That's what woke me up. I thought it would be exciting to watch the lightning, so I pulled back my curtains and knelt on my bed, looking up at the sky. I remember Granddad saying that you had to count the seconds from the sound of the thunder until the lightning, or maybe it was the other way round. Anyway, that told you how close the storm was. So I was counting slowly and when I got to three, the lightning came and suddenly it was as if it wasn't night anymore. I could see everything, but only for a second or two. I looked across our garden and into the garden of Mr Swain's house and that's when I saw them.'

Giuseppe sat very still, watching Stevie's face.

'Bravo, Stevie. You are doing really well. You say you saw *them*. Who was it you saw?'

'I saw a lady in a dressing gown - just like the dressing

gown that Grandma wears. And I saw Mr Swain. He was in his pyjamas.'

Christina swallowed hard, putting a hand out to Stevie as if to stop him from continuing. But Giuseppe took her hand and pushed it aside. 'Let him continue, Christina. And then what happened, Stevie?'

'The lady stood near the door, she was pointing, almost like she was stabbing the air. She looked really upset. And then she put her hand on Mr Swain's arm and kind of pushed him forwards, then she turned around and went back indoors.'

Giuseppe closed his eyes. He needed to hear the boy's words, but wished he had not heard them.

'Then it went dark,' Stevie continued. 'And when the next flash of lightning came, that's when I saw the summer house all broken and smashed. The tree fell, didn't it? It fell on the summer house and fell on Mr Swain too, didn't it?'

The confidence in Stevie's voice was wavering now, his bottom lip began to tremble and Christina pulled him onto her lap. 'Ssh, Stevie. You don't need to think about it anymore.'

'It was very sad, wasn't it, Auntie? Mr Swain was a very brave man, going into the summer house like that. And whatever that lady said to him, well it must have been really important, mustn't it?'

CHAPTER 29

They waited until after supper before returning to Claremont Lodge. Christina spent a little longer settling Stevie, reading him his favourite bedtime story. *Countryside Companions* told a tale about farmyard animals who between them looked after the farm when the farmer and his wife were poorly. She'd read it to Stevie so many times he knew most of the words by heart, saying them before she turned the page.

'And the dog looked after the sheep and the sheep looked after their lambs,' he said, as she had almost reached the end.

'That's right, Stevie. And then when Mr and Mrs Farmer were well again, they had a big party for all their animals, with their favourite treats.'

'Like ice-cream,' Stevie said, a mischievous grin on his face.

'I'm guessing that would be your favourite treat. How about we go out together over the weekend, maybe we could ask *Zio* Giuseppe to join us?'

'Does he like ice-cream too?'

'He loves it,' she said, wrapping her arms around her nephew and holding him tight. 'And now, it's time for you to go to sleep.'

'There won't be a storm tonight, Auntie, will there?'

'No, Stevie. You don't need to think about storms anymore now. Only ice-cream.'

She left the landing light on and Stevie's bedroom door slightly ajar, and blew him a kiss. 'Night night.'

Downstairs in the back kitchen, the mood was sombre. Anne had a few sharp words with Giuseppe when she discovered he had been quizzing Stevie about the night of the storm.

'You shouldn't have reminded him of it. The poor lad. He'll be having nightmares again. You know how he was when there was all that trouble with poor George Leigh.'

'This is very different,' Giuseppe was quick to defend his actions. 'Stevie remembers the storm as a great adventure, he has talked about at school, his teacher praised him for his account.'

'Well, I'm not happy about it,' Anne said, turning her back on Giuseppe and continuing to mash the potatoes. 'And you'd better make sure your cousin doesn't hear about it, or it will only lead to more arguments between you.'

Supper was a simple affair, with sausages, mash and peas being dished up, despite English sausages being Giuseppe's least favourite meal. As a result he spent most of the meal time, picking at the edges of the food, pushing the peas around and barely lifting the fork to his mouth.

Christina sought to introduce a neutral topic by mentioning the latest news on the election. Instead, her comment generated a fierce response from Mario. 'I'm sick of hearing about politics. It's as if nothing else is happening in the world, bar the preparations for the United Kingdom general election.'

'You have to admit, it's a pretty important event, Dad.'

'Whoever wins it will lead to some difficult times ahead, you mark my words.'

'They can't be much worse than the difficult times we've lived through until now,' Christina said.

'When you've lived through a world war, then you'll know what difficult is.' Mario glared at Christina until Anne put her hand on his arm, causing him to turn away.

'Your Dad's had a trying day. Haven't you, love?' Anne said.

'Sorry, Christina. I don't mean to take it out on you. It's just this business with the Council. They won't give me a straight answer and until I know one way or another...'

'Yes, well, we've all had a trying day,' Christina said, pushing her plate away and glancing sideways at Giuseppe, who until now had remained silent.

Little was said as they all helped to clear away the dishes and no explanation was given when Giuseppe and Christina took their leave to make their return visit to Claremont Lodge.

It was as if Lorna had been waiting for them as the door opened just moments after Giuseppe pressed the doorbell. She waved them in, without any greeting and this time no offer of refreshments.

'You've come to see Danny. I'll call him, shall I?' Without waiting for an answer, she left them in the sitting room, and stood at the foot of the stairs, calling up. 'Danny, you'd better get yourself down here, you're wanted.' The confidence was back in her tone, as if she was comfortable with the way the next hour would play out.

She returned to the sitting room, choosing the chair she had sat on earlier. The settee that Giuseppe and Christina were sitting on was low, the cushions soft as they sank back into it, which meant Lorna was looking down on them. Her raised position seemed to reinforce her self-assurance that all would be well.

Several minutes passed before Danny joined them and during that time nothing was said. Lorna looked down at her hands, inspecting her nails, which Christina noticed were now painted scarlet to match her dress. Christina fidgeted a little, moving one of the cushions behind her so that she was propped further forward, closer to the edge of the settee. Giuseppe kept his eyes directly focused on Lorna, hardly blinking, almost daring her to look up, certain that if she did, she would choose to look away again.

Then Danny sauntered into the room. 'Hey there. Good to see you again, Mr Bianchi.' He pulled a footstool over from the bay window and perched on it. 'Lorna says you wanted to talk to me about something?'

'*Buonasera, Signor* Forrest.'

'Danny, please.'

'Now that you are here, Danny,' Giuseppe continued, 'I think *Signora* Warrington would like to tell us exactly what happened on the night *Signor* Swain died.'

Giuseppe now had Lorna's attention. She looked up at him, then at Danny and finally at Christina, as if she was trying to determine how to respond.

'You know what happened. You were here,' she said to Giuseppe.

'I was here later. But earlier, *Signora* Warrington. Can you tell us what happened before I arrived?'

Lorna looked again from Giuseppe to Danny, and then she stood, walked to the bay window, keeping her back to them.

'Danny's the one you should be asking. I told you about the argument. Well, I reckon Danny wanted to pay the old man back for accusing him. So he got him out into the garden somehow and then the tree fell, the roof of the summer house collapsed with the old man inside and that was that. That's when Danny scarpered.' As she spoke she traced a pattern on the window with her finger.

'What are you talking about?' Danny strode towards Lorna, putting his hands on her shoulders, forcing her to turn around to face him. 'I wasn't even here that night.'

'Get your hands off me.' She pushed him away and he stumbled a little, but quickly regained his balance.

'I think you should sit down, *Signora* Warrington. You too, Danny. When we are seated, *Signora* Warrington will tell us again what happened the night of the storm, but this time she will tell us the truth.'

Everyone in the room looked at Lorna and waited. In the silence Giuseppe noticed the tick of the clock that hung on the wall above the fireplace. He began to tap his fingers on the arm of the settee in time with the ticking. It was as if he was counting down to a moment when many questions would finally be answered.

Lorna remained silent. She had returned to her chair, her fingers gripping either side of the seat, as though it might give her some stability in an otherwise turbulent situation.

'No matter,' Giuseppe said. 'I can tell you.' He stood, moving to the bay window, turning to face into the centre of the room. 'Do you know Christina's nephew, Stevie Rossi?' His question was directed at Lorna.

She shrugged her shoulders.

'He is a bright young boy. Just six years old, with sharp eyesight and a taste for adventure.' Giuseppe paused, letting his words sink in. 'On the night of the storm, Stevie was woken by a great clap of thunder. Watching a storm can prove exciting for a small child, and so he pulled back his curtains and looked out into the night. Soon after the thunder came a flash of lightning that lit up the back garden of Bella Café and the garden of Claremont Lodge. We are neighbours of sorts, our gardens back onto each other, do they not?' He gave a polite smile, nodding towards Lorna, who looked away from him.

'And what did young Stevie see during those few seconds?' Giuseppe continued. 'He saw a woman come out from the back door of Claremont Lodge, a woman in a quilted dressing gown, accompanied by *Signor* Swain. He saw the woman point excitedly and push *Signor* Swain into the garden.'

'That's right, I'd forgotten,' Lorna said suddenly. 'Well, such a dreadful thing like that, you can't always remember things exactly as they happened. So, like I said, Danny was out in the garden, I saw him and I told Mr Swain he'd better get out there to make sure Danny was okay. But I didn't think it would end up like it did, did I? I mean, how could I have known? And it was Danny's fault for being out there.' She folded her hands in her lap as if she had completed a difficult task and was pleased with the result.

'Hang on a minute,' Danny said. 'I wasn't even here that night. I keep on telling you. After we had the argument I left. Mr Swain apologised, said he was sorry he'd doubted me. But I was so het up about it all I couldn't bear to be here, so I went over to Eastbourne like I told you, Mr Bianchi. And Mickey, he confirmed that's where I was.'

'*Si*. What Danny says is true, *Signora* Warrington. He was in Eastbourne that night. And so now we are waiting once again for you to tell us the truth.'

Lorna jumped up, stamping one foot as she did so and holding her arms out, her palms flat as if she was finally ready to admit to the very worst of things - causing a man's death.

'I told you what Edward Swain did to my family.'

'You told us that *Signor* Swain was your father's accountant and that you believe he stole from your father.'

'Oh, I believe it alright, because it's true. And it wasn't just the money he stole, like I told you, he was after my mum too. So I decided I'd track him down. It wasn't that hard. You detectives make out everything is so difficult, but all you need to do is ask the right people the right questions.'

'You discovered he had moved to Bexhill?'

'This is a small enough town, he wasn't hard to find.'

'You took a room in his lodgings and he did not recognise you?'

'I never went to Dad's work. I'd never seen Mr Swain, all I had to go on was a name.'

'And you married, so you had a different surname.'

'I didn't marry. That was a lie. Not likely to trust a man, am I? Not now I know what old man Swain did to my family. I don't think he ever guessed who I was, although when I arrived and gave my name he told me he knew of another Lorna. *The daughter of a friend*, he said. He'd never met her, but he knew she was much loved. That's what he said. How dare he say those things.'

'Didn't that make you question what you believed? If Mr Swain talked about your father as a *friend*, surely he would never have done the things you're accusing him of?' Christina said.

Lorna waved her hand at Christina, as if brushing aside the argument and continued. 'He was no friend to my dad and we all know the kind of friend he wanted to be to my mum.'

'Did you ever speak to your mother about *Signor* Swain?'

'Not likely to admit to it, was she? Anyway, none of it was her fault, she was true to my dad, even after he died. Old man Swain might have got the money, but he never got my mum.'

Lorna had everyone's attention. They waited for her to continue.

Her tone was almost wistful as she recounted the rest of her story. 'After Mum died I got a job in Woolworths, lived in a house share for a while. Then I had this idea I'd take a ten pound passage to Australia. I kept imagining what it would be like to live under blue skies every day, but then I saw an advert in *The Lady* magazine, a family looking for a nanny. I recognised the surname, Mr and Mrs Ingram. It felt as though I'd been given a sign. They'd been friends of our family, from years back. I remembered some talk of them moving to Italy. So I got in touch, they offered me the job, but I knew I couldn't start a new life until I tidied up the past, until I sought retribution for what that man did to my family, to me. I had to pay him back for what he'd done. You can't destroy a family like that and expect to walk away scot free. So, yes, it's true. I wanted something bad to happen to old man Swain. But I didn't want him to die.'

CHAPTER 30

Giuseppe was quiet. He kept shaking his head, as if the unravelling of Lorna's story was more than he could bear. There was no glory in being right. Edward was still dead. Whether Lorna had intended for it to end this way or not made no difference.

'How did you persuade Mr Swain to go outside?' Christina took up the questioning.

'I told him Danny was out there. I banged on Mr Swain's bedroom door. Do you know I think he was actually sleeping through that storm. Can you believe it? When he answered he sounded half asleep still. He mumbled something about getting a coat and I told him there was no time, that Danny had come back, that he was in a state and now he could be in danger. When we got downstairs, he went to grab a mac from the hall stand and that's when I shouted at him. *I saw him go into the summer house,* I said. We all knew how dilapidated that old place was, I can't believe it hadn't collapsed years ago. You could stand inside and look up through the roof to the sky, it was nothing but holes. *If something happens to Danny just because you want to put your coat on, well think how that will look.* That's what I said. So he opened the back door and stumbled out into the rain.'

'You must have known you were putting him in danger?'

'I thought, great if he gets a good soaking, that's just what he deserves.'

'*Signora* Warrington, when I arrived that night the key was hanging beside the back door and the door was locked. I had to unlock the door to go into the garden. And so, after you had pushed *Signor* Swain out into the storm, you came back into the house, locked the back door, and you waited. And you saw the tree fall and you knew his fate.'

Christina and Danny were staring at Lorna now, both of them wide-eyed, as though they were struggling to comprehend what Giuseppe was saying.

'How could you do such a terrible thing? To stand by and watch a man die,' Christina said.

'What he did to my family killed any emotions I might have had, all I wanted was revenge. And you,' Lorna pointed at Giuseppe. 'What kind of detective makes friends with a criminal, eh?' Her laugh was coarse, her voice flat, as if all the energy had gone from it.

'Edward was going to tell me something. The last time I saw him he asked me to come to the lodgings the next day and he would explain everything, but by the next day Edward was dead.'

'And if he'd told you how he'd got away with it? What would you care? You're retired, you've walked away from your responsibilities.'

Lorna had taken it upon herself to seek revenge for her father's death. Her actions were misguided, Giuseppe was certain of it. He had always trusted his intuition, and right now his intuition was telling him that even if Edward had had feelings for Lorna's mother - for Josephine - he had never acted on those feelings, and what Giuseppe was even more certain of was that Edward could never have been guilty of embezzlement, of stealing from his employer and standing by when the man took his own life. There had to be another explanation.

'You found nothing in *Signor* Swain's room when you went looking?' He directed his question at Lorna.

'It was you who rifled through his things,' Danny said,

lurching forward towards Lorna as if he was going to shake her again. 'You let him think it was me.'

'No smoke without fire, eh?' Lorna gave a hollow laugh. 'You told me yourself how your brothers are forever nicking stuff, stands to reason it runs in the family. Leastways, that's what I persuaded old man Swain to believe, although between you and me he didn't take much persuading.' She took a step back, as if she was goading him to take a swing at her. 'Anyway, no, I didn't find anything. Not that I really knew what I expected to find.'

'Christina, I am going upstairs to look in Edward's room. You go home now, I will be with you soon. Danny, do not let *Signora* Warrington upset you. When someone is full of anger, they will search for anyone and everyone to be their... how do you say it in English... their punchball.'

'Yeah, well, I don't intend to be anyone's punchball, so I'm off out. But don't think you can scare me, Lorna. I'll be back to sleep here tonight and tomorrow night. I've got just as much right to be here as you have. More probably, given that you were the one who killed our landlord.' Danny picked up his jacket and left the room.

Giuseppe didn't wait for Lorna's response. Now, as he climbed the stairs to the attic room, he reflected on her words. She had been just fifteen years old when she found her father's body; the pain would still linger. And if the police had confirmed the death as suicide, they would have had no further interest on the whys and wherefores. Giuseppe knew all about the anger and hurt that lingered after a tragic death, the need for answers, for some sort of explanation.

The only time he had been in Edward's bedroom was on the night his friend lost his life. He had pushed open the door, hoping to find Edward sleeping through the worst of the storm, to find that he had already plunged into the very heart of it.

Stepping into the bedroom now felt like an intrusion. The heavy damask curtains were closed, providing no opportunity for the bright autumn sunshine to filter in. The stale smell of unwashed bedlinen, mixed with a fusty odour coming from the damp patches around the eaves, led Giuseppe to pull back one of the curtains. Using all his strength, he tugged at the bottom sash window. It lifted about two inches, but enough to let in a blast of cold air. The view from the window was of the back garden of the lodgings, the fallen tree and decimated summer house. A little over a week had passed since the night of the storm and the only timbers that had been shifted were the ones that the ambulance men had eased aside in order to lift Edward's body out.

Giuseppe shook the thought away and moved to the wardrobe. The attic room was larger than Giuseppe's bedroom above the café, but here the ceiling sloped down sharply on either side of the bed, leaving little room for tall furniture. A squat wardrobe had been chosen to fit the space at the foot of the bed. Giuseppe opened one of the doors, glancing at the neatness of jackets paired with folded trousers. Several ties were draped over a hook on the inside of the wardrobe door and on the floor of the wardrobe were three pairs of leather shoes. They must have been recently polished as the smell of wax still lingered.

A gilt carriage clock sat on the small table to one side of the bed and on the other side was a tallboy with six narrow drawers, which Edward opened in turn, starting from the bottom. The contents of each drawer mirrored the neatness of the wardrobe. Paired socks, folded vests and pants, shirts looking as if they had barely been worn, with their shop creases still in them. It was the top drawer that piqued Giuseppe's interest. He removed each item, laying it on the candlewick bedspread to take a closer look. A Bible. A well-thumbed copy of *Moby Dick*, with an inscription on the flyleaf, *Dear Edward, may all of your adventures be happy ones. Love Mother and Father.* It was dated 5th June, 1921 - a birthday gift, perhaps? The last item he removed from the drawer was a soft leather pouch. A ribbon was tied around it, keeping the letters that it contained from spilling out. Giuseppe untied the ribbon and lifted the letters out. Each one still in its envelope and from the postmarks they appeared to be in date order. They were each addressed to Edward, but not to Claremont Lodge. The address read, *84 Melbourne Road, Margate, Kent.* He sifted through the pile until he found the earliest date, 1st September, 1957, slid the single sheet from the envelope and read.

Dear Edward

Thank you for your kind thoughts and your offer of help. Lorna and I are still reeling from the shock of losing Keith. You know well enough what a proud man he was. You have always been a dear, dear friend. Perhaps in another life we could have been more than friends, but I know that both you and I respect Keith too much to ever want to hurt him. I believe his actions were due entirely due to the shame he felt as a result of the bankruptcy. He never gave me reason to think he doubted my love for him, or your friendship. The only transgression you and I were guilty of was in thought alone, never in deed.

But all of that is in the past, and now it is for us to try to bear a future without him.

I hope you are keeping well.

Kind regards

Josephine

Reaching the end of this first letter he continued to read several more. Each one was signed Josephine, each with a similar tone as the first. The letters confirmed what Lorna had guessed, and went some way to explain Edward's last words - an apology to Josephine for loving her - even though he had never acted on his feelings. And then, after Keith's death, Edward had offered the family some kind of assistance, but it had been declined.

The next envelope he picked up was still sealed. It was addressed to Mrs Josephine Chaney and had been marked 'Return to sender'. The postmark was dated 10th December, 1963. Lorna had said that her mother had died in July 1963. Lorna may have left the family home by the time this letter arrived. More likely though, she had seen the sender's address, which was written on the back of the envelope. The letter had been sent from *Claremont Lodge, Sea Road, Bexhill*. So, Lorna had told another lie. She hadn't had to 'discover' where Edward had moved to. She had his address right there.

Giuseppe looked inside the top drawer of the tallboy again. There was a silver letter opener lying right at the front of the drawer. He used it to slit across the top edge of the envelope, taking out the two folded sheets, smoothing them flat on the top of the tallboy and began to read.

Dear Josephine

I'm sorry it's been a while since I last wrote. I hope you and Lorna are well. In all your replies to my letters, you have never mentioned how you are managing? These past years must have been so difficult for you, not just dealing with the grief, but also your financial situation. I have wished so many times that I could turn the clock back. I tried so hard to persuade Keith not to make those investments, but he was convinced they were sound. He was excited about being able to expand the business, get another printing press, take on more staff. The day his broker told him the news Keith came to see me. He sat at my desk and wept. At that moment I knew it could only go one way. I had been doing the bookwork for long enough to know how little there was in the current account, how much was owed to the bank, as well as the loans for all the machinery. It was just a matter of time.

The thing is, Josephine, I have recently sold my house in Margate and plumped all my money, as well as the few savings I had, into a house near the seafront in Bexhill-on-sea. It is a delightful place my dear, albeit a little ramshackle. There are rooms here for you and Lorna. It would be wonderful if you could come and join me, it's too large a house for just one person and I'd love to be able to share it with you both. I understand that there can never be anything else between us, other than friendship, but I believe that Keith would rest easy knowing you had someone to look out for you, rather than see you struggling on your own. I wasn't able to help Keith, but if I can help his family, then I will feel I have gone some way to repaying the friendship he offered me during the many years we worked together.

Do say you will think about it.

Yours

Edward Swain

Giuseppe folded the letter again, put it back in the envelope, and slid the envelope into his jacket pocket. He couldn't return to the sitting room just yet. All he could think about were the tragic consequences of misunderstandings, lost opportunities, and wasted lives.

CHAPTER 31

Lorna Warrington was alone in the kitchen when Giuseppe reached the ground floor of the lodgings. He could hear her humming a tune to herself, making him wonder how she could be so calm in the face of all she had done. But perhaps, like his tapping, the humming was a nervous reaction. Maybe she didn't even know she was doing it.

As he walked along the hallway, he reflected on all that he had learned about Lorna Warrington. Her ability to switch off one part of her personality to display another was a skill that any actor would treasure. The difference being that Lorna's actions were not part of a fictional drama, they were rooted in reality.

Of course, her father's suicide and subsequently her mother's death would have left Lorna not just alone, but wounded, struggling to understand how and why it was that she had lost both parents. She would have been looking for answers and the one person who could have given her those answers was the one person she chose to blame. If only she had opened Edward's letter, she would have been given an inkling that her father had been dreadfully unlucky, he had invested unwisely. Far from being the one to take money from his employer, Edward had tried to save Keith Chaney from making a foolish decision. And six years after Keith Chaney's death, Edward was still offering a hand of friendship to his widow and daughter. It appeared that news of Mrs Chaney's death had not reached Edward. When his letter was returned he must have thought it was an act of pride on behalf of Lorna's mother, that she wanted to continue struggling alone.

Hearing his footsteps, Lorna turned to face Giuseppe,

a challenging expression on her face.

'Found anything?' she said.

'*Si.*'

He took a couple of the early letters that Mrs Chaney had written to Edward, laying them out on the kitchen table, waiting for Lorna to read them. Instead she turned towards the sink, turning on the Ascot water heater and running some water into the bowl.

'Your mother wrote these to *Signor* Swain. They confirm that Edward did care for your mother, but both he and your mother cared too much for your father to do anything to hurt him. And when your father died Edward offered a hand of friendship to you and your mother.'

She turned the water off, picked up a tea towel and dried her hands. She glanced down at the letters, then picked one up, scanned its contents and put it down again.

'That just proves he had a guilty conscience,' she said.

Giuseppe tutted, picked up the letters, then placed another envelope onto the table. This was the letter that had been returned to Edward unopened. He turned it over, pointing to the sender's address.

'This is how you found *Signor* Swain.' It was a statement, not a question.

'So what if it was?' She pushed the envelope back across the table, as if it was contaminated in some way. 'Mum died just months before this letter arrived. Not likely that I'd want to read anything he had to say, was it?'

'You decided to visit *Signor* Swain, confront him perhaps?'

'I could have done that. But he would have just denied it, wouldn't he? So I took a room here, gave a different name, and bided my time.'

'Your grief had turned to anger.'

'Of course I was angry, you'd be angry too if you'd had to live my life.'

Giuseppe pulled a chair out from the table and sat down, picking up the envelope and tapping it slowly on the edge of the table, as if considering his next move.

'You were never inquisitive about the contents of this letter?'

'Why would I be?'

'No, you are right. You were certain that *Signor* Swain had not only stolen money from your father but he had also tried to steal your mother. And yet after your father died your mother made no attempt to develop their relationship.'

'I told you, that just proves old man Swain was doing all the running. I don't care what Mum said in those letters. I know how much she loved my dad. She'd never have cheated on him.'

'We will never know the truth about the relationship between Edward and your mother. But I believe that if Edward had stolen money - if there was even a possibility of truth in your accusation - then surely your father would have confronted his accountant, rather than taking his own life? Did you ever consider that it might have been something that your father did that caused him to take that decision?'

'You're saying my father was a criminal now, are you?' She stepped towards Giuseppe, her eyes lighting up with fury, her cheeks a fiery red. 'How dare you.' She held a hand up as if to strike him. It hovered in the air above his head. He sat very still, holding her gaze.

'*Signora* Warrington, I think you should sit, calm yourself and read this letter, the letter that you returned to *Signor* Swain unopened. If only you had opened it…'

Giuseppe felt a weight of sadness wash over him as he passed the envelope back across the table towards her.

Lorna slumped down on a chair opposite Giuseppe as if all her energy was expended. She hesitated for a moment, then slid the two sheets from the envelope and read in silence.

As she read, Giuseppe watched her eyes flicking across the lines, from left to right. She reached the end of the letter, paused, then began to read it again from the beginning, as if doubting all that she had read. When she had finished the second read through she stayed very still, her hands holding the sheet of paper, looking at it and then looking up at Giuseppe.

'And so, you see, *signora*, sadly your father made some bad decisions, and it was those decisions that led him to lose all his money. *Signor* Swain did not steal from him, on the contrary he tried to give him advice, to warn him that the investments presented too much of a risk. But often we think we know what is best. I too have been guilty of not listening to the advice of friends and colleagues.'

Everything in Lorna's posture and her facial expression reflected someone who had finally admitted defeat.

'*Signor* Swain wanted only good things for your family,' Giuseppe continued. 'He tried to help your father, then when he could no longer help him he extended a hand of friendship and support to your mother.' Giuseppe paused. 'I believe he cared very much for your mother, but I also believe he was a man of integrity, that the friendship he offered would have been respectful. You and your mother could have lived a more comfortable life. Perhaps your mother would still be alive today.'

Giuseppe knew much of what he was saying was based on supposition. He had known Edward for a short time, he could never be certain of his intentions regarding Lorna's mother - Josephine. He knew too that telling Lorna about Edward's final words would only feed her suspicions that there was more to the relationship. But nothing that Edward had done deserved the punishment that Lorna had meted out. Not a life sentence of bitterness and acrimony, but the ultimate sentence of death.

'*Signora* Warrington. You are guilty of causing the death of an innocent man.' Giuseppe spoke slowly, with precision. A judge pronouncing his verdict.

'There's no court that will find me guilty. What proof have you got, eh?' She stood, stabbing her finger towards him. 'He walked into the garden, into that dilapidated old summer house. You can't blame me for the whole thing collapsing. They call it an act of God, don't they? Well, that's about right - he got his just desserts, didn't he?'

When Giuseppe arrived back at Bella Café, Christina was standing in the shelter of the doorway. She grabbed at his arm, stopping him in his tracks.

'What happened? Did you find anything useful in Edward's room? I couldn't bear to stay in that woman's company for another minute. Lies seem to trip off her tongue as easy as a sharp knife going through butter. As soon as you went upstairs Danny scarpered too. After everything he's been through with that bully of a stepfather, even he was shocked as to the lengths she went to implicate him, when she was the guilty one.'

'Come, let us walk a little and I will explain what I have learned. It is a very sad story, Christina. The sadness made worse because there is a chance that at least two people's lives could have been saved.'

They crossed over to the seafront and stood at the

railings looking out towards the horizon. The tide was on the turn, churning up the shingle with each wave. For a few moments Giuseppe said nothing, absorbed by the movement of the water and the shuffling of the stones as they created ever-changing patterns on the shoreline. Several small birds were pecking at bits of shell and seaweed, their colouring was so similar to the greys and browns of the shingle that it was only when they moved that Giuseppe noticed them.

He tucked his arm through Christina's, gesturing to a nearby bench.

'You're not too cold to sit?' she said.

'It seems I am becoming accustomed to the English weather.'

She glanced sideways at him to see he was smiling.

'Wait until Dad hears you say that.'

'It may have to remain our secret for now,' he said, lifting one finger to his lips.

'What's the truth then? Was it as Stevie said?'

'*Signora* Warrington believed Edward was a thief, that he had stolen money from her father - his employer - and that he also wanted to steal the love of her mother. And when her mother died it was... how do you say it?'

'The final straw?'

'*Si*. Perhaps she had seen earlier correspondence between her mother and Edward, perhaps she had to find someone to blame and he was the only person she could think of. Whatever her reasons and with no proof, she wanted to see Edward for herself. Remember, she had never met him all the time he worked for her father. When she came here to Bexhill, found Edward settled, living a comfortable life, the bitterness she felt at the loss of both her parents suddenly had a focus. And then perhaps during the night of the storm she saw a chance to punish him.'

'Do you think she meant for him to die?'

'I really don't know. She locked the kitchen door and when the tree fell onto the summer house, she knew that Edward was inside and that at the very least he would have been badly injured. But she stayed inside and only when Stevie alerted us and I went to the lodging house was she forced to go back out into the garden with me. At that point she knew for certain he was close to death.'

'But even then she showed no remorse,' Christina said. 'Just the opposite, she tried to blame Danny for it all. It's scary to think how grief and anger can eat away at a person. To lead to such a dreadful thing, to be completely calm when you've caused someone's death.'

'She has convinced herself she did not cause it. That it was an act of God, the storm, the fallen tree. She believes she is innocent.'

He ran his hand along the edge of the bench, scanning the further stretches of beach. 'Come, let us walk.'

'You said earlier that two people's lives could have been saved?'

'Si. If Mrs Chaney had accepted Edward's offer of help, she would not have had to struggle to bring up her daughter alone, cope with being penniless, maybe she would not have become ill. *Signora* Warrington would have learned the truth about her father's bankruptcy. And so Edward's life would also have been saved.'

'We have a saying in English, *pride comes before a fall*. If Mr Chaney hadn't been too proud to accept Edward's advice…'

'It is too late to change what has passed.'

'You're not thinking about Mr Swain now, are you?'

'Your instincts and intuition are wasted on the

Eastbourne Herald.' Giuseppe smiled, pulling his jacket collar up and tucking his scarf in a little tighter. 'I am feeling cold now. Shall we return?'

They had reached the westerly end of the seafront, having had the wind in their face as they walked. Now, as they turned, the strength of the wind increased, pushing them forward.

'What will happen to Lorna now?'

'I must inform the police. They will interrogate and make their own decision.'

'Giuseppe, if it goes to trial… Stevie…'

'He is just a child, he will not be expected to give evidence. It will be for me to give an account of that night.'

'But you won't be here. Will you?' There was a ring of hope in her question.

'If there is a trial, I will have to return.'

'It's all such a mess, Giuseppe.'

'Life is never neat and tidy. If it was you would have nothing to write about and I would have nothing to investigate.'

CHAPTER 32

Early on Friday morning, Giuseppe was the first to hear the results of the United Kingdom election. Mario's wireless was on in the back kitchen as Giuseppe made his first espresso of the day. The BBC announcer explained that Labour MP, Harold Wilson, would visit the Queen later that day to ask for permission to form a government. The first Labour government for thirteen years. Apparently Labour had achieved a slim majority, beating the Conservatives by just five seats. Not much, but enough.

Only two days had passed since Giuseppe had contacted the police regarding Lorna Warrington's part in Edward's death. He presented all the information he could to the senior office at Bexhill police station - an Inspector Morris - and then followed up with a phone call to Inspector Pearce.

'From what you're telling me, I'd say it's far from an open and shut case,' Pearce said. 'She's got motive, I'll give you that. And opportunity, but whether that will be enough to make a solid case…'

'The back door key. Remember, the door was locked when I arrived that night. The key was hanging beside the door. It could only have happened that way if *Signora* Warrington intended to leave *Signor* Swain to his fate.'

'Yes, I understand your reasoning. Well, Morris is a good man by all accounts. If you've given him all the details then you can trust him to see it through. I still think they'll struggle to get it to court though. And if they do? These things take time, you know, and they'll need you as a key witness. Are you going to stay on in England until then?'

It was one of many questions Giuseppe had been asking himself. The first concerned the Forrest family. Surprisingly, a conversation with Mario went some way to providing an answer. It was late evening, after Giuseppe's final conversation with Lorna that he seized the opportunity to speak to his cousin. Christina and Anne were up in the flat, but Mario had remained down in the cafe, making further adjustments to the shelf that he thought he had fixed days ago.

'Mario, do you have a moment to talk with me? I would like your help.' Giuseppe said.

The cousins sat at one of the tables, but not before Mario poured two glasses of vermouth from a bottle that Giuseppe had gifted him a few days earlier.

'I told you I'd keep it for special occasions,' Mario said, smiling. 'I'm not sure we can describe your success discovering the truth about Mr Swain's death as a *special occasion*, but you must be pleased that at least you have the answers you were searching for.'

'*Grazie, sì*. I am relieved. Not pleased though. It is very sad to think that such hatred exists in anyone, enough to take a life.'

They clinked glasses and each took a sip of vermouth, putting their glass down at the same moment.

'But there is another matter I hope you can help me to resolve. *Signor* Swain's other lodger - Danny Forrest. His family are living in dreadful circumstances in Eastbourne.'

'Poor housing conditions? Well, there's not much I can do about that. It's true for so many families, I'm afraid.'

'It is not the condition of their home that concerns me. They are living with a brutal man who is putting their lives in danger. I have promised to help them.'

'I don't see what I can do.'

'Your acquaintance, Councillor Rogers. Would you be able to speak to him? I do not know how these things work here in England, but if the council are preparing new homes, it must be possible to recommend a family who is in desperate need.'

'I'm more than happy to speak to him, there's a chance I guess. At the very least he'll know who to approach and what the protocol is.'

They continued sipping their drinks for a few moments, each absorbed in their own thoughts and then Mario said, 'What will happen to Claremont Lodge? Did the local police give you any idea what happens in these cases. Is it right that Mr Swain had no family?'

'While I have been investigating Edward's death, it seems the police have been investigating his life. Edward has a brother. They have contacted him. He lives in Scotland.'

'He'll be here in time for the funeral?'

'*Si.* Then it will be for him to decide what happens to the lodging house. He will sell it, I expect.'

'Unless the council want to knock it down.'

'I hope they do not. With some attention it could be a very beautiful home for someone.'

'There you are. Perhaps you should buy it.' Mario looked up from his glass, his expression suggesting he was as surprised at his sudden idea as Giuseppe was to hear it.

On Friday evening the Rossi family gathered around the dining table for supper, bar Stevie who agreed to an early night with the promise of a Saturday morning outing with Tony, which was bound to involve ice-cream.

'Did you persuade your editor to cover the election result?' Anne asked.

'He didn't need much persuasion. If we didn't cover it, then our readers might think we didn't care. The electorate will be hoping for change, whether they voted Labour or Conservative.'

'Or Liberal?' Mario added.

'Or abstained,' Anne quipped.

'Anyone who didn't vote should be ashamed of themselves. Women especially. When you think of what the Suffragettes sacrificed in order to get us the vote…'

'Here we go, off on one of your campaigns again,' Mario said, a lightness in his voice that Giuseppe hadn't heard in weeks. 'I've spoken to Councillor Rogers, by the way. He's going to do what he can for the Forrest family. It sounds hopeful that he'll be able to help them.'

'That is excellent news. *Grazie*.'

'They'll need money coming in, though. I don't expect Danny will be able to sell many typewriters, bless him,' Anne said.

'I've got some good news there,' Christina said. 'I've persuaded Charles to buy one, to replace the one he let me bring home.'

'Goodness, your powers of persuasion really are working,' Anne said.

'I caught him on a good day, I think. But speaking of powers of persuasion… Giuseppe, you've got something to tell Dad, haven't you?'

All focus was on Giuseppe, who began tapping the edge of the table, then drew a breath before speaking.

'I have booked my ticket. I am going home.' He directed his announcement at Mario, watching for his reaction.

'When?' Anne said, a flutter of anxiety in her voice.

'Two weeks from today.'

Mario pushed his chair back from the table and stood. 'I'll clear away.' He gathered up some of the empty plates, but was stopped when Anne put her hand on his arm.

'Sit down, love.'

'I know what you want and the answer is no,' Mario said, the lightness in his tone that was there moments ago now replaced with quiet defiance.

Giuseppe stopped tapping and once again directed his words at Mario. 'When I learned the truth about *Signor* Swain's death, the unspoken accusations, the assumptions that led to the waste of a life, I was reminded again that we all have to face our fears. I must sit with Carlo Prezzi, look into his face and ask him to tell me the truth about the day his grandson died. Perhaps I must also meet Rosalia and lay to rest the bitterness between us. And you, Mario, there are things you also need to lay to rest. Come back with me, please. I will stand beside you while you revisit the events you have tried for years to forget. We will do it together.' There was silence in the room, the only sounds coming from outside. The wind had been building all day, rain threatening. Now the first raindrops fell, hitting the window and changing the sound of the passing traffic as their tyres met with the wet tarmac.

'I'm not leaving Anne. The café. There's too much for one person.'

'Of course you won't leave Mum,' Christina said. 'The two of you must go. I'll take a couple of weeks off, Charles owes me holiday, anyway. Tony will help at the weekend.'

'*Signora* Forrest?' Giuseppe said.

'Of course. Why didn't I think of that?' Christina said, her eyes brightening at the thought. 'She could start straightaway. Once she's got the hang of things you two could actually have an afternoon off together, imagine

251

that.'

'What about your sister?' Anne said. 'Do you think Flavia would like to help at the weekend, when she's not working in her bookshop?'

'No, Mum.' The enthusiasm in Christina's voice was replaced with a flat, dull tone. 'Flavia has made it clear she's not interested in us. Let's keep it that way.'

'I'm not so sure, darling,' Anne said. 'It felt as if your sister was holding out a hand of friendship when she was here last weekend. You need to give her a chance, we all do.'

'Let's forget about Flavia for now, shall we? The main thing to decide is if you and Dad agree to go to Rome and for how long. Then, it's just a case of booking the tickets, and I'll help you pack.' The brightness was in Christina's eyes again.

Throughout the conversation Giuseppe sat back in his chair, closed his eyes, to remove himself from the family discussion. The signs were positive, he could envisage a time very soon when his cousin and wife would sit beside him on the long train journey to Rome. On their arrival there would be much to face. Edward had said that a storm leaves devastation in its wake and Giuseppe had replied by suggesting that from the ruins often comes new growth.

There had been much devastation, in Italy, in Bexhill, in the past and more recently just days ago. But Giuseppe needed to believe that something good could be salvaged from the ruins. This evening he would listen to the shipping forecast on the wireless. Perhaps there would be the promise of fine weather ahead.

Thank you

It's been fun discovering more about Giuseppe Bianchi and, as ever, I have my great writing buddies, Christoffer Petersen and Sarah Acton, to thank for continuing to support me on my writing journey.

I have also been lucky to team up with the most wonderful narrator - Charles Johnston - who did the most excellent job at bringing Giuseppe alive in the audiobook edition of *Crossing the Line*. Charles is a trained opera singer and was kind enough to cast an eye over my mentions of opera in After the Storm as we learn more about Giuseppe's passion for music.

Thanks also go to Janice Paiano, one of my lovely readers, who suggested some wonderful Italian names for me to choose from for my characters. One of the names I chose from her suggestions - Filomena - is briefly introduced here in After the Storm but we will learn much more about her in the next novel.

Writing *After the Storm* during 2020 - a strange year indeed - has reminded me how lucky I am. As an author I have the chance to escape the realities around me - if only for a few hours a day. And although I am cocooned here at home, rarely seeing another person face to face, I have a lovely warm feeling that I am part of a wide circle of friends - spanning continents - every time someone reads one of my books.

Thank you to all my readers and here's to a brighter future for us all.

Isabella Muir
December 2020

As a reader your words make all the difference

Honest reviews of my books help other readers find them. As an independent author I don't have the backing of a publisher or a team of publicists. I can't advertise in the traditional way, but I do have one thing going for me, and that's a group of engaged readers. If you enjoyed this book, I would be very grateful if you could spend just five minutes leaving a review (as short as you like) on Goodreads or your favourite online book review websites, book groups, your own blogs and social media sites.

Thank you!

www.isabellamuir.com

About the author

Isabella is never happier than when she is immersing herself in the sights, sounds and experiences of the 1960s. Researching all aspects of family life back then formed the perfect launch pad for her works of fiction. Isabella rediscovered her love of writing fiction during two happy years working on and completing her MA in Professional Writing and since then has gone to publish five novels, two novellas and a short story collection.

Her first *Sussex Crime Mystery* series features young librarian and amateur sleuth, Janie Juke. Set in the late 1960s, in the fictional seaside town of Tamarisk Bay, we meet Janie, who looks after the mobile library. She is an avid lover of Agatha Christie stories – in particular Hercule Poirot – using all she has learned from the Queen of Crime to help solve crimes and mysteries. As well as three novels, there are three novellas in the series, which explore some of the back story to the Tamarisk Bay characters.

Her latest novel, *After the Storm*, is the second in a new series of Sussex Crimes, featuring retired Italian detective, Giuseppe Bianchi. The first Giuseppe Bianchi mystery - *Crossing the Line* - introduces us to Giuseppe on the day he arrives in the quiet seaside town of Bexhill-on-Sea, East Sussex, to find a dead body on the beach and so the story begins…

Isabella's standalone novel, *The Forgotten Children*, deals with the emotive subject of the child migrants who were sent to Australia – again focusing on family life in the 1960s, when the child migrant policy was still in force.

www.isabellamuir.com

By the same author

BRAND NEW SUSSEX MYSTERY SERIES
Featuring retired Italian detective - Giuseppe Bianchi
BOOK 1: CROSSING THE LINE*
(Also available as an audiobook.)
BOOK 2: AFTER THE STORM

THE SUSSEX MYSTERY SERIES
Featuring young librarian and amateur sleuth - Janie Juke
BOOK 1: THE TAPESTRY BAG*
BOOK 2: LOST PROPERTY*
BOOK 3: THE INVISIBLE CASE*
(All available as audiobooks.)

THE SUSSEX CRIME MYSTERIES
A Janie Juke trilogy - box set

SUSSEX MYSTERY NOVELLAS
Featuring characters from the Janie Juke novels
DIVIDED WE FALL
MORE THAN ASHES
WAITING FOR SUNSHINE

THE FORGOTTEN CHILDREN
(Also available as an audiobook.)
A story about a mother's search for her child

TWELVE AT CHRISTMAS
An anthology of twelve Christmas-themed short stories

IVORY VELLUM
An anthology of short stories

*Isabella's novels are also available as Italian editions.